A SEASIDE
MURDER

BOOKS BY ALICE CASTLE

A SEASIDE
MURDER

ALICE CASTLE

bookouture

Published by Bookouture in 2024

An imprint of Storyfire Ltd.
Carmelite House
50 Victoria Embankment
London EC4Y 0DZ

www.bookouture.com

ISBN: 978-1-83525-267-3
eBook ISBN: 978-1-83525-266-6

To Ella and Connie, with love

ONE

Very early one bright morning in May, Sarah Vane realised she had abandoned her alarm clock, along with most of her old city habits. Nowadays she relied either on the cries of the Kent coast seagulls to wake her up, or Hamish, her little black Scottie. He was strongly of the opinion that no one should lie around in bed after dawn had broken. On this particular day, the gulls just managed to beat Hamish to it, but that didn't stop him leaping out of his snug tartan basket in the corner of her room and onto her floral sprigged coverlet, to make sure both her eyes were open.

'Come on now, Hamish, what time do you call this? And you know you're not allowed on the bed,' Sarah said fondly. Once, in her busy life as a London doctor, she had been a bit iffy about dogs, but it was fair to say she was now a total convert. She gave him a hug and popped him back on the floor.

She supposed she was also gradually getting used to the loss of her late husband, Peter. She still spoke to him often, though, as she pottered around her delightful fisherman's cottage by the sea, and she would always be heartbroken he hadn't lived to enjoy the retirement they had planned so meticulously together.

Not that things had exactly gone by the book since she'd been in Merstairs, Sarah recalled as she pulled on her pink dressing gown and went downstairs, Hamish trotting importantly in front of her. But, after the first murders in Merstairs in over half a century, the dust had now settled. Everything was ordered and calm once more.

Sarah unlocked the back door, letting in a gust of tangy seaside air, and put Hamish out in the garden. Immediately he rushed to trample all over her newly planted flowerbeds of irises and agapanthus.

'Hamish,' she remonstrated, but after a guilty glance over his shoulder, the little dog ploughed on, scampering over the lavender bushes and peonies she'd spent so much time putting in. He must be on the scent of his nemesis, Mephisto, the enormous marmalade cat who lived next door. That was a David and Goliath battle this underdog was never going to win.

Pets aside, things were beautifully peaceful. Perhaps... too peaceful? Sarah loved the place, and already felt as though she'd lived here all her life. But somehow, that wasn't quite as satisfying as she knew it should have been. After running a GP practice for many years in one of London's busy suburbs, spending her days deducing people's health problems and her evenings battling with mountains of paperwork, her sharp mind now felt almost as though it was rusting with all this sea air and relaxation. There was no doubt about it, if she wasn't careful she could find herself at a bit of a loose end, she realised as she tucked into a slice of toast with lush golden apricot jam and sipped a cup of her favourite English Breakfast tea, good and strong.

She washed and dried her plate and mug while watching Mephisto sneering at Hamish from the branches of her lilac tree, which was just coming into bloom. Then she put the dishes away, and after that, she stood in the middle of the kitchen. The entire cottage was pin-neat and organised down to the last spoon, and she didn't want to spend the day twiddling her thumbs. Then she had a brainwave. She was going to do her friend Daphne Roux a *very* big favour.

Daphne, her old schoolmate, was Mephisto's owner and Sarah's next-door neighbour. Warm and generous to a fault, she made friends effortlessly wherever she went – unlike Sarah, who tended to be more reserved and analytical. Daphne constantly gathered and shed hobbies and interests, but the one thing she'd never wavered on was her enthusiasm for clairvoyance. She even had a shop on the Merstairs promenade, Tarot and Tealeaves, where she gave consultations facing one of the most beautiful sea views in England. Not that you could see it. Daphne's windows were filthy.

Sarah looked out a plastic bucket from under her sink, quickly filled it with cleaning products and an assortment of sponges and cloths, then whistled to Hamish. The little dog, who'd just got within a whisker of his enormous ginger prey (or so he thought), appeared at the back door with a 'What is it now?' look on his little face. But then Sarah said the magic word that overrode all other considerations.

'Walkies!'

A few minutes later, they were striding along the coastal road into the heart of Merstairs, with Sarah admiring the cresting waves and Hamish keeping a weather eye on a large tern flying overhead. One minute more, and they'd reached the promenade, deserted at this very early hour. Hamish paused outside the antiques shop, which had become a frequent haunt. Its owner, Charles Diggory, had very blue eyes and looked like a long-legged cross between Lord Peter Wimsey and Sherlock Holmes. He was separated from Francesca, the mayor of Merstairs, and he half-owned a Chihuahua that Hamish loved with every particle of his huge Scottie heart that didn't have his mistress's name on it. Today, however, Sarah carried straight on, her step purposeful. When she came to a halt outside the dusty Tarot shop, Hamish looked up at her as though to say, 'Really?' It was clear to him the awful cat who sometimes frequented this place was currently back in his garden at home, so there was no need to hang around here at all. But then he got a whiff of something rather odd.

At the same moment, Sarah gasped. Then she moved forward carefully. There was something in the recessed shop doorway, something she'd initially taken for a pile of rags dumped on Daphne's doorstep. That wouldn't have particularly surprised her – Daphne might even have put them there herself, you just never knew with her magpie ways. It could have been finds from her frequent forays to the local charity shop. But something told Sarah this wasn't rags.

Carefully, Sarah bent down, ignoring her creaking knees, and leant forward. The more she scrutinised it, the more she realised the pile had a distinctly human shape. This was a huddled figure. She had never seen anyone sleeping rough in Merstairs, but it was still very early in the morning. Perhaps any poor homeless souls normally moved on before the tourists and shopkeepers were up and about. Well, she hated to wake anyone living in such awful circumstances, but she did need to get into Daphne's shop. She had the keys in her hand, the spare set her friend had given her in case of emergencies. Daphne was going to be thrilled with this surprise, she was sure of it. Now all Sarah needed to do was to tactfully move this unfortunate person on, then she could get on with her planned clean-up.

'Excuse me,' she said as gently as she could. She didn't want to give them a terrible shock. 'You can't really sleep here. I need to get past, you see. I have to get into the shop. If you'll just get up, I can offer you a cup of tea.'

As soon as she'd said it, Sarah realised it wasn't the wisest suggestion she'd ever made. This person could be anyone, they could have a multitude of problems that would be beyond her to solve. What if they were aggressive, for instance? While she had compassion for anyone in need, people could be unpredictable and, after all, she was now a lady of a certain age. She wasn't frail, but she was no Mike Tyson either. And she was on her own.

At her side, Hamish let out a whine, as if to remind her of his presence. She patted him and reconsidered. All right, she wasn't totally alone – but with the best will in the world, her tiny dog might not be a match for whoever this was.

'Sorry, I hate to wake you, but I really do need to get on,' Sarah said more firmly, using the no-nonsense tones that had usually served her well, whether with her own daughters – now both grown up and with children of their own – or with tricky patients. There was no response at first, then she heard a faint moan. It sounded like a woman's voice. Emboldened, Sarah stuck out a hand and shook the person's shoulder gently. They were covered up, she could now see, with coats and sweaters. Was it someone moving out of Merstairs? But if so, why on earth had they stopped here? Something didn't add up.

'Um, come on now, wake up,' Sarah said, a little more loudly. She was about to put her hand out again, when she looked down at it, and realised there was something red on her fingers. What was that? Paint? Or...

Horrified, she peered at the huddled figure, and started throwing off the sweaters. Sarah hadn't been a GP for so many years without recognising blood when she saw it. She could feel her own pulse ramping up with urgency and her breath becoming panicky, as she finally uncovered long, sandy-coloured hair flopping forward. She parted it, to see the pale face of a young girl, eyelids fluttering feebly as she fought to regain consciousness.

'You're all right,' Sarah said, doing her best to keep her voice gentle and reassuring despite the shock she was feeling. 'Don't worry about a thing, you're going to be fine. I'm calling an ambulance,' she said, reaching for her bag and pulling out her mobile phone.

Hamish, by her side, whined again. His day wasn't shaping up the way he'd expected at all, and now he was getting very worried about his mistress's new friend.

TWO

Sarah was sitting in the doorway, next to her patient. She tried a bit of delicate probing, to locate the wound, but the girl winced. Sarah realised she was pulling at a necklace, caught in her blonde hair. She tried to untangle it, noticing it was an ornate two-tone crucifix, the cross in rose gold, the figure in silver, but she got a low moan for her pains. Better to leave things alone for the moment, she decided, wadding up one of the cleaner-looking sweaters instead and using it to staunch the flow of blood. It was hard to be completely certain without a proper examination, but this looked very much like some sort of stabbing. She pressed the makeshift dressing to the wound as firmly as she could and tried to keep the poor thing conscious. It was all she could really do until the emergency services arrived. The girl needed sterile dressings, a drip, antibiotics... a host of things that the doorway of Daphne's shop could not provide.

'Come on, my dear, stay with me. Stay awake,' said Sarah urgently. The girl's skin was now becoming waxen. A fine sheen of perspiration had broken out on her unlined brow. She couldn't be more than twenty-five, Sarah reckoned, and was a pretty little thing. So young. She shook her head in horror.

What on earth had happened here? As the minutes ticked by, with no sign of an ambulance, and nothing else stirring on the deserted street, the pad Sarah was holding to the wound slowly began to feel damp. It was becoming saturated. She hated this: the sense of impotence, the worry about every passing second leaving the girl's chances worse as the head lolling on her shoulder became heavier.

Was this really the Merstairs that Daphne talked about, a sleepy little place where nothing much happened? Nirvana by the sea? Sarah was beginning to think her friend couldn't be more wrong about her home town. Just as she was despairing of help ever arriving, she felt a change in the girl. She seemed to be struggling to sit upright.

'OK, careful now,' Sarah said, trying to help her into a more comfortable position. 'Easy does it. Is that better?'

She propped her a little more snugly against the doorway, supporting her head. The girl's eyelids fluttered.

'Hey, don't worry about anything, you're safe,' said Sarah gently, keeping her own anxieties out of her voice as she had so often done in the past. She smoothed the hair off the girl's forehead as the blue eyes fluttered open again, and then widened in alarm, or maybe pain.

'Nothing to worry about. Help is on the way,' Sarah said gently. 'Can you tell me what happened? Who did this to you?'

Again, the girl struggled a bit and Sarah held onto her as she opened her mouth and croaked out a word.

'What was that?' Sarah said, stooping closer to try and hear. The girl's voice was very faint.

'Wits...' she said.

'Wits, did you say?' Sarah bent even closer, to get her ear as close as possible to the girl's mouth. 'Was that what you said?'

But when she straightened up again and looked at the young face, she realised a change had come over it. The features were now relaxed, the eyes closed once more, the mouth was still. There was no more panting for breath, no panicked attempt to communicate. The struggle was over. The poor girl would never speak again.

* * *

It was a relief when Sarah saw the ambulance speeding towards her. The coast road was still clear of other traffic and the flashing lights of the vehicle were garish in the early morning light. For once, she was happy to let the paramedics take over. The girl seemed light as a feather as they expertly moved her onto a stretcher and, after a few checks, confirmed Sarah's diagnosis by drawing a sheet over her pretty face. One of them came over and laid a hand on Sarah's shoulder. 'You did your best, love.'

'Have you checked the wound?' she asked.

The burly man, whose padded high-vis jacket and trousers made him look even larger, shook his head. 'Time enough when we get her back to base. You can talk to that lot about it, though,' he said, nodding his head in the direction of the police car which had just drawn up.

As the doors of the ambulance slammed shut on the girl, and it was driven away at half the speed of its arrival, Sarah turned to face two familiar figures.

'Aha, Constables Dumbarton and Deeside,' said Sarah wearily.

'Keep turning up like a bad penny, don't we?' said Dumbarton, a heavy frown settling on his beetle brow.

'Well, now you mention it...' Sarah answered.

'No, I meant *you* do,' said Dumbarton, looking crosser.

'Oh I see, but you said... Oh well, never mind. I expect you'll want to know about the time of death, all that sort of thing.'

As Sarah spoke, Deeside stepped forward, right into the

space so lately occupied by the dying girl, jabbing at the jumpers on the ground with the toe of his boot. She frowned in surprise. Surely he should be treating the crime scene with a bit more caution.

'We'll be getting all that information from the experts... don't you worry your head about it,' said Dumbarton dismissively.

'Um, but should he be...?' she started, then faltered. She was only going to get on the wrong side of the duo if she criticised their work. But on the other hand, valuable clues could be being trampled... She looked down and saw there was actually something under Deeside's boot.

Just then, there was a crackle on their police radios, and they went into a huddle over by their car, presumably so she'd be out of earshot. Sarah darted forward and pocketed the small square navy blue card and slip of white paper that Deeside had been standing on. She didn't feel bad about it, as the man had clearly destroyed any forensic evidence it might have borne with his huge feet.

'Right, got to tape up this area,' said Dumbarton importantly, turning back to Sarah. 'Just move along there, can you?' he said to her, as though she was some random rubbernecker.

Sarah did as she was asked, just as another car drew up. The plume of red hair as the driver got out was as good as a Tannoy announcement: Mariella was on the case. Sarah sighed in relief. Mariella was Daphne's daughter, and a fledgling member of the Merstairs police force. She was eager to become a detective – but Sarah had seen at first-hand how keen some of her colleagues were to sideline her.

Now Mariella shook her head at Sarah, then gave her a huge hug. 'Looks like you've had quite a morning,' she said, getting out her notebook and pen, and gesturing towards the nearby Jolly Roger pub. 'What do you say we get them to open up early and do us a cup of tea? You can tell me everything. I've already rung Mum. Well, it's her shop, so she'll need to be questioned too. I'll be killing two birds with one stone.' Sarah gritted her teeth, and Mariella apologised. 'Sorry, I wasn't thinking. Not the most tactful expression. Here, follow me and let's get sorted out.'

Sarah felt quite comforted, letting Mariella take the lead. Though she'd been present at more than her fair share of deathbed scenes, thanks to her profession, this morning had been a horrible shock. The poor girl had been such a pitiful scrap, much too young to die.

Mariella rapped on the pub door and they were soon sitting with piping hot cups of tea. It was just what Sarah needed.

The pub was under new management these days but the replacement landlady, Claire Scroggins, had apparently fallen madly in love with the bizarre décor introduced by the previous owners, Trevor Bains and the late Gus Trubshaw. The dark interior was still dotted with an assortment of plastic fish, pirate flags, rubbery fake sea urchins and lots of netting draped here and there, which Mariella ignored as she led Sarah through the events of the morning, making quick notes in her book.

Sarah had just got to the part where she'd accidentally pulled the girl's hair and noticed her crucifix necklace, when there was a rattle at the door. It was Daphne, with a worried frown in place of her usual joyful greeting of 'Coo-ee!'

She hugged Sarah to within an inch of her life, then said, 'Well, what a horrendous morning! I can't believe what's happened! It's like a nightmare. I came as soon as Mari rang,' she said, looking anxiously at her daughter. 'Darling, I really don't like you getting mixed up in stuff like this.'

'I feel I should be saying that to you, Mum – after all, it was your shop doorway the victim was found in,' Mariella replied drily.

'Well, it was nothing to do with me! And Sarah, I don't understand what you were doing outside Tarot and Tealeaves

anyway?' Daphne's lurid pink scarf, wrapped around her head
like a homage to a 1980s fitness video, clashed frantically with
her scarlet linen tunic. Hamish, under the table, turned away as
though to spare himself the sight – though he was fond of
Daphne, who was as liberal with chips from her plate as she was
with pats and belly rubs.

'Oh, well... It was supposed to be a surprise,' Sarah faltered,
now the moment had come to explain herself to Daphne. 'Or a
bit of a treat,' she shrugged.

'And I don't know why you've got that bucket of cleaning
stuff with you, either. You're not hiring yourself out as a Mrs
Mop now, are you? You can't be finding retirement that dull
already!' Daphne shook her head, her magenta drop earrings
quivering like tall trees in a storm.

Sarah shrugged and decided to come clean. 'Well, I just
thought I'd spruce your shop up a bit for you... I thought it
would help business. You did say you hadn't had much interest
recently. Then I spotted the poor girl, huddled in the doorway.
She was covered with clothing spilling out of a black bin bag.
At first, I thought someone had just left stuff from the charity
shop round the corner on your step. But why would they do
that?'

'Oh, people are always leaving donations there. They seem
to think my doorway is a dumping ground. So bizarre when it's
in constant use. But hang on one minute,' said Daphne, holding
up her palm like a police officer directing traffic. 'You mean you
were just going to break into my shop and, and, *clean* it?' She
could hardly have been more outraged if Sarah had announced
she'd been planning to steal all her Tarot treasures and flog
them on eBay.

Sarah sighed. It was clear that the little favour she'd
intended to do for her friend would not have been appreciated
at all. 'I think you're missing the point, Daphne. The girl died.
Right on your doorstep.'

'You're right,' Daphne said, looking anguished. 'Who on earth was she, do you know?'

'I haven't a clue,' said Sarah, remembering again the floppy dark blonde hair and the china blue eyes that had flickered open briefly – and were now closed for good. 'And who on earth could have done that to her?'

'Done what to her? What on earth do you mean? I thought she'd just died,' Daphne spluttered.

'People in their twenties don't just *die*, Daphne. Or at least, not very often,' Sarah said, remembering a couple of cases when unsuspected heart issues had felled apparently healthy patients without any warning. That kind of unfortunate sudden death was emphatically not the case here, however. Not with all the blood she had seen.

Daphne stared at her, with a rather anxious look in her eye. 'Don't tell me... No, I don't want to know.' At that moment, Hamish got to his feet a little stiffly and shook himself all over. 'And Hamish doesn't want any of that nasty stuff happening again, do you, Hamish boy?' Daphne said, bending down and patting him lavishly.

'Well, I think you're going to hear all about it, whether you want to or not,' said Sarah. 'Oh, not necessarily from me,' she clarified, as Daphne gave her an affronted look. 'But obviously Mariella has questions to ask you.'

Daphne looked at her daughter with mingled annoyance and affection. 'Well, fair enough, if you suspect, what do you call it? *"Foul play"*,' Daphne said, making ironic quote marks round the words as though she thought Sarah and Mariella were just getting carried away. 'I know it's good for you to get interesting cases, and I know Sarah wants to help you progress, but not everything's a murder, you know.'

Sarah and Mariella looked at each other. 'Well, unfortunately this looks very much like one,' said Mariella. 'Anyway, Mum, just to clarify – it's not your stuff in the bags outside?'

'I certainly didn't leave anything there,' Daphne shrugged.

'And Sarah, you didn't see anything, um, sharp left in the doorway?'

'A weapon, you mean?' Sarah asked Mariella. For the first time, it struck her how odd it was that she'd seen nothing of that kind. 'No, I'm sorry.'

'All right, then,' said Mariella. 'Well, if you've nothing else to add, Aunty Sarah?' She started putting her pen and notebook away.

'Well... just the girl's last words.'

'Last words?' Mariella's head shot up and she flipped her notebook open again, ready to write everything down. 'Tell me exactly what was said.'

'Well, the poor girl – she wasn't conscious when I got there. Then maybe she realised she was dying, I don't know. Anyway, she opened her eyes... they were so blue. And then she spoke.'

'What did she say?' Mariella asked gently.

'Her voice was very quiet. I had to lean right down towards her to hear her. That's how I got...' Sarah gestured to the rusty marks on her jumper.

'We'll need to bag that up,' said Mariella.

'Don't tell me that's blood!' shrieked Daphne.

'Yes of course. What did you think it was?' Sarah replied.

Daphne tutted. 'Well, keep your ghastly stains away from me, for goodness' sake. So? What on earth did the girl say?'

Sarah leant towards her friend. 'It was very odd. It was just one word. "Wit".'

'What?' asked Mariella.

'No, "*wit*",' corrected Sarah. 'Well, actually, come to think of it, it was "wits". Plural.'

'Wits,' said Mariella slowly, writing it down.

'Wits? Just that? What on earth does that mean?' Daphne looked thunderstruck. 'I thought you were going to say she'd told you why she was there, at the very least. I mean, in my shop doorway, of all places.'

'Well, sorry to disappoint you. It was just that word.' Sarah sat back again.

'OK,' said Mariella. 'So, definitely nothing else?'

'No,' said Sarah – though there was something niggling at her. She just couldn't quite remember what it was.

'I'll be off, then,' Mariella said, shutting her notebook for the second time and taking leave of the two ladies. 'You know where I am if you need me.'

Both assured her they did. Once the door had banged shut again, they were left looking at each other over the rims of their teacups.

Just then, a woman drifted into the pub in a floral dress and nodded to Daphne. A moment later, a curly-haired young man went and sat down with her. Sarah wondered if they'd heard the terrible news already. They had their heads close together and were murmuring in low voices.

She dragged herself back to the matter in hand. 'I wish I knew what that word meant,' she said, feeling exhausted all of a sudden. 'Wits.'

'Word? That's probably not even a whole word. It's more like a syllable.' Daphne took a sip of her drink.

'A syllable? That's an interesting idea. You think she might have meant, I don't know, Whitstable, maybe?'

Daphne spilt her tea down her front. 'Sarah, that's a brilliant idea! Whitstable is only a little way down the coast from here. She's bound to have meant that. You look done in, I vote we go home and rest now. But the moment you're feeling better, let's go there and see what we can find out.'

THREE

By the time Sarah and Daphne reconvened the next morning, Sarah was even less sure a trip to Whitstable was the right course of action. After a listless day and a sleepless night, she felt like a limp rag, not a dauntless investigator.

'We don't know what the poor girl meant at all, Daphne, or even if she really meant Whitstable. What are we going to do, wander up and down the high street there and ask people if they stabbed a girl yesterday morning?'

'You know, she could have just fallen on a knife, if she was even stabbed at all,' said Daphne mulishly. 'It doesn't have to be one of your grim murders.'

Sarah thought back to the blood seeping from the girl's chest. It was very hard to imagine any sort of accident that could possibly have led to such an injury.

'Well, if she fell, where is the knife?' Sarah asked. 'Because I didn't see it.'

'I don't know, maybe under one of those jumpers you were talking about,' said Daphne, throwing up her hands.

'There was nothing there,' said Sarah – but then she remembered that wasn't true. She'd found that blue card, and also a white piece of paper. She now fished them out of her handbag and looked at them. 'Drat, I can't believe I forgot to mention these to Mariella. Never mind, I'll do it as soon as I can. There won't be any proper forensic evidence to compromise, as that massive constable was clod-hopping all over it already.'

'What on earth have you got there?' asked Daphne, craning forward.

They both looked at the two objects. The card had been roughly torn in half. The shiny blue side was blank, but on the reverse was a telephone number. Next Sarah smoothed out the slip of paper. It looked like a till receipt, also a little torn and covered in boot prints. It was hard to make out the writing, particularly if you were a lady in her sixties who was slightly in denial about growing increasingly long-sighted, but she could make out a tiny design at the top, featuring a cute boat bobbing on some waves.

'What do you think this is?' she asked Daphne, handing her the paper.

'Looks like a bill for something... Does this say "sandwich"?' Daphne peered at the scruffy, smeared handwriting.

'Could be,' said Sarah doubtfully. 'I wonder if it's a restaurant receipt.' Then she looked at the minuscule writing printed at the bottom. 'Wait, look at that. Is this some sort of serial number?'

'CT5 something something something – the last bit is too blurry to read.' Daphne wrinkled her brow. Then her expression transformed into an ear-to-ear grin. 'You know what, Sarah? CT5 is a postcode – for Whitstable. I knew it, "*wits*" means Whitstable!' Daphne was triumphant. 'We should get going straight away.'

'But there must be loads of places where you can buy a sandwich in CT5.'

'Probably, but we'll never know which one this girl went to

unless we try and find it,' said Daphne. 'We'll just make some discreet enquiries.'

Sarah raised her brows. She knew how Daphne conducted herself during an investigation, and she was about as subtle as a two-ton sledgehammer in pink fluffy mules. Still, looking into the poor girl's death would make Sarah feel she was doing something useful. The police might well think they had everything in hand – and Mariella was bound to tell them both not to interfere – but the authorities in Merstairs could do with all the help they could get. Mariella was highly competent, but those two constables seemed as bumbling as ever, and the fact that the detective in charge of the station favoured them over Daphne's daughter said all you needed to know about him.

She couldn't bear to think of that unfortunate girl, little more than a child, bleeding out on Daphne's shop doorstep, and no one being held accountable for the crime. Well, it wouldn't happen on her watch.

FOUR

In no time at all they had jumped into Sarah's trusty Volvo and were speeding along the coast road with the windows down, while the ends of Daphne's pink scarf fluttered this way and that in the delicious sea breeze.

Hamish, on the back seat in his comfy harness, tilted his head to one side thoughtfully. If he'd been a betting dog, he'd have said that the chip lady's scarf was going to hit the floor... around now. There was a slither of pink and a loud wail from Daphne. Hamish sat back and, in the mirror, Sarah saw what looked very much like a satisfied grin on his dear little doggy face.

'Oh, drat this thing,' said Daphne, bending with some difficulty, the seatbelt cutting into her generous midsection as she fished around her feet for the slippery silk.

'Maybe leave that for when we get there,' said Sarah. 'It'll only fall off again and it would be a shame to shut the windows on such a lovely day. Listen, I know you're upset about what's happened, and you hate the idea that there's been another, um, murder,' she said carefully.

'I don't know how you can be so relaxed about it,' Daphne wailed.

'I'm not,' Sarah said. 'But anyone would think it was you, not me, who'd discovered that poor girl.'

'I suppose it's what comes of being a professional,' Daphne sniffed.

'Well, my profession isn't finding bodies, that's for sure,' said Sarah, feeling a little irked with her dear friend. 'And it was ghastly, if you must know.' The discovery of that dying waif had brought back all the pathos of her husband's deathbed, and reminded her of the many other times when, despite her expertise as a GP, she had been unable to save a patient.

Daphne sighed almost as gustily as Hamish. 'All right. That was unfair of me. I know there's a lot going on behind that calm exterior of yours. But it's just such a shame all this is happening again.'

'I agree with you there,' said Sarah. 'That's why I think it's so important to try and help... But let's think about cheerier things. Mariella seems to be getting on so well with the police. You must be thrilled.'

It was the right thing to say. Although it could be a dangerous job, and would bring Mariella into prolonged contact with so many of the issues her mother could hardly bear to contemplate, Daphne's pride at her clever daughter's progress outweighed any misgivings. 'She thinks it really won't be long before she's out of uniform,' she confided.

'That's splendid news,' said Sarah. 'Hopefully we can root out something on this trip that will help her with this case... Just think, Daphne, that could be a real boost for her career.'

'Yes. Yes, let's hope so,' said Daphne, turning to stare out of the window. They were just coming to the outskirts of Whitstable now. On Sarah's right was a flourishing caravan park, while on the left there was a dark blue sign for a new luxury hotel.

'OK, the search is on for a parking spot,' Sarah said, looking from left to right as they drove slowly down the picturesque winding streets leading towards the sea. 'Then we need a plan.'

'Oh, we'll just have a wander, shall we, and see what leaps out?' said Daphne, craning from the window. 'Look, there's a shop with dreamcatchers in the window. We must pop in there.'

'Hmm. We're not on a shopping trip, you know, Daph,' said Sarah. 'We're looking for a sandwich place in CT5, with a boat logo. Hopefully the restaurant can then tell us a bit more about our poor victim – or even the murderer.'

'Well, I dare say we'll have to pass a shop or two while we're doing that,' said Daphne. 'And it won't hurt to nip in if we want to. Wouldn't it be lovely if someone just came up to us on the high street and said, "I did it, it's a fair cop"?'

Sarah smiled. 'I bet that's Mariella's colleagues' game plan.'

'Dumbarton and Deeside?' Daphne shuddered. 'I asked Mari to get them round to my place... I thought it would really help them if I did a quick reading, sorted out some of their misaligned energy streams. But she said they simply don't believe in that sort of thing,' she said in astonishment.

Sarah could see both sides of this particular problem and decided that an understanding nod was the best response. 'Ah, there's a space.'

With a bit of careful manoeuvring, and some helpful yips from Hamish, Sarah finally shoehorned her car into the tiny space between an SUV and a fancy BMW. Judging from the cars on this street alone, it looked as though Whitstable was even more upmarket than Merstairs.

'Let's look on the bright side, Sarah,' said Daphne determinedly. 'Even if we came here for a pretty grim reason, a change of scene can still be a tonic. Besides, it's nearly time for lunch,' she added, while Sarah locked up the car and put Hamish on his lead.

They were soon strolling up the high street, admiring the

pretty pastel-painted façades of the shops with their jolly striped awnings. There was everything on sale here, from chi-chi homewares to covetable fashions. Daphne stood, entranced, in front of a traditional sweet shop selling pear drops and aniseed balls from huge old-fashioned jars, while Sarah scanned the shopfronts for sandwich places and boat signs. But even she couldn't help checking out a lovely toyshop full of all kinds of handmade doll's house furniture that would be perfect for her little grandchildren.

'I have to admit, this is really charming,' said Sarah, gazing up and down the street.

'Isn't it lovely? Of course I prefer Merstairs,' Daphne said, ever loyal to her home town. Then she stopped abruptly and gasped aloud. 'Oh! Just look at that, Sarah!'

For a second, Sarah's heart leapt. Had her friend spotted something crucial? 'Is it the ship logo, Daphne?' she asked breathlessly.

'What?' Daphne looked round at her friend, surprised. 'Oh, no – but Pat from the book group said this is a great place to eat.' With that, she dived into the turquoise-painted interior of a little café.

Sarah was left standing on the pavement, tutting. If they were going anywhere for lunch, it should be the place the receipt came from. Surely Daphne saw that? Also, having had a run-in with Daphne's chum Pat not so long ago, she wasn't sure she totally trusted her suggestions. But there were a few seats outside, which meant the place was dog-friendly... and it was a gorgeous sunny day. There were certainly some very tempting aromas drifting out onto the pavement. Hamish put a paw on Sarah's leg as if to endorse the idea.

'Oh, all right then, boy. I'll just tie you up here, then, and Daphne and I will grab a quick bite to eat. I won't be a second.'

Hamish, while not thrilled at being left outside, decided it wasn't worth making a big fuss. He curled up peaceably on the nice warm pavement and enjoyed the feel of the sun's rays stroking his tufty black fur. Suddenly he opened one eye again. An irresistible scent of lady dog was wafting down the street towards him. Then he heard a tappety-tap of little paws and a familiar set of pins appeared in front of him. His heart fluttered and he sat up. There was only one pooch he knew who could sport a diamante collar with such élan. His pink tongue unfurled of its own volition and he panted like a chap who'd walked through burning deserts and was now presented with a tall glass of cool water.

Charles Diggory bent down from his great height and secured his Chihuahua, Tinkerbell, to the chair leg next to Hamish's. It wasn't easy, sharing custody of the animal with his ex, former mayor of Merstairs Francesca – not least because she had a tendency to dress the creature up on the days when he was taking her out. Today Tinkerbell was wearing a miniature T-shirt in shrieking pink with the words 'Boy Toy' emblazoned across it in rhinestones. It made no sense, as Francesca's own style was strictly tweedy with Princess Anne-style scarves clamped under her chin. He would have taken the outfit off before coming out, but Tinkerbell wasn't above giving him the odd nip. Now he patted the tiny dog on the head. 'You play nicely, now,' he said, then turned to Hamish and gave him a stroke. 'Hello there, boy. I'll just pop in and see where your mistress has got to.'

Hamish put his head on one side, in a position that Sarah had assured him was extremely cute, but Tinkerbell took one look and turned her back on him, sitting up straight on her matchstick legs. Hamish sighed gustily and rested his head on his tufty paws. She was playing hard to get, but he'd win her over in the end. He just knew it.

FIVE

The meeting in the café was somewhat awkward, partly because the place was little more than a corridor, but mostly because Sarah really wasn't expecting Charles to appear, with that languid look in his blue eyes. With everyone simultaneously saying their hellos, perusing the menu and making an order, it soon became claustrophobic. Sarah was glad to get outside again and take her glass of sparkling mineral water over to their table on the pavement.

When she sat down, her cheeks were rather pink – from the heat inside the café, she told herself determinedly, and *definitely* not from close proximity to Charles. Hamish barely glanced her way. He was lying with his head on his paws, gazing soulfully at Tinkerbell's trim back view. The reverse of her hideous little T-shirt said 'Toy Boy?' in diamante and Hamish looked as though he'd put in a very earnest application for the post and been summarily rejected. Sarah wondered about Charles's taste. His own clothes were always immaculate, but he seemed to go quite potty when dressing his dog. And why on earth did the creature need garments anyway?

Daphne bustled out next. 'Isn't this just marvellous? And

wonderful to bump into Charles like that. Though I hear you've been, er, bumping into each other quite regularly?'

Sarah blushed even more furiously. Really, she thought, fanning her hot face, global warming was a terrible thing. 'I don't know what you mean,' she protested. 'Unless it's walking the dogs? We've occasionally been on the beach at the same time...'

Charles's emergence from the café put paid to that discussion. He sat down on the third chair, arranged his long legs in their fine linen trousers to his satisfaction, and smiled at the two women. 'So, what brings you to Whitstable on this lovely day?'

'We could ask you the same question,' said Daphne a little archly.

'Or we could just tell you that something else has happened, something that's just so awful you really won't believe it,' Sarah rushed in.

Charles looked from one to the other. 'I'm just here to scout for antiques for the shop. No secret there. But what on earth do you mean? Are you all right?' He bent towards Sarah, then realised what he was doing and included Daphne in the gesture. 'Both of you, I mean.'

'Thank you,' said Sarah, looking down at her lap. 'I'm, we're fine. There was an incident... It was... a bit distressing.' Suddenly she felt her face crumple.

Up until the moment she'd come out with that, she hadn't realised what a toll the whole thing had taken on her. It had been so sad, so awful, to hold that poor creature as she took her last breath. She'd tried her best at the time, but she still heartily wished she could turn back the clock and do something more positive for the girl. More pressure on the wound, a faster call to the emergency services... In her heart of hearts, though, she knew she'd done everything possible, and it was just a sense of helplessness making her doubt her actions. She almost wished she hadn't been going to clean Daphne's shop at all – but then that woebegone child would have died alone, which would surely have been worse. At least the girl had breathed her last with concerned arms around her.

Wordlessly, Charles handed Sarah one of his beautifully starched handkerchiefs and she raised it to her eyes, this time scarcely even bothering to note the embroidered monogram entwining his initials with Francesca's. He really ought to update his hanky drawer.

This thought served to pull her out of an emotional tailspin, and she was grateful, too, when a waitress came out loaded with plates for them. Once everyone was settled with the sandwich of their choice – egg salad for Sarah, roast beef for Charles and tuna mayo for Daphne, with a large order of chips for the table – she felt bold enough to continue.

'Sorry about that. It was, well, it was a bit of a facer. I'd decided to spring-clean Tarot and Tealeaves—'

'Excellent idea, it could do with a spruce-up,' said Charles, at the exact moment that Daphne shook her earrings emphatically and said, 'For the record, against my wishes!'

Everyone was silent for a beat, then Sarah continued. 'As I was saying, I got there and then saw a girl on the doorstep. Well, not at first, I just thought it was a lot of abandoned clothes. She was in a bad way.' Sarah looked down again, remembering the pallor, the fast and thready pulse. 'The worst thing was that there was so little I could do.'

'At least you were there,' said Daphne kindly. 'That must have been a comfort.'

'Thanks, Daphne.' Sarah gave her a small smile and drew a breath. 'Then, at the end, she was struggling so much to tell me something, and then she just, well, died. I feel awful that it means nothing, really. Because here we are in Whitstable, and there hasn't been anything that's clicked.'

'Not yet, anyway,' said Daphne. 'Maybe after lunch it will.' She took a huge bite of her sandwich and, as Hamish had hoped, a chunk of tuna fell out and hit the floor. Before he could get to it, though, a tiny paw had reached out and scooped it up. A second later, Tinkerbell was looking very smug. Now it was Hamish's turn to present his back view. That tuna had had his name on it. Love was one thing – food was quite another.

'Wait a minute,' said Charles, looking at Sarah. 'This is awful. I was in Margate all yesterday, I got back late. I haven't heard a word about all this. And do you mean to tell me the dying girl said, "Whitstable"?'

'Well, no, not exactly,' said Sarah, toying with her egg sandwich. 'She just said, "Wits".'

'*Wits*? I wonder what on earth she meant by that.'

'It was heartbreaking. She was so hoping I would understand. The look she gave me... it was sort of beseeching... and then, well.'

'All right, all right, she died,' said Daphne. 'Let's not labour the point. The thing is to concentrate on solving that clue. "Wits" has surely got to mean Whitstable, hasn't it?'

'But nobody shortens it, do they? I've never heard it called "Whits",' said Charles.

'Perhaps she didn't have enough breath left for the whole word,' Sarah shrugged. Though nothing was leaping out in this pretty little street as an obvious reason to murder someone. Rather the reverse, it couldn't have been more charming if it had tried for years.

'OK,' said Charles, very much as though he was humouring Sarah. 'Well, I vote we finish our lunch, then go for a wander, and maybe, you're right, something will strike us.'

'Oh, but we do have something else to go on,' Sarah said, remembering the snippets she'd picked up. She fished the card and the paper out of her pocket. 'We think this is a sandwich receipt,' she said, spreading out the slip.

Charles puzzled over it, then picked it up. 'Um, I don't want to be a spoilsport, but shouldn't this be with the police?'

Sarah looked a little shamefaced. 'Well, they were both stuck under one of those constables' shoes. And I forgot to mention it to Mariella. The thing is we're here now, we might as well just see if we can find the place. We should look out for this,' she said, pointing the boat out to Charles.

'All right. On your own head be it,' said Charles, with a mock-strict expression. 'Perhaps we should get a move on before I get cold feet.'

Hamish, sitting by Daphne's chair, and ever hopeful that a second dollop of tuna would make its way straight to him this time, was disappointed that lunch seemed to be over without another crumb coming his way. He got up cheerfully enough, though, when Sarah leant down to ruffle the tufty fur on the top of his head and explained they were off. Tinkerbell, he noticed, got quite different treatment. Charles didn't bother to speak to her, but just scooped her up and popped her under his arm.

'That's a great way to carry her, Charles,' Daphne said approvingly. 'And even better, we can't see her dreadful outfit like that,' she added, with one of her trademark laughs that started way down in her purple sandals.

Sarah shook her head as she left a little tip under her plate for the girl clearing the dishes. 'Now then, which way shall we go?'

'Let's carry on down here. This is the main street for restaurants and bars,' said Charles.

It was hard to keep Daphne on track – a couple of times Sarah and Charles peered into likely-looking places only to find she'd disappeared into a shop selling crystals or wind chimes – but they had soon covered most of the street. None of the eateries had 'boat' in their names, much less on their receipts.

'This is the last place,' sighed Sarah, looking at the sign swinging in the fresh breeze. It depicted a seagull, and the place was called the Sailor's Rest. 'There's no chance, is there?' she said wearily.

'We won't know until we've tried,' said Charles. 'Come on, let's give it a go. Daphne, could you just hold the dogs' leads for a second?'

Daphne seemed to weigh up a grumpy response, but realised she could spend the time gazing happily into a home-wares store so held out her hand for the two leashes. Sarah gave them to her with a smile.

Inside the Sailor's Rest, the lunchtime rush was over and a waitress was spritzing and wiping down the tables, watched by a slightly dour woman in her forties. She put on a mega-watt smile when Charles and Sarah approached, which dimmed when she heard what they were after.

'Are you kidding me? Of course we've had young people in here eating sandwiches – what kind of place would it be if we hadn't?'

'You're right,' said Sarah. 'This is pointless. The place we want has a boat logo on its receipts, anyway,' she shrugged.

The effect on the woman was electrifying.

'Like this, you mean?' the woman said, taking a receipt out of the pile in front of her and shoving it across the counter to Sarah and Charles. 'We've only just changed our name.'

'Look! It's identical,' said Sarah. 'That's amazing. Did you see a young girl, a few days ago, blonde hair, in her early twenties...'

'Yes. I've said. We see people like that every day. Don't you remember anything else about her? Anything distinctive?'

Sarah thought back. It was so hard. The poor girl had been so swathed in old clothes, and had hardly been at her best... 'Well, she had very blue eyes.'

'Like half the UK population,' sniffed the woman.

'Her hair was a bit like yours, a lovely dark blonde,' Sarah added desperately.

'Riiight,' the woman said, starting to look very fed up.

'And there was another thing, if I could just remember...

give me a minute,' Sarah said, gritting her teeth as Charles looked on, bemused. She gazed at the woman again, hoping for understanding... and her eye snagged on the chunky silver necklace she was wearing. 'That's it! She had a chain on.'

'Oh, well in that case...' the woman said, then as Sarah looked hopeful, she added, 'no, obviously that means nothing.'

'Just a second. It was gold, it was a delicate chain, it was something religious, Catholic... that's right, it was a crucifix. In two colours, rose gold and silver. I remember thinking I hadn't seen one like that before.'

'Well, it doesn't ring a single bell. Sorry about that,' the woman said, with an on-off smile that suggested her patience had run out. 'Got to serve my customers,' she said, indicating two holidaymakers who'd strayed in for a coffee.

'Can I ask your staff member?' Sarah said, pointing to the girl cleaning tables.

'Knock yourself out,' the woman said with a shrug.

But the story was the same with the teenager. She was happy enough to break off from her task but could shed no light on customers with necklaces and big blue eyes. 'We're quite busy, you see,' she said, scurrying off to get menus for the new arrivals.

'Well, that was a damp squib,' said Sarah, when they were outside again and had relieved Daphne of her dog-sitting responsibilities.

'In one way, perhaps – but Sarah did come up with more detail on the girl's description – she was wearing a crucifix,' Charles said to Daphne.

'Unusual,' said Daphne. 'Most people are attuning to the universe these days,' she said, with a mystical look in her eye. 'Let's go and sit by the sea, now. It's just up this way. Don't worry, Sarah, we'll reach enlightenment soon, I feel it in my bones.'

Daphne strode off, with Tinkerbell and Charles at her

heels. Sarah followed more slowly, feeling she was missing something vital, but no matter how hard she tried, she couldn't quite think of it. Hamish looked up at her, begging her to pick up the pace. His lady-love was halfway to the beach. There was really no excuse for dawdling.

SIX

Although the Whitstable coastline was every bit as pretty as that of Merstairs down the road, with wide blue skies rolling as far the eye could see and waves bobbing up to meet them, there was one thing that was in precious short supply on the shingle beach. Answers.

The little trio stood in a clump while the dogs frolicked at the edge of the sea. Then Tinkerbell slipped on the stones and fell in. Hamish grabbed her by the scruff of her neck and brought her back, shaking droplets everywhere.

'Eww! Well, thanks very much, Hamish,' shrieked Daphne, brushing down her raspberry-coloured tunic. Sarah tried to look sternly at her dog, but he seemed so crestfallen that she couldn't resist a loving pat. He was getting the cold paw again from Tinkerbell, who was quivering even more than usual in Charles's arms and whimpering in a very weedy fashion, given that it was all her own fault in the first place.

'Let's move a bit higher up the beach and sit on one of those benches,' said Sarah practically. 'The dogs can dry out and we can keep on thinking what to do about this poor girl. At least we know she really was here, I suppose.'

'Yes, but who isn't?' said Charles, gesturing at the packed beach, full of tourists scrunching up and down on the area's distinctive stony beach. His shirt was now pretty damp from Tinkerbell burrowing under his arms to keep warm. He tried to put her down but she refused to unfurl her tiny legs and take her own weight. Really, she was the most absurd creature, Sarah found herself thinking. She patted Hamish fondly again. He'd saved Tinkerbell from being dragged out to sea, and he wasn't getting a word of thanks. Well, she decided to put that right.

'You were very brave in the sea, Hamish,' she said, smoothing his ears.

Then Daphne joined in, having apparently forgiven the dog for her drenching. 'You were a good boy, Haims, saving that little rat from the water,' she crooned loudly.

Charles coughed but, before he could say a thing, Daphne's mobile rang. After delving in her bag for what seemed an age, while her *Twilight Zone* ringtone blasted out at top volume, she finally found it and strode off down the beach to answer the call.

'It could be a client,' she said importantly over her shoulder.

Meanwhile Charles attempted to put Tinkerbell down again, but she was hanging on like a bushbaby in a storm. He sighed and looked rather bleakly out to sea. 'Isn't all this a bit of a waste of time?'

It was Sarah's turn to feel tetchy. 'Well, do you have a better idea? The poor girl's last word was "wits". It must mean Whitstable, mustn't it? Given that it's so near to Merstairs.'

'Well, no, I don't agree. It could mean anything. It could just be her mispronouncing *wits*, maybe she meant, *what's* – as in, "What's the matter with me?"'

'Maybe,' Sarah conceded unwillingly. 'That would be quite an odd accent, though.'

'She could have been South African,' Charles said. 'They

really clip their vowel sounds. I should know, Francesca has a lot of relatives from Cape Town.'

'But then, if *wits* was actually *what's*, that would be the start of a sentence... and it didn't feel like she was about to embark on a big speech,' said Sarah. 'She knew she was very ill, probably dying. The way she gathered all her strength... it was important to her, to get this one word out. And that word was *wits*.' She kicked at a pebble on the beach. 'I don't know, Charles. This is so hard. I want to do her justice, to honour that dying effort, to find out what she meant. It feels wrong just to dismiss it as something she mispronounced.'

'I understand,' said Charles, gazing out to sea. 'But *wits*... if she knew she was speaking her dying words, wouldn't she have tried to make them more understandable? That makes me think *what's* is still more likely.'

When Sarah didn't answer, he went on. 'So for now it's a toss-up between her saying "what" in an accent of some sort, or maybe referring to this place. And, even though we know she was here, we don't know what she was doing or why. So I know which alternative I prefer.'

'Right,' said Sarah quietly, hunching her shoulders a little. She would have liked him to agree with her, but she'd done her best to put her point across. Only time would tell which of them was right. She certainly wasn't going to agree with him for the sake of it. And if that was what he was expecting, he was doomed to disappointment – and they weren't compatible at all. Not that she thought they were, anyway, she hurried on with her thoughts.

They both sat in silence for a minute, as if mesmerised by the sight of the sea heaving up and down and sending the odd wave forward to lick the stones on the edge of the beach.

Then Sarah shook her head and snapped out of it. There was no earthly reason why they should be at daggers drawn over this. Neither of them really knew what had been in the girl's

mind when she'd spoken, and arguing about it was just ridiculous. She turned to Charles. 'Look—'

'Sarah—'

Charles had swivelled round to face her. Now they both
laughed.

'Sorry,' he said gently. 'That all got quite heated, I'm not
sure why. I've had a difficult morning, maybe that's it.'

'Oh dear,' said Sarah, instantly sympathetic, although she
doubted it would have been quite as harrowing as the last
couple of days had been for her. 'What's the matter?'

'I shouldn't bother you with it,' Charles said, eyes facing
front again.

'Well, if you don't want to...' Sarah shrugged her shoulders.

'Francesca is being tricky about the divorce,' Charles said
quickly – just as Daphne lolloped back to the bench and
flumped down in between them, looking pale and shaken.

'You'll never guess what I've just managed to find out,' she
said, looking somehow several years older. 'Only the name of
the poor victim.'

SEVEN

Instantly, Sarah put the interesting matter of Charles's divorce to one side. 'You've found out the girl's name? Goodness, Daphne. How?'

'It was Mariella on the phone,' Daphne explained.

Sarah was glad the poor thing had been identified – even though it must mean that a family somewhere must have had its happiness shattered forever. 'So who is she?' she asked. 'And should Mariella be telling you? Actually, forget I said that,' she added quickly.

The Met police officers she'd encountered over the years in London had been as tight-lipped as any of the oysters Whitstable was famous for, but Mariella's candour was definitely to their advantage. And in a place like Merstairs, the news would always get out somehow. Someone could sneeze in the morning by the clock tower and, by evening, everyone on the crazy golf course would know they had flu.

'Honestly, Sarah, you know Mari is the soul of discretion,' said Daphne, flapping her hand to bat away any suggestions to the contrary. 'I've lost count of the number of people who've told me so. Anyway, that's not important. The dead girl... it's only Abi Moffat!'

With this, Daphne clasped her hands to her mouth, her eyes as wide as saucers above her fingers. She was obviously expecting an enormous reaction from Sarah and Charles, who carried on sitting there, a bit stumped. Then a change crept over Charles's face.

'Hang on, no! Abi Moffat? You mean... *Miss Moffat?*' The colour drained from his cheeks and his mouth worked in distress. Sarah was still none the wiser and was now feeling distinctly out of the loop.

'Who on earth is Abi Moffat?'

'Miss Moffat. Hell's bells,' said Charles, still miles away.

'Charles! Don't say hell and Abi in the same sentence,' Daphne hissed. 'If there's one thing I know, it's that girl has gone straight to heaven. She was just the nicest, kindest...'

'The sweetest...' Charles picked up the thread as Daphne started to cry. 'Most caring.' He twisted his linen handkerchief between his long fingers, and looked very much as though he might break down too.

'She was obviously very special,' Sarah said gently. 'How do you both know her?'

'She was in charge of the reception class at Merstairs Primary,' sniffed Daphne. 'Mari is friends with her big sister, Veronica. They were at school together. And their mum, Jennie, works in the Seagull Bakery.'

Sarah wasn't familiar with the local schools, but she certainly knew the bakery. It was famous for its buttery croissants and delicious sourdough bread, and was one of the many reasons she might possibly have put on a pound or two since moving to Merstairs.

'Abi teaches – taught – my grandchildren, Calista and Max,' Charles said, still sounding stunned. 'She was so patient, just a dream teacher, really. She knew all their names after the first day, and really made the twins feel welcome. Francesca was so resistant to them going to the local school – she felt they needed the individual attention they'd get at a private place. But our daughter, Arabella, was adamant. She's separated from her husband, Piers. And even though he's as rich as Croesus, he's been very difficult about the settlement. She said the twins might as well get used to it and, do you know, they've actually thrived there.'

Charles seemed astonished at the thought. Sarah, whose own daughters Becca and Hattie had both shone at their local inner-city comprehensive school, suppressed a bit of a tut. It was also the first time she'd heard anything much about Charles's daughter, and she tucked the information away to consider later. The girl seemed practical, at least, which was something she always approved of.

'Abi sounds marvellous. What a horrific thing to have happened. And why would anyone want to kill such a lovely girl?'

'You're really sure it was murder, are you?' said Charles, raising his eyebrows at her. 'I didn't doubt it before, but I just can't understand how anyone would do this to Miss Moffat.'

Sarah considered the matter. It was hard to see a motive for killing such a popular teacher. And admittedly she hadn't been able to investigate the wound as thoroughly as she would have liked. But what could have caused it, apart from a human hand with malign intent?

'I'm sure,' she said. 'Daphne, what did Mariella say about it?'

'She said it was a stabbing,' she confirmed, stifling a sob. 'Some weird kind of puncture wound, but they don't know what caused it. Who could have done such a wicked thing?'

Sarah sighed. It was desperately sad. 'I can't sit by, having seen Abi die like that. I have to try and help find the killer and get them to justice. But I'll understand if this feels a bit close to home, and you two don't want to get mixed up in the whole business.'

'Are you kidding?' said Daphne, looking at her friend in amazement. 'Normally I don't want to touch stuff like this with a barge pole, you know me, Sarah. But this time of course I'm involved. And you too, Charles, surely? We can't just sit by while someone like Abi is bumped off. It isn't right. This is our grandchildren's beloved teacher we're talking about. We need to stop this sort of thing happening in Merstairs, once and for all, and the sooner we get our hands on the person who did this...' Daphne held her arms out in front of her and mimed throttling someone, which Sarah didn't think was a good look. Neither, apparently, did Charles.

'Easy, tiger,' he said, putting a hand on Daphne's sleeve to restrain her a little. 'I think we need to be a little careful – certainly no "eye for an eye" stuff. We're not vigilantes, Daphne my dear.'

'Aren't we? Well, maybe we should be. I'm not one for violence, of course, but I must say I'd like to get to grips with whoever did this...'

'Yes, yes, we know,' said Charles again. 'Hopefully we'll get to the bottom of this quickly – and then whoever perpetrated this evil crime will be put behind bars for a thousand years, where they belong,' he added.

Sarah looked at both her friends in surprise. Feelings were running high on the bench, amongst civilised beings. Goodness knew what would happen in Merstairs proper, when the news got out. People would be rightly furious that a lovely young girl, a lynchpin of the community, had been senselessly killed right on their doorsteps. The faster Sarah and her friends found the perpetrator, the better – for Abi's family, and for Merstairs as a whole.

EIGHT

The knowledge that it was Abi Moffat who'd died cast a pall over proceedings. Sarah sat on the bench, between her down-cast friends, and tried to think of anything that might either cheer them up or push their search onward. It was getting chilly. She shook her head and buried her hands in her pockets. Her fingers closed over the restaurant receipt, which had got them exactly nowhere – and something else. She drew her hand out. Clutched in it was the navy blue card with the ripped top which had also been with Abi.

'Wait a minute, you two. This number... Do you think it's worth me ringing it? I found it with the receipt.'

'You mean you've had that all along and not said anything?' Charles was aghast.

'Well, we were following up on the receipt first, it seemed a bit more of a lead.' Sarah couldn't help sounding defensive. 'Why, does this mean anything to you?'

'A random number on a card? No.'

Sarah wasn't loving this side of Charles. She stood up, and Hamish panted at her. 'Let's go up the beach a bit and we'll try the number,' she told him.

She crunched her way through the stones, marvelling at the difference between shingle and sand, and now less surprised Tinkerbell had come a cropper earlier. Manoeuvring on the slippery pebbles wasn't that easy. Once she was a few feet away from Charles and Daphne, she dialled.

'Wittes Hotel, how may I help you?' a seductive voice purred. Sarah almost dropped the phone.

'Sorry, *Wittes*, did you say?'

'Wittes Hotel, that's right,' the receptionist said again, her tone maybe a tad less welcoming.

'Thank you, wrong number,' said Sarah, and cut off the call. She rushed back to the bench, brandishing the card. 'You'll never believe it,' she said frantically. 'This card is only for a hotel called the Wittes.'

Charles and Daphne gazed at her dumbly, both still in their cocoon of grief for Abi. Then Charles's eyes widened. 'You don't mean...'

'Well, I think we should go and find out,' Sarah said, slinging her handbag onto her shoulder.

'Hang on a minute, find out what?' asked Daphne, rubbing her eyes.

'Whether there could be a clue at this Wittes Hotel that could tell us who killed Abi, and why, of course. Wits was Abi's last word, remember,' Sarah said. 'What are we waiting for?'

NINE

After biting her tongue as Daphne, Charles and both the dogs trudged back to the car, then took what seemed like an age to do up their seatbelts, Sarah buckled up in seconds flat and quickly turned the key in the ignition. Then she shoved the car into reverse, took off the handbrake – and shot backwards, hitting the car behind with a sickening crunch.

'Why on earth did you do that?' wailed Daphne. She'd been thrown back against her seat and was rubbing her neck. Sarah hoped she hadn't got whiplash. Charles, in the passenger seat, seemed unharmed, but turned to look at her with raised eyebrows. Sarah was already halfway out of the car door. The vehicle behind was a flashy and immaculately shiny dark green Jaguar, and she saw to her mortification that its bumper was badly mangled. Even worse, a red-faced man was clambering out onto the pavement, swinging his car keys and looking furious enough to burst. He stared at her with a malevolent gleam in his eye.

'For goodness' sake! I might have known it would be a blasted woman driver,' he growled, striding towards Sarah, who was in the road by her Volvo. 'What the heck did you think you were playing at?'

Sarah, who could almost see the steam coming out of his ears, took an involuntary step back – and got beeped at by a passing car for her pains.

'Now she wants to get herself run over! That's no way to get out of this mess, my good woman. I want your insurance details, pronto,' the man shouted.

Just then, Charles unfurled himself from the passenger seat. 'Goodness me. If it isn't Rollo,' he said, with every appearance of delight. 'What brings you to Whitstable, old boy?'

The man paused, his face morphing comically from anger to disbelief. 'Old Digger Diggory. Well, I'm blessed. Washed up in this area, have you?'

Within seconds, the two men were embroiled in a round of hearty back-slapping, interspersed with obscure schoolboy insults. Sarah bent down to the car window and exchanged a grimace with Daphne. 'Are you OK? Does your neck hurt?'

'I'm fine,' mouthed Daphne, but Hamish, seeing his mistress and not enjoying being cooped up in the car, whined to come out. Sarah opened the door, undid his harness and led him over to the pavement.

The red-faced man, catching sight of Sarah and Hamish, slapped Charles on the shoulder. 'Digger, you dark horse, thought you were married to that uptight Francesca, what? Anyway, keep the new woman under control, would you? See the damage she's done to the old bus?'

'So sorry, Rollo, let me...' Charles started patting down his jacket pockets, as though about to flourish a chequebook and pay for the damages.

Rollo immediately waved him away. 'No, no, old man. Let's say no more about it. Just don't let the little lady drive again, eh?' He nudged Charles and laughed heartily, they both said they must meet up soon, and with that the man got back into his car and zoomed off, his bumper looking decidedly the worse for wear.

'Good grief, who was that dreadful man?' said Sarah, furious at being called a 'little lady' and equally annoyed that Charles had apparently really enjoyed the encounter.

Charles grabbed her arm and said out of the corner of his mouth, 'Rollo Wentworth. Schoolfriend, and I mean that in the loosest possible way, though I did spend a bit of time with him in the holidays now and again. Look, here he comes again. Just keep smiling!'

Sarah obediently fixed a rictus grin on her face and the shiny Jaguar sped past them for a second time. 'What on earth is he doing?'

'Oh, I think it's some sort of victory lap,' said Charles, dropping her arm as the car vanished round the corner. 'Ghastly man. I can't believe how well he's done. He's absolutely loaded. But of course he had pots of money to start with. I think his father made sausage rolls or something,' he added with the inbuilt snobbery of the landed classes. 'Anyway, your car looks fine, so shall we make a move?'

Sarah, blessing the fact that her beloved runaround was made of sterner stuff than a top-of-the-range Jaguar, but feeling a tad bereft now that Charles's arm had been removed, secured Hamish in the back. Then she got into the driving seat in silence.

Daphne, meanwhile, was agog at developments. 'Who *was* that chap, Charles?'

Charles shook his head as Sarah eased off the handbrake. 'We were at school together. He's a hotel tycoon now, I believe.' Then, just as Sarah was pulling out of the parking space, he yelled out, 'Oh my goodness!'

For the second time that afternoon, there was the horrible sound of gears grating against each other. The car lurched forward, though this time thankfully Sarah didn't hit anything. 'What?' she spluttered, as soon as she'd turned the ignition off.

'I say, Sarah, are you feeling all right? Your driving's all over the place today,' said Daphne.

Sarah gave Daphne a very stern look via the driving mirror, but her friend was blithely unaware, as she was patting Hamish.

Meanwhile, Charles was smacking his forehead with his palm. 'Wittes!' he kept saying.

'Charles, what on earth are you doing? You'll hurt yourself,' Sarah remonstrated.

Charles turned to her. 'I've just realised. Rollo owns the Wittes Hotel.'

'You're kidding!' piped up Daphne from the back seat. 'Well, let's get a move on, then. If you can get the car into gear, that is, Sarah!'

TEN

The Wittes Hotel was about equidistant between Whitstable and Merstairs and, once they had pulled up in the car park, Sarah couldn't understand how she had driven straight past it before. The signage was in the same luxurious dark blue as Abi's card. Below the name, there was a list of amenities, including a spa, golf course, tennis courts and fitness centre.

'Right, well, here we are,' said Sarah, as they all got out of the car, leaving Tinkerbell asleep on the back seat with the window open. It wasn't a hot day so she'd be fine. 'What sort of connection do we think Abi had to this place?'

'Let's ask a higher power,' said Daphne, getting that faraway look in her eye again.

'Or, alternatively, we could go through everything we know so far,' said Sarah in matter-of-fact tones. 'Abi was a teacher, she was well liked—'

'Loved,' chorused Daphne and Charles together.

'Yes,' said Sarah thoughtfully. 'But someone also hated her enough to kill her in Daphne's doorway. Sorry, Daph,' she added. 'We have to stick with the truth. She had a lunch receipt on her, and this card for the hotel.' She got it out of her pocket again. 'And that's pretty much it.'

'There'll be something here, I can just feel it,' said Daphne, closing her eyes again. 'I think we should just breeze on in and look around.'

'Trouble is, I do know the owner,' said Charles. 'And, having just seen Rollo for the first time in years, it's going to look a bit weird if I suddenly turn up, isn't it? Bad penny and all that.'

'I vote we say we're scoping the place out for a big occasion. Like your seventieth birthday, Sarah,' Daphne said excitedly.

'But that's not for ages! Well – quite a few years anyway,' said Sarah, blushing as she realised it wasn't as far away as she perhaps would have liked. 'What about *your* seventieth, Daphne?'

'Oh, no one would believe that,' said Daphne blithely, resettling her scarf around her ears.

Charles put his hand briefly on Sarah's arm, as she stared at Daphne. 'I'll just say Francesca's sent me to see about a venue for Arabella's birthday, or something, shall I?'

'Better not,' said Sarah crisply. 'I hardly think she'd back you up if anyone rang her to check. Not if what you were saying earlier is true,' she added pointedly. Now it was Charles's turn to blush. 'Maybe we should pretend we want to use the spa?'

It wasn't until someone coughed that they realised a stranger was in their midst. Sarah shot round to find a man standing right behind them in a dark blue uniform, matching the sign. He had a slightly amused look on his face.

'Can I help you, ladies and gentleman?'

Daphne stepped forward and Sarah inwardly braced herself. 'Yes, yes you can. We were just wondering if we could pop in and have afternoon tea here? I often have visitors and this would be a good way to see if your hotel might be a suitable place for them to stay.'

Sarah breathed out. Daphne had played her hand magnificently. She had come over with just the right touch of the grande dame, added to her usual warmth. Little did the man know that when anyone visited Daphne, they had to cram into the ramshackle spare room of her cottage with her extensive collection of garden gnomes, and usually had to sleep with Mephisto on top of them for good measure. And then Daphne spoke again.

'And, of course, this could be just the spot for my next séance.'

Immediately, the man's face became shuttered. 'You'd have to speak to the manager about that,' he said, in tones which suggested they'd be doing a roaring trade in ice creams in the underworld before such a thing came to pass. 'But if you'd like to join us just for the afternoon tea, I'm sure we can accommodate you.'

'Let's have it on the terrace,' said Charles airily.

'How do you know there's a terrace?' said Sarah in surprise.

'Knew this place before Rollo turned it into a hotel. It was his family's home, you know, for a while. Beautiful old pile, been here since before the time of the Cavaliers and Roundheads.'

As they turned the corner, leaving the uniformed man behind and seeing the house for the very first time, Sarah couldn't help gasping.

'It's such a beautiful building.'

The Elizabethan house, in mellow creamy stone, stretched in front of them. The façade was covered by Virginia creeper, which Sarah knew would turn to a flame red in the autumn. Even now, as they edged towards summer, its verdant green was a vivid contrast to the old stonework. To either side of the impressive entrance were low hedges, immaculately clipped and interspersed with rose bushes in velvety dark crimson.

'I wonder if we're really dressed for tea in a place like this?'

said Sarah. She'd felt quite fresh and pretty this morning – but that now seemed like quite a while ago. Hamish, enjoying his liberation from the back seat, jumped up at her and deposited a few more black hairs on her skirt, which didn't help matters.

'Nonsense, Sarah, you look fine, you honestly won't be letting us down at all,' said Daphne, settling her scarf more securely on her dyed locks and shouldering her lime patchwork handbag. 'People always say linen creases, but I've never found that myself,' she said, striding off in flapping trousers that looked as though they'd been used for origami.

Charles and Sarah shared another brief smile but Charles, Sarah noted, looked as immaculate as ever, his shirt as fresh as though it had been ironed only a moment before and his jacket unrumpled even after being folded up in the back of the car and sat upon by both dogs.

'You'd better go first,' Sarah whispered to him as they followed Daphne down the path to the house. 'You look the most respectable. And you know the owner.'

'Always happy to oblige, dear lady,' he said, crinkling his eyes at her. That smile, thought Sarah. It really was quite something.

But she wasn't as thrilled when he deployed it, to great effect, on the very attractive thirty-something lady at the reception desk a couple of minutes later. Immediately, the receptionist was eating out of his hand and leading them past the indoor tea room, where Sarah spotted a woman of about seventy-five in a beautiful floral dress. It was the lady from the pub yesterday, with the same curly-haired male companion.

'Why on earth would you tell her something like that?' the man was saying rather tetchily, while the woman sought to placate him. There was no time to ask if Daphne or Charles knew them, as the receptionist marched them onwards to the spacious terrace. In no time at all the little trio were seated, with Hamish slurping gratefully from his own bowl of water.

'This is quite the view, isn't it?' sighed Charles, stretching out his long legs.

Sarah wasn't quite sure whether he meant the rolling Kent countryside in front of them, or the receptionist walking swiftly away to order their teas.

'Oh, it's gorgeous,' said Daphne, every bit as at ease as Charles.

The sun was warm on the terrace, but not ferocious, and the easy chairs they were in were very comfortable. This really was the most pleasant spot. Sarah felt herself relaxing at last, only to bring herself up short. 'We can't let ourselves drift off like this. We're here to find out more about Abi Moffat.'

'Shh,' said Daphne, as an obliging young thing in a Wittes uniform unloaded their tea, and a plate of tempting-looking shortbread biscuits too.

'I must say, they have done everything very tastefully here,' said Charles, twisting his cup round to admire the gold band on its rim and the stripes of rich blue, which matched the signage and the livery of the staff. He busied himself pouring his Darjeeling tea, plopping a slice of lemon into his cup.

'Hmm,' sniffed Daphne. 'Bit boring, I think. Queen Elizabeth I would never have gone for that dull navy. She liked a big ruff, a bit of glitz. And I think red was more her colour,' she said, absently patting her own scarlet locks. 'But still, probably best to play it safe. That way nobody gets offended. What happened to this house after her reign? You were talking about Cavaliers, Charles. That's my favourite era. So romantic.'

Daphne had never paid much attention in history at school, Sarah remembered. The English Civil War had been a particularly bloody period of history, with the country bitterly divided between Catholic royalists and Protestant republicans. 'Terrible, all those families at odds with each other over religion. Very sad.'

'Yes, yes, awful. Of course the family here have always been

Catholic. But at that time people were switching faith almost as often as they changed underwear,' Charles drawled, taking a sip of his tea.

'So how did the family who lived here survive, if they stayed true to their religion?' Sarah asked.

'Simple. They hid in plain sight. They pretended to become Protestants but conducted Catholic masses in secret.'

'Really? How fascinating,' said Daphne. 'Did Rollo tell you all this?'

'Even better. When I used to come over in the school holidays, we would play in the old priest's hole, you know, a little secret room, left over from the times when the family would have to hide the padre, his Bible and all the paraphernalia for the mass.'

Sarah sat up, her cup clattering on its saucer as she hastily put it down. 'Oh my goodness! That's it. Don't you see?'

'See? See what?' said Daphne, raising a hand to her brow and searching the horizon like a lookout in the crow's nest of a ship.

'Not out there, Daphne. Inside – inside the house!' said Sarah. 'Abi was wearing a crucifix, don't forget. She was Catholic. And this is a Catholic house. There must be a connection. We have to find that priest's hole. Come on, you two!'

ELEVEN

'Well, I don't know, Sarah. It's a bit of a stretch, being killed over something in a country house hotel,' said Charles.

Sarah rounded on him. 'Do you have any better ideas? No? Well then, let's test my theory.'

'I suppose it's worth a try. OK, then,' said Charles, slurping down his tea.

'Do we have to go now? We haven't even finished the biscuits,' said Daphne. Hamish, too, was sitting close to the plate and looking at Sarah with huge eyes.

'Put one in your bag for later if you must,' said Sarah impatiently, while she picked up the dog and held him firmly under her arm.

Daphne needed no second invitation. She opened her patchwork bag and tipped the entire plate of shortbread into it, then shut it quickly and patted it in satisfaction. 'There. Good to go now,' she smiled.

Sarah just looked at her. 'I have no words,' she said. 'Right. Let's get to it.'

Back inside the hotel, and moving quietly to avoid attracting the attention of any of the diligent staff, Sarah, Daphne and

Charles found themselves in a lushly carpeted hall, not far from the reception area.

'I think... if we just go down this way...' Charles started loping along, beckoning to the others to follow. Just then, a woman in her twenties came round the corner, pushing a trolley laden with dirty dishes.

'Are you lost?' she said brightly. 'Reception is just down there,' she added with a smile.

'Oh, er, no, we were just looking for the library,' said Charles. 'Thinking of having a drinks reception there. Just wanted to check it out,' he added with a wink.

The girl giggled. 'Of course, sir. If you'll just follow the corridor, first left then straight ahead, you can't miss it.' With that, she wheeled her trolley in the direction of the kitchens.

Charles watched her go, then at a dry cough from Sarah, he plunged forward. 'Well, you heard the girl, it's this way.'

A few moments later they turned the corner and, up ahead, saw a set of impressive oak double doors.

'Aha, here it is,' said Charles. 'Hope it's not locked.'

But they were in luck. The doorknob, carved to resemble a lion's head, turned easily and Charles strode forward confidently into the room, Sarah and Daphne following behind. It was clearly the library, the walls lined with bookcases in wonderful burnished wood, filled with leather-bound volumes whose gold-tooled covers gleamed against red damask walls. But, before the women had got properly inside, Charles came to an abrupt standstill, and they both cannoned into the back of him. Sarah peered round him in surprise and found herself meeting the eyes of four bemused men, sitting at a long table. They were facing a small audience of what looked like sales representatives, all wearing name badges, clad in suits, and sporting eager expressions. Most of them were now craning round to look at the new arrivals.

'Aha,' said one of the men. 'This must be our keynote

speaker. You're very early... and the photo you sent must be from a couple of years ago?' He squinted at the brochure in front of him. 'Well, never mind, it's great that you're here. And these are, erm, your assistants?'

'Oh, er, right,' said Charles, to Sarah's horror. 'Yes, these are my... staff.'

What on earth was Charles playing at? Sarah looked at Daphne, who raised her eyebrows and shrugged very slightly. But Charles walked forward, sat himself down in the empty front row, and was now gesturing to them to join him.

'Won't interrupt you,' Charles said in a jocular tone. 'I'll just wait for my moment until I give my, er, speech.'

'Very good,' said the chairman, though looking a little surprised that Charles had brought not one but two assistants with him, and the blonde one appeared to be carrying a dog, of all things, while neither seemed to have any notes. He clearly decided to let it go and started speaking again. 'As I was saying, it's been a spectacular year for the industry. And it's largely thanks to all of you that we've done so well in challenging economic conditions. You'll be aware that the market position in some respects may be said to have slipped...'

Despite herself, and the very peculiar circumstances which had brought them there, Sarah felt her eyelids growing heavy. They'd been on their feet most of the day, and she had just eaten quite a lot of shortbread. Plus it was terribly stuffy in this room. Hamish, who was enjoying being on Sarah's lap, was very warm. As the pompous man at the top table kept on droning about his market reach, she couldn't help it, she began to drift off... Daphne, sitting next to her, felt Sarah's head drooping onto her shoulder and started feeling a little heavy-lidded herself.

Charles looked ruefully at his companions. He would have loved to have joined them in a little snooze. There was just the small matter of his keynote speech on who-knew-what keeping him awake.

A smattering of applause and then a dry cough from the chairman told Charles that the moment of truth had now come. Why on earth hadn't he just said, 'Wrong room!' when he'd first set foot in the library? But no, in his blessed arrogance he'd thought he could style this out... and now look where that supposition had led him...

When Charles got rather reluctantly to his feet, he inadvertently jogged Daphne, who in turn shifted and woke Sarah. So, by the time he was in position at the top table, taking a sip of water and nervously shuffling the papers he'd found in front of him on the table, he was being regarded with some interest not just by the audience of delegates but also Sarah and Daphne. Daphne was smiling seraphically, but Sarah's eyes were wide with anxiety. Charles gave her a pleading look and coughed to clear his throat. The chairman looked over to him with a 'What's the hold-up?' expression on his face.

'Ladies and, er, gentlemen,' Charles started reluctantly. 'We are gathered here today...'

At this point, Sarah shot to her feet and made for the door, leaving the surprised Daphne, and a roomful of murmuring audience members.

Charles straightened his papers yet again, before reluctantly starting to speak. 'As I was saying—' he began, and then an ear-splitting alarm shrilled out.

TWELVE

In the library, the company chairman looked at his colleagues anxiously. 'That's the fire alarm,' he said, getting up and addressing the audience. 'We weren't warned there would be a drill so it's safe to assume this is the real thing. If you'd just leave your belongings where they are, and form an orderly queue...'

But at the first mention of the word 'fire', the audience leapt to its feet. Within seconds it was pandemonium, with as much pushing and shoving as the first day of the Harrods sale.

Charles and Daphne stood looking at each other, taking shelter by one of the walls of books. Eventually, the scuffles died down and they were alone, with just a few overturned chairs and abandoned notebooks lying around.

'Shouldn't we be running to the fire exit too?' Daphne said, wild-eyed.

At that moment, Sarah sauntered back into the room. 'No need,' she said with a smile.

Charles laughed. 'You didn't!'

'I had to. I couldn't listen to your speech on... what were they even here to discuss?'

'Who knows?' shrugged Charles. 'But thank you. That was a very lucky escape. Well done.'

Daphne looked from one to the other. 'Will someone tell me what's going on?'

'I set off the alarm,' said Sarah. 'Two for the price of one – Charles is off the hook with his "keynote speech" and now we've got an empty room so we can search for this priest's hole. Now, let's not waste another second.'

'Ah yes,' Charles said slowly. 'If only I could remember where the deuce it was...' He turned around slowly, wrinkled his forehead... then shrugged. 'No. It's gone.'

'You're kidding!' said Sarah.

'Well, no,' said Charles. 'The whole idea was that they were secret rooms – otherwise they wouldn't have made great hiding places, would they?'

Sarah stared at him. 'So what on earth do we do now?'

'I've got it,' said Daphne happily. 'We can tap the panelling, like they do in the movies!'

'But there are hardly any panels, it's all bookshelves. Charles, do you seriously not remember where the entrance was?'

Charles scratched his head and looked blankly around him. 'I was probably about six, don't forget.'

'Come on, we don't have much time. Once the hotel people discover there's no fire, the conference delegates will be back in here and then you really will have to make a speech about widgets, or whatever they're selling.'

'All right, Sarah. That calming thought does nothing for my powers of recall,' said Charles a little tetchily. He put his hands to his head, clearly trying to think. 'God, I'm sorry, this place looks very different – and come to think of it, it was always Rollo who opened up the priest's hole.'

'But weren't you watching? You were in the room with him, I take it.'

'Again, not that helpful, Sarah.' Charles, looking weary, went over to stand by the mantlepiece. While it was made of marble, around it was an intricate carving of grapevines and musical instruments. It was very beautiful.

'Oh, come on now, Charlie boy,' said Daphne heartily. 'It's not like you to get in a state. Think back. Where were you when the hole opened?'

'I suppose I'd be around here, and Rollo would be...' Charles put his elbow on the mantlepiece, and his hand knocked a bunch of wooden grapes. Immediately, there was a grating noise – and a panel next to the fireplace popped open.

'The priest's hole!' said Sarah.

'I told you we should have tapped the panelling,' said Daphne, as they all rushed forward to peer into the space. 'I can't see a thing.'

'Wait a second,' said Sarah, grabbing her mobile. 'Let's all use our phone torches. See if we can't make things a bit brighter.'

They fiddled with their phones, Daphne in particular needing a helping hand to get the correct swiping motion, and then all three of them shone the beams into the dark, dark secret room that lay before them.

THIRTEEN

The priest's hole wasn't even really a room, more of a wardrobe-sized space. And, worst of all, it was filthy dirty and full of dust. Nevertheless, Sarah insisted they each clamber into it to have a proper look around. After a thorough inspection, there was no doubt. It did not contain the secret to Abi Moffat's death, unless that was somehow inextricably mixed up with a lot of spiders' webs.

'Well, that's a disappointment,' said Charles, brushing dust from his trousers.

'Yes,' said Sarah. 'No leads at all. And no religious element, either. I was expecting at least a gorgeous seventeenth-century chalice or something.'

Daphne was shaking her head, her scarf drooping deject-edly, when there was a noise from behind them. It was the company chairman, advancing upon them with a very cross look on his face.

'I think you lot have got some explaining to do,' he said, grit-ting his teeth. 'Our keynote speaker has just turned up! What's more, that fire evacuation was a false alarm, and the alert came from right outside this room. What do you have to say about that?' he said, directing his question straight at Sarah.

'Well, only one thing springs to mind,' said Sarah, grabbing Hamish as she strode towards the door out of the library, then taking Daphne by the arm and hauling her along too, dodging through the returning clumps of delegates. 'And that's – goodbye!'

'Yes,' said Charles, who was also beating a hasty retreat. 'And farewell from me too. Do enjoy the rest of your conference.' With that, he shut the door with a decisive snap and the three of them scurried down the corridor, dodging several blue-coated members of staff, one of whom turned to glare suspiciously at them.

'That was all quite exciting,' said Daphne breathlessly in the car park a few minutes later. 'Has it got us any further on, though?'

'I don't know,' said Sarah, unlocking the car and letting Hamish greet a still-sleepy Tinkerbell excitedly. 'But I vote we don't hang around discussing it, as it looks like the hotel manager might be coming out to have a word with us.'

No one needed telling a second time – in short order, they crammed themselves into the Volvo and were speeding off, crunching merrily over the gravel, before the cross-looking man in a dark blue suit could reach them. Sarah kept her foot on the accelerator until they were safely back on the Merstairs road.

'Phew, that really was a bit of a close one. What would you have done if I hadn't set the fire alarm off?' Sarah asked Charles.

'Simple. I was preparing to rehash the last keynote speech I gave.' Charles smiled.

'Really?' Sarah was surprised. 'What was that about, then?'

'Ah well,' chuckled Charles. 'It was to Tinkerbell, and I was just summing up a few behavioural changes I thought she might wish to consider... I would have adapted it to suit the occasion, obviously.'

'Obviously,' echoed Sarah drily, thinking it was a jolly good job she'd pressed that alarm when she had, though it had seriously gone against the grain for her to commit an offence like that. 'And we never found out what that conference was about, did we?'

'Oh, I spotted a sign on the way out. As we were running past it,' said Daphne excitedly. 'You'll never guess what they specialised in.'

'Just tell us, Daphne, I can't play any more games today,' said Sarah, concentrating on the road ahead.

'You'll love this,' her friend said, already starting to chuckle. 'They were only a fire safety company.'

Sarah, remembering the pushing and shoving which had broken out as soon as the siren had begun to shrill, couldn't help herself. She started to giggle, and before she knew it, Charles and Daphne had joined in.

By the time they drew up outside the Jolly Roger in Merstairs, Sarah's stomach muscles were aching from all the laughter, and tears of mirth were streaming from her eyes.

But then something happened that wiped the merriment away in an instant. She caught sight of the wreaths piling up in the doorway of Daphne's under-used shop, Tarot and Tealeaves. There was even a makeshift shrine, with candles arranged in a heart shape around a photo of the dead girl. The little flames flickered in the breeze.

Sarah parked the car and walked along the street as though on automatic pilot.

'Where are you going?' Daphne called, and Charles shrugged his shoulders when she just kept on walking.

When she reached Daphne's shop doorway, she knelt down, looking at a rather blurry photograph of a cheerful, pretty blonde girl with big blue eyes – eyes that had been scrunched up in pain when Abi lay dying. The sight was like a bucket of cold water thrown over her, a reminder of the true importance of what they were doing. Abi Moffat had also no doubt enjoyed a laugh with her class, and her family. All that had been taken away from her by whoever had so cruelly killed her on Daphne's doorstep. She closed her eyes, and saw the girl lose her fight for life once again. When she reopened them, Sarah realised that, now more than ever, she would leave no stone unturned trying to find out what had happened to the girl.

Sarah turned to Daphne and Charles. 'I really thought Abi's crucifix would lead us to something. It was so unusual, the two colours of metal...'

'Wait,' Daphne said, electrified. 'Was it... a kind of pinkish gold, with the Christ figure in silver?'

'It was,' Sarah nodded.

Daphne put her hands to her temples. 'Why didn't you say so before? You do know what that means, don't you?'

FOURTEEN

'I haven't the foggiest idea what you're on about,' Sarah said to Daphne.

'Oh my goodness, I suppose you haven't been here long enough to know about the Church of All Saints.'

'Isn't that just the Catholic church near the train station?' Sarah wrinkled her forehead.

'It's very strict, though, Sarah. And special members of the congregation are given those crucifixes. I know that because Mariella was really envious of Veronica's, and I had to explain it was to do with her religion, so Mari couldn't have one. Abi was Veronica's little sister, you know. I wonder if Abi was just having a quick pray in that priest's hole.'

Sarah sighed. 'It's another dead end, then, surely? No one is going to get killed over a crucifix – not in England, surely. We'll just have to sleep on it and see what else we can come up with as a motive.'

* * *

Sarah sat at her small kitchen table the next morning, clutching a cup of tea as though her life depended on it. She hadn't slept well, going over in her mind again and again Daphne's revelation, as well as all the possible meanings of the word 'wits'.

There weren't that many, as far as she could see. They'd tried Whitstable and found it totally devoid of leads. The Wittes Hotel had been a washout too. And now she was back at square one, trying to remember Abi's exact tone of voice when she'd said the word, thinking desperately whether or not there had been some sort of gesture which might have given emphasis or thrown much-needed light on the matter. But Abi had been so close to death. The simple word had taken all her energy – the last of her life force. It seemed so disrespectful that Sarah was signally failing to interpret what she'd said.

By the time she'd fallen asleep last night, Sarah's eyes had felt gritty with tiredness. Now she sighed and drank up the dregs of her tea. Hamish, in his basket, seemed subdued this morning too. He'd enjoyed all the shenanigans yesterday, especially cuddling up to Tinkerbell, who'd been rather groggy after her long snooze in the car, but she knew he sensed her listless mood today. As she watched, he put his head on his paws and sighed almost as deeply as Sarah.

'Right, that's it! Enough of this moping around, boy. We're going to get out and about and enjoy some fresh air before we meet Daphne.' With that, Sarah fetched Hamish's lead from the hook by the side of the fridge. Instantly, all his woes were forgotten, and he leapt to his feet, wriggling his body enthusiastically to show how very thoroughly he approved of this development.

'It's only a walk, Hamish,' Sarah said, bending to pat him. But she knew exactly how he felt. There was something about being outside, especially in beautiful Merstairs, that could really buck you up. She took a brief peep out of the kitchen window, facing onto her rather squashed flowerbeds. She hadn't had a chance yet to undo the damage after Hamish's recent incursions. Well, it would have to wait. The May skies were streaked lightly with wisps of cloud, and she was keen to see how the breeze was affecting the sea.

They pottered out of the front door, and picked up their pace as they walked along the sea road, Sarah's silver-blonde hair and Hamish's tufty fur being ruffled by a few boisterous gusts of wind, while the waves looked choppy out to their left.

Sarah's newly buoyant mood faltered a little as she neared Daphne's Tarot and Tealeaves shop, but she kept on going, not ignoring the growing shrine but at the same time trying not to let it throw her too far off balance. She was soon crossing the road and turning right, away from the seafront, where Madame Grimaldi, Daphne's only competitor in the seaside psychic stakes, had already set up her fortune telling tent, patterned with gold and silver moons and stars. Sarah strolled on, past the estate agency that had sold Daphne her infamous beach hut. Then she was in the maze of back streets leading out of Merstairs. It didn't take many more minutes before she halted again, in front of a pleasant low brick building surrounded by railings.

Merstairs Primary School had a jolly little playground, complete with games of snakes and ladders drawn out on the tarmac, a wooden shop for the children to play in and a climbing frame in one corner. Sarah couldn't help but smile. It took her back to those early days with her daughters, Becca and Hattie. Becca had loved school but Hattie had been more hesitant, and Sarah was forever grateful to the kind teachers who'd encouraged her sensitive child to blossom. She walked over to the railings. Near the gates, a heap of bouquets had already formed. Cards had been taped up, too. The wonky handwriting and heartfelt messages of the children Abi had taught brought tears to Sarah's eyes. She had clearly been one of those precious teachers no one can afford to lose.

She was just bending to see the wording on what was obviously a beloved teddy that had been tied to the railings with a yellow ribbon, when there was a voice at her side. 'Know her, did you?'

Sarah straightened up. The woman looking at her was in her late forties, her mouse brown hair dragged back anyhow into a ponytail. She was wearing an oversized jumper, despite the spring warmth, and her blue eyes looked very tired. Something about the way she held herself so rigidly told Sarah all she needed to know about the agonising pain and extreme stress she was feeling.

'I was the one who found her,' Sarah said gently, touching the woman's arm. 'And you must be... Abi's mother?'

''Sright. Jennie Moffat. You'll be the doctor lady, then.' It wasn't a question.

'Yes – well, I'm retired. I did my best to make Abi comfortable, though... I don't think she was in any pain,' Sarah said, mentally crossing her fingers. She was sure being stabbed wasn't exactly a blissful experience, but it was true that Abi hadn't complained at all – possibly because she hadn't had the strength. 'She seems to have been very much loved. You must have been so proud of her.'

'I was that,' said Jennie Moffat, turning away and getting a soggy tissue out of her coat pocket. Sarah delved in her handbag and proffered a fresh one, which Jennie took. 'Thanks, love. Just the three of us, it was. Her and Veronica's dad took off years ago. I've always done my best for them. And now this.' The poor woman dissolved into sobs again.

'I'm very sorry for your loss,' Sarah said quietly. 'Please let me know if there's anything at all I can do. Did you know... I wonder if you realise that Abi said something before she died.'

Jennie wheeled round to face Sarah. Her tired face scrunched into a mask of fury. 'Said his name, did she? Blamed him. That blimmin scumbag. He's evil, right enough.'

'Who is? She didn't say a name,' Sarah said, but Jennie Moffat was still muttering.

'Worst day of her life when she met that low-life, it was. Why they haven't banged him up yet beats me. Don't know what those clowns in the police are doing... it's not like they don't know what he's been up to.'

'Do you mean Abi's... boyfriend?'

'Boyfriend? He should be so lucky. Stalker, more like. Just wouldn't leave her alone. Twice her age, and not good enough to lick her boots, disgusting man...' Jennie was almost shaking now with anger.

'How awful,' said Sarah carefully, not wanting to inflame the poor woman further but needing to show some sympathy. 'Um, who would that be?'

'Don't tell me you haven't heard? You'd be the last person in Merstairs, in that case,' Jennie shot Sarah a look that was full of scepticism.

'Well, I only moved here a short while ago. I don't know everyone yet,' Sarah said apologetically.

'Josh Whittsall, that's the toerag's name,' said Jennie Moffat, her face twisting as she pronounced it.

'Josh *Whittsall*. I see,' said Sarah thoughtfully.

'He's the one. He's the one that done it,' Jennie Moffat said, almost vibrating now with pain. Then suddenly her features looked angry and set again. She dived into the little clutch of floral tributes near the railings and picked up a supermarket bouquet of rather sorry-looking red roses. There was a card attached.

Sarah just had time to read *Forever in my thoughts, all my love, Josh* before Jennie Moffat yanked it from the cellophane-wrapped bunch of flowers and ripped it in two, hurling the bits onto the pavement. Next she started on the flowers, tearing the petals off each bloom and letting them rain down like sinister blood-coloured confetti. 'He took my little girl away,' she said, as the tears streamed down her face.

Sarah automatically put her arm round the distraught woman, and murmured to her, calming her, as Hamish wagged his stumpy little tail in a vain attempt to cheer things up. After a few minutes, the poor woman's sobs stopped and she started hiccoughing. Sarah carried on patting Jennie Moffat's back gently – but her mind was working at a hundred miles an hour.

Josh Whittsall. Now there was a name to conjure with.

FIFTEEN

That afternoon, Sarah sat at a table at the Beach Café and frowned, staring at the waves lapping the shore. Jennie Moffat's pain had been terrible to witness. She didn't even want to think about how she would react if one of her own girls was killed, a superstitious dread making this most rational of women shy away from something so awful. No mother should have to bury her baby. It was an abomination against the natural order of things. Sarah scanned the horizon instead, and tapped her foot under the bench until Hamish nudged it with his nose.

'All right, boy,' she said, leaning down to smooth his ears. 'I know I'm being impatient. But where on earth are they?'

When she raised her head again, she was glad to see a large purple shape on the horizon. 'Thank goodness. That has to be Daphne.'

'Talking to yourself? They say it's the first sign of madness,' came a drawl at her elbow. She looked up into the blue, blue eyes of Charles Diggory.

'Where did you spring from?' She felt quite disconcerted at being taken unawares.

'Had some business in the town. And I just passed the

school. Someone's made an awful mess of the tributes to Abi. Shocking behaviour.'

'Oh, I think I can shed some light on that,' said Sarah, waving in vain to Hannah Betts, the café manager, who was busy with some tourists. Charles raised one long finger and she trotted right over. They ordered a round of teas and some of the café's wonderful teacakes. 'You must tell me how you do that some time,' Sarah said mulishly.

'Do what?' Charles arched a brow. 'Ah, here's Daphne. Dear lady, do take a seat. You look a little puffed, if I may say so.'

Daphne was indeed puce in the face, and so short of breath that it was several seconds before she could speak. She slung her large velvet bag onto the table, took a hefty draught of Sarah's glass of water and then finally stopped waving her arms around and burst into speech.

'You'll never guess what's been going on. The police have spent ages questioning me *again* this morning. They seem to think I'm their prime suspect!'

Sarah wrinkled her brow. 'Was it Mariella who questioned you?'

'Of course not. It was those idiots, Tweedledum and Tweedledee.'

'But why on earth would they think you had anything to do with it?' Sarah was baffled.

'Well, because it all took place literally on my doorstep,' said Daphne, pointing over the road to her shop, which still had crime scene tape across the frontage. 'I told them about that till receipt and the hotel card you found, by the way, but they weren't interested at all. They brought up that business about my beach hut instead.'

Daphne seemed most affronted, but what were the odds, really, of her shop being involved in a second crime, just after a body had been found in the hut she owned?

'I have to say, they do have a point. If you think about it,' Sarah said.

'Thank you, Sarah. Well, I like that.' Daphne crossed her arms over her ample chest and only the arrival of the toasted teacakes cheered her up. She dragged the plate towards her as if she had never seen food before. 'They had me locked up for hours, without so much as a crumb of nourishment,' she said, homing in on the largest teacake.

'Look, don't worry, Daphne. We'll soon get this latest murder cleared up, and then you can tell those idiotic PCs where to, um, stick their enquiries,' said Charles bracingly.

Daphne, who already had butter running down her chin and was about to take a second teacake from the plate, nodded. 'Well, that's all well and good, but we don't even know if my clever idea about Abi's connection to the church is going come up trumps, do we?'

'But that's why I asked you to meet me here,' said Sarah eagerly. 'I'm really keen to investigate your suggestion, Daph. But I think I've found us a proper suspect, as well.'

Daphne turned wide eyes to her and even Charles looked impressed. Sarah carried on, unconsciously leaning low over their table, though there were only a few visitors sitting near them, and they looked more interested in admiring the buckets of small crabs they'd caught from the pier than in eavesdropping. 'I was talking to Jennie Moffat this morning—'

'Poor Jennie,' broke in Daphne. 'What that woman must be going through!'

'Well, exactly,' said Sarah, trying to get back on track. 'She told me—'

'She must be in agony. Imagine, Sarah, if it was one of our girls! Or even your daughter, Charles,' she tacked on as an afterthought.

'It doesn't bear thinking about.' Charles shook his head.

'Max and Cali are devastated anyway, they adored Abi. They don't want to go back to school if she's not there.'

Daphne patted Charles's arm. 'It's so sad, isn't it?'

'Yes, it's a tragedy for the community. But I also think that Francesca might be using it as an excuse to get the twins into private education. She's, erm, in a funny mood at the moment,' he added, glancing Sarah's way.

Sarah, who thought she'd got Francesca's measure by now, certainly wouldn't put it past the woman to use any pretext, even murder, to get what she wanted. The mayor of Merstairs was a massive snob and seemed to enjoy nothing more than bullying her (apparently) soon-to-be-ex-husband. 'But wouldn't that cost a fortune? They're so young, you'd just be paying through the nose for them to play in the sandpit.'

'Tell me about it,' said Charles ruefully. 'And it's not as if I'm in any sort of position to shell out. But never mind that. What's your piece of news?'

'Well, it could help all of us. Charles, if we solve this quickly, Francesca might calm down about the schools thing. And the police can't keep bothering you if we've caught the real killer, Daphne.'

'So who do you think it is?' Daphne asked, putting one hand up to her scarf, which was listing badly to the left.

'Jennie Moffat let slip, while I was talking to her outside the school, that Abi had an admirer. Well, really more of a stalker, she said. And his name was Whittsall. Josh *Whitt*sall,' Sarah finished excitedly.

'Oh I see! Josh Whittsall... well, I did wonder about him and Abi, I suppose. He was in school sometimes, helping her stick up the kids' artwork,' Daphne said slowly.

'You didn't mention that,' Sarah pounced.

'Well, come on Sarah, not everyone who helps people out is a homicidal maniac,' Charles said with a laugh.

'True. But maybe this Josh is. I think we should go and check him out,' Sarah said, a determined look on her face.

'When you put it like that, going to see Josh seems quite scary,' Daphne said, suddenly seeming hesitant.

'We'll have Charles with us. Won't we, Charles?' Sarah raised an eyebrow.

'Of course. If you really feel it's necessary...' Charles's gaze was a little shifty. 'I had promised to see Francesca. Some, ah, paperwork to chat through, you know,' he said with another significant look at Sarah.

'Oh, I'm sure all that can wait,' she replied airily. 'This feels a lot more urgent. Jennie Moffat is adamant that Josh Whittsall killed her daughter. And I'd say she's keen to get her revenge. She ripped the heads off his bunch of flowers, then stamped them into the ground. It wasn't pretty.'

'Jennie's state of mind sounds quite worrying,' said Charles, his high forehead wrinkling.

'Gosh, yes,' said Daphne. 'We don't want any more trouble. I wonder when we should go?' She grabbed the last teacake and shoved it into her mouth whole.

'Daphne! I think that was mine,' said Sarah.

'Sorry,' Daphne mumbled through a mouthful of crumbs. 'You know I always have to eat when I'm stressed.'

'And also when you're not stressed,' Sarah muttered darkly. She'd been looking forward to that teacake, it had been particularly well-buttered.

'What was that?' Daphne asked.

'Nothing, Daph,' said Sarah. There was only one thing that was important right now. She stood up and untangled Hamish's lead. 'Right, come on, then,' she said to her surprised friends. 'What on earth are we waiting for?'

Charles dabbed his mouth with his napkin, then threw it down onto the table and got up decisively. 'Right, Daphne. We all want justice for Abi, don't we? And Jennie seems to be on the warpath. Those scrunched-up rose petals... I saw them outside the school too and, well, I didn't like the look of them.'

At this, Daphne snorted. 'Honestly, all this fuss about a few flowers.'

'You wouldn't say that if you'd seen them. Jennie gave me Josh's address, he lives with his parents,' Sarah said as she left a couple of notes under the glaringly empty teacake plate to pay the bill. 'Are you coming, Daph?'

SIXTEEN

Passing Tarot and Tealeaves, with Daphne huffing behind her, Sarah couldn't help but notice the impromptu shrine had grown and was now spilling over onto the pavement. As well as the tealights and cards, there were balloons and sweets, left by children Abi had taught. It was a poignant sight. Then her eye was caught by something else – a flyer taped to the window of the shop. She crossed the road to read it.

Daphne stood uneasily, with her back to the doorway where Abi had lost her life. 'I hate this, Sarah. It's doing no good at all for my psychic vibrations. There's a lot of disturbance in the Beyond because of what happened to Abi.'

'Well, there's going to be a disturbance in Merstairs as well, according to this,' said Sarah, pulling the handwritten notice off the window and showing it to Daphne and Charles. 'Look, it says there's going to be a torchlight procession through the town to commemorate Abi... tomorrow night.'

'But that's rather sweet, isn't it?' said Daphne, not understanding Sarah's urgent tone.

'In theory, yes... but it looks as if feelings are really running high. What if Jennie manages to convince people that Josh

Whittsall is the killer? Everyone will be out on the streets, at night, in the dark... anything could happen.'

'You're right, Sarah. Good job we're going to see him. This way we can either warn him – or make sure he gets what he deserves,' Charles said, a determined look on his face.

* * *

The Whittsalls' place wasn't far from the school. It was in a small estate of new-build houses. Their neighbours' homes were light and bright, their flowerbeds bursting with jolly spring bulbs. Josh's was superficially similar, with a front garden every bit as neat as the others. But there were no tubs of bright flowers, and the rectangle of lawn lacked even a fringe of shrubs. It had also been mown to within an inch of its life. The place had a utilitarian, almost unloved feel. Sarah began to wonder about the Whittsalls' religious beliefs. Just how fervent were they?

Sarah hardly had time to ring the bell before the door swung open and she found herself staring into the pale, lined face of a woman in late middle age, her hair ruthlessly scraped out of sight.

'Yes?' the woman enquired, in a flat-sounding voice.

'Um...' Sarah dithered uncharacteristically. Just as she was wondering how to frame her request to come in and throw a verbal hand grenade into this quiet – too quiet – home, there was the thunder of feet on the stairs and a good-looking man in his late thirties appeared, with a fully laden rucksack, which he left by the bannisters.

'Oh hello,' he said, also taken aback to see the little delegation on his doorstep. 'Can we help you with something?'

Charles stepped forward, to Sarah's relief. 'We were just wondering if we might come in and have a word?'

'About church matters?' the young man said. Luckily he

didn't wait for a reply, ushering them in while the silent woman stood by and allowed them to parade into her home.

They followed the man – who was clearly Josh Whittsall – into a kitchen at the end of the passageway. The other door along the way was firmly closed, and the only pictures on the hall walls were religious scenes: Christ on a donkey, and a group of pious-looking men who Sarah guessed must be apostles. The kitchen was a white-walled, square room, and the sole decoration was a calendar bearing a picture of Jesus suffering on the cross. Everything was surgically clean, down to the plain white tea towel hanging over the sink. It was a bit like being in an operating theatre: sterile, functional, used by many but personal to none.

Josh Whittsall gestured to the trio to sit at a scrupulously scrubbed pine table with matching high-backed chairs. His mother slunk into the free seat, folding her hands in her lap and looking silently and incuriously at her uninvited guests.

'Tea?' Josh said, in a rather desperate voice.

Sarah, Charles and Daphne, affected now by the strange atmosphere in the house, just nodded, and you could have heard a pin drop as Josh got out (plain white) mugs, found teabags in a (plain white) cannister and put a (white) sugar bowl on the table.

'Do we have any biscuits?' he asked his mother in an undertone.

At first, it looked as though she was going to ignore the question. Then she simply shrugged her shoulders. Josh sighed and then started opening and closing cupboards, giving glimpses of sparse stacks of plain crockery, a minimum of foodstuffs and certainly no biscuits.

'Sorry,' he said to the visitors. As there were only four chairs around the small table, he stood awkwardly, leaning against the kitchen units, while the kettle started to shrill. It was the only sound in the quiet house.

Once everyone had a mug of tea in front of them, Josh finally addressed the elephant in the room – a white elephant, of course. 'Um, what exactly can we help you with? You don't really look like you're from the church,' he said, his pleasantly modulated voice rising at the end in question.

Sarah spoke up. 'We're not. In fact, we've come because... well, this is rather difficult, but it's in relation to Abi Moffat.'

At once, Josh's open face became shuttered, and he turned away and busied himself with washing up the spoon he'd used to remove the teabags from the cups. It hardly warranted that much scrubbing, Sarah felt. She spoke up above the sound of the running tap.

'Jennie Moffat, Abi's mum, well, she seems to have got a rather odd impression about you...'

At that, Josh whipped round and faced them all. 'Mum, would you please go and sort out my ironing? You know I'm going to need that shirt. I've set up the ironing board upstairs,' he said, twisting the tea towel in his hands.

His mother looked at him silently for a moment. 'All right, son,' she said, and took herself off. Immediately, the atmosphere in the kitchen lightened. Josh took the chair his mother had vacated.

'Look... the thing about me and Abi...' he started, toying with his mug. 'Well, it's difficult to put it into words. We'd known each other for years. We met at church...'

'And you resented her trying to move on when your relationship ended. You can say it, we already know,' Sarah urged him, leaning towards him.

Josh immediately reared back in his chair. 'No! No, it wasn't like that. Not at all. That's why I sent Mum upstairs... The thing is, well.' He took a deep breath. 'The thing is that I'm gay.'

'Gay?' Daphne repeated.

'Shh!' Josh said, looking hunted. 'My parents can't know. They wouldn't understand,' he said, rubbing his hand across his face. 'It was Abi's idea, to get them off my back. They've been going on at me to marry a good Catholic girl for years, settle down, have kids. She knew how hard it was for me. She'd always known. She was younger, but we were always friends. She was a good, kind soul. She was trying to help me.'

'I don't understand, how was all this supposed to help?' Sarah asked.

'We pretended we were going out, which calmed Mum and Dad down. But then Abi met someone in real life – she was really crazy about him. She didn't feel right about us, after that. Not when it got serious. But she didn't want to leave me in the lurch, so she said why didn't I make out I was pining for her and couldn't get over the break-up. That would buy me some time.'

Sarah glanced at Daphne and Charles, thinking furiously. Did this sound plausible? Or was this young man making the whole thing up on the spot, to try and get out of the frame? As though he'd read her thoughts, Josh pushed his phone towards her.

'Go ahead,' he said. 'Take a look. There's all my messages with Abi. The whole thing is on there, from the start of our "relationship", to when Abi said it had to stop. She was an angel, throughout the whole thing. I bought her a special All Saints crucifix, to say thank you. I miss her so much,' he said, hand over his eyes again.

Sarah scanned the texts wordlessly, then passed the phone to Daphne, who craned over it with Charles. It all checked out. There was one last question she had to ask, though.

'Do you know who Abi took up with? This man she was so keen on?'

'No,' shrugged Josh. 'As you can see, she was pretty cagey about him. It wasn't like her. But I didn't want to press. She'd been so marvellous to me.'

'You realise Jennie Moffat actually thinks you were stalking Abi?' Sarah said.

Josh nodded. 'But I have an alibi. I've heard Abi died early in the morning... Well, I was with someone.'

'Can you say who? Tensions are running high, you know. Abi was very much loved and a lot of people have got the impression that you weren't over her. If you can say where you were, it would really help.'

Josh looked down at his hands, clutching the almost empty mug. 'All right, then. I suppose there's no way of avoiding saying it. I was with Mitch Crowley. He's our priest's nephew,' he added.

'I'm sorry I had to ask,' said Sarah.

'That's OK, I suppose. Mitch and I are leaving Merstairs anyway, ditching our jobs. We both work at the new Wittes Hotel.'

Here, Charles, Daphne and Sarah exchanged glances. That explained the card at Abi's feet.

'What choice do we have but to go?' Josh stopped speaking for a moment, as emotion threatened to overwhelm him. He took a breath and went on. 'Abi always tried to protect me, but now her going means everything will come to light. It won't do any good if we try and tough it out.'

'Listen, do I have your permission to, well, to tell Jennie about this? If anyone can get the message out, that you're not to blame, she can,' Sarah said. 'It's a lot to ask, I know.'

Josh was silent for a moment, weighing things up. At last he spoke. 'At this point, why not? I wish it could have been another way. I'd rather have told my parents myself, got their support even, but that's not an option. This way they'll still find out... but Mitch and I will be long gone by the time they do. We'll be safe.'

There was a sound from the hall, and Josh jumped. Mrs Whittsall had come down the stairs.

'Right, son. Your dad will soon be home.'

Josh looked at her for a second longer, then stretched out a hand. For a moment, his mother grabbed it convulsively, cradled it, and pulled it to her lips. Then she opened the front door. 'Best get going.'

Josh didn't need a second urging. He shot into the hall, picked up his belongings, and the front door banged shut behind him.

Sarah, Daphne and Charles were left looking at each other. 'Well, that went well,' said Daphne drily.

Mrs Whittsall seemed to rouse herself at the sound of Daphne's voice. 'It's time for you all to leave.' She stood, face as blank as ever, while Sarah, Charles and Daphne shuffled past her in the narrow passageway. In a matter of moments they were out of the front door. As it slammed behind them, they all turned to look at one another.

'Don't say a thing. Not until we're well clear,' said Sarah, as they hurried up the path. Just as they were leaving the cul-de-sac, a large man with the sort of red face that usually betokened dangerously high blood pressure shoved rudely past them, nearly knocking Sarah over.

'I say,' Charles remonstrated, but the man took not a bit of notice. He just pounded towards the Whittsall house with a set look on his face.

'I bet that's Mr Whittsall,' said Daphne with a shudder. 'I'm getting a really bad feeling about him, his aura is seriously dissonant.'

'I think we've had a bit of a lucky escape – as has Josh Whittsall,' Sarah said. 'I feel so sorry for him – and his mother.'

'I couldn't agree more,' said Daphne. 'I wish there was something we could do for them. At least he's getting away. She really needs some colour in her life,' she said as she adjusted her scarf headband. 'I knew that church was strict, but this is ridiculous.'

'I don't think it's All Saints at all, I think it's Mr Whittsall,' said Sarah. 'But I've still got some contacts with an organisation that helps women in difficult situations. Maybe I'll pop by the church and see if there's a moment when I can give her a leaflet. You never know, it might get her thinking.'

But, even as the words left her lips, she knew the chances of Mrs Whittsall seeking help were slim. She had even made the ultimate sacrifice, and let her beloved son go, to keep him safe. And, even more depressingly, Sarah realised something else. Another clue had bitten the dust. Josh wasn't, and never had been, stalking Abi. In fact, they were friends. Friendships could go sour, of course, but not in this case. And, most crucially of all, Josh appeared to have an alibi for the time of Abi's death. He didn't have her blood on his hands.

But at least Josh had given them vital new information – Abi had a real boyfriend, someone she was genuinely keen on. Now there was another burning question they had to answer. Who on earth was he?

SEVENTEEN

'We need to find out who Abi was really seeing,' Sarah said as they took stock, just out of sight of the Whittsall house. 'But I think we need to talk to Jennie Moffat first.'

'That poor grieving mother? Should we be intruding on her at a time like this?' Charles was looking at his most fastidious.

'I think we've got to. There's going to be a vigil, and we know that Jennie thinks Josh is responsible for what happened to her daughter. She won't be the only one. But we know he's innocent. We need to tell her. And you never know, she might even have some ideas about who the real boyfriend could be.'

'Well, you could be right,' said Charles. 'But where on earth do we find her?'

'Just round the corner, silly,' said Daphne. 'Mari used to go over to play at Veronica's all the time, when they were small.' She led them to the next cul-de-sac along. Jennie Moffat's house turned out to be number fourteen, with a cherry red front door.

'Who's going to be the one to ring?' Daphne said, shifting from foot to foot.

Sarah sympathised with her friend's uncharacteristic reticence – intruding on a bereaved parent was not on her top ten list of activities, either. But she passed Hamish's lead to Daphne and marched up to the door.

The bell had a jolly 'bing-bong' chime which seemed out of keeping with the friends' mission, and with the sad period of mourning no doubt enveloping all who lived within. For a moment or two Sarah was sure no one was going to answer and was feeling a mixture of relief and anticlimax. Then she heard slow footsteps and the door opened a crack.

'Mrs Moffat? I'm Sarah Vane, we met outside the school earlier. I wonder if I could come in for a moment? I have something to tell you about Abi that might be... well, a relief, I suppose.'

Jennie Moffat looked at Sarah a little wildly, then saw Daphne, Charles and Hamish behind her. 'Here, what is all this? What's going on?'

'It'll be easier to explain if we come in,' Sarah said gently. Jennie thought about it for a moment and then stepped away from the door wordlessly, trudging towards the back of the house. Sarah took that as an invitation and gestured to the others to follow.

A minute later they were all seated around Jennie Moffat's kitchen table, with Sarah firmly grasping Hamish on her lap.

'I suppose you want tea?' Jennie said listlessly, clasping a crumpled tissue in her hand and gazing round at them with red, sore-looking eyes.

'Let me make it,' said Daphne, jumping up. Sarah wished she'd had her hands free to do it, as Daphne was sure to add a dash of exuberance to the operation, but keeping Hamish nice and quiet seemed more important.

Sure enough, Daphne was soon asking a stream of questions about the whereabouts of tea, mugs and the kettle, even though the answers to most were pretty evident, and with a sigh Jennie got up to do the honours herself. In a way it was quite useful, as going through the familiar routine seemed to keep her mind off her woes a little.

'I'm sorry we've burst in on you like this. It's just that there's something we feel you should know,' Sarah started.

'Right,' said Jennie, opening cupboards and clattering around, assembling mugs, spoons and milk. 'Anyone take sugar?'

They all shook their heads, and Sarah started again. 'The thing is, Jennie, we think you may have got the wrong end of the stick about your daughter...'

It was totally the wrong thing to say. Jennie immediately slammed the cupboard door shut, and turned to confront Sarah, who was now holding onto Hamish even more tightly to reassure him.

'How dare you come here and think you can tell me stuff about my own daughter? Think I don't know what she was? She was an angel, my Abi. And if that toerag hadn't—'

Charles put up his hand. 'If you're referring to Josh Whittsall, there's... new information we ought to share.'

Perhaps it was Charles's commanding manner that instantly calmed Jennie down, or maybe it was the tantalising way he'd dangled the news all three of them were now longing to impart, so they could be on their way.

'Well. What is it, then?' Jennie snapped.

'You see, it's like this, Jennie...' Sarah began in soothing tones.

Now Daphne leapt in. 'Oh, for goodness' sake, Sarah. She isn't one of your patients, you don't have to break it to her gently. The sooner we tell her, the sooner Josh'll be off the hook.'

'I should have known it! You're on his side, trying to help him escape. Well, let me tell you, Josh Whittsall is going to get what's coming to him at the vigil, you see if he doesn't,' said Jennie fiercely.

Sarah rolled her eyes at Daphne. 'I think what my friend

meant to say is that we've spoken to Josh and got his permission to explain something to you. He is gay. He wasn't going out with your daughter at all, much less stalking her. They were just friends. He was hiding his true nature because he felt his parents would never accept it.'

Jennie, who was holding the cannister of teabags, and had looked for a moment as though she was about to launch it at Daphne's face, now put it down carefully on the side. She looked from Charles to Sarah and back again. 'What? What are you saying?'

* * *

'I don't know why Abi wouldn't have told me. She heard me sounding off about Josh often enough. And as for her having another boyfriend, well, that's news to me,' Jennie said a while later, shaking her head and wiping her eyes again. It hadn't been an easy conversation, but at least the poor woman now seemed in a much less martial mood.

'It's simple, Jennie. She'd given Josh her word. And you know what an honest, pure soul she was,' Daphne said, her own eyes filling up as she gave Jennie a tight hug.

'It's so like our Abi, to do something like that, helping someone out when they're in a pickle. It's just, well. I wish she'd trusted me with it.' Jennie started to sob again, and this time it was Sarah who stepped in with words of sympathy.

'You know, she really couldn't tell you and I bet she found that hard. But she knew you loved her, and she loved you. At least you've got that to hold onto.'

'Yes... but when it looked like Josh had done it, I thought I'd have justice for my Abi. Now he's in the clear, it could have been anyone. They're out there, free, while my girl will soon be in her grave... It's not right,' she wailed.

'And you're sure you have no idea at all who her real boyfriend could be?' Sarah probed gently.

Jennie shook her head. 'I'm that upset about it. It wasn't like her to sneak around.'

'I suppose the boy had asked her to keep quiet, for whatever reason... and of course she had to honour her promise to Josh as well.'

'Poor Abi. She didn't seem herself, the last couple of days. And no wonder, with all this on her plate.'

'She wasn't well?' Sarah pressed her. 'What sort of symptoms?'

Jennie looked up. 'Oh, she wasn't ill, as such. More like she had a lot on her mind.'

'I expect she was finding it hard, not being open with you,' said Daphne kindly.

'Well,' said Sarah, looking round at her friends. 'I think it's time we left you to it, Jennie. But do ring us any time if you need anything – or think of who Abi's boyfriend might be.'

'Don't you worry, Mrs Moffat,' said Charles, getting up with Sarah and Daphne. 'These ladies and I will be doing all we can to bring the killer to light.'

'We will,' said Sarah. 'It's not that the police aren't up to it – as you know, Daphne's Mari is on the case – but we've got time to dig around and we'd like to do it to honour Abi's memory.'

Jennie sniffed. 'All right. I don't mind telling you, when you lot turned up I was ready to throw you out straight away. But it's kind of you to try to help. I feel bad now for all the things I've said about Josh, poor man. Seems like he'll have been suffering too. I'll see to it that the vigil tomorrow is a peaceful affair,' she added, looking a little shamefaced. She was probably remembering how she had whipped up ill-feeling against an innocent person.

They left her standing on the doorstep, looking aged beyond her years. Sarah shook her head as soon as they were out of sight. 'That poor woman. What she's been through doesn't bear thinking about.'

The trio walked back to town rather silently, preoccupied with their own thoughts. As they passed the antiques shop, Charles peeled off. 'Well this is where I leave you two,' he said. 'Unless you'd like to come in for a nightcap?'

Despite her tiredness, Sarah was tempted for a moment. This, surely, would be the moment for Charles to get all kinds of things off his chest – news about his divorce would be top of her list – but then a yawn sneaked up on her out of nowhere.

'Oops, sorry, Charles, I need my bed,' she said. 'And so does Hamish.' Indeed, the little dog seemed to have gone to sleep where he stood. Sarah hoped she wouldn't have to carry him all the way home.

'I'm tired too,' said Daphne, quite subdued for once. 'But listen, let's meet up tomorrow.'

'Yes,' said Sarah. 'We really need to brainstorm any potential boyfriends Abi might have had. How about meeting in the Jolly Roger before the vigil, so we can work out what we're looking for?' She thought about everything she needed to get through at home – including sorting out those squashed flowerbeds. 'Say, early afternoon?'

'Agreed,' said Charles. He gave the ladies a mock salute, and they parted ways.

EIGHTEEN

The next day, with the mud from replanting the peonies and irises Hamish had trampled carefully washed from her hands, Sarah greeted Daphne and Charles outside the Jolly Roger. Once, she would have found it daunting walking into a bustling pub, but with Daphne and Charles by her side, she really felt like a regular. Even the fact that there were some tourists sitting in their usual seats didn't matter a jot.

'Gosh, it's busy today. You two get settled somewhere and I'll fetch the drinks,' Sarah said. 'The usuals?'

Both Charles and Daphne nodded in agreement and started to scan the bar for free places. As well as a motley crew of tourists and locals, there was a big group of darts fans clustering around the board at the back, and two tables of women laughing and joking nearest the doors.

By the time Sarah had been served – it took longer than usual, thanks to the press of people – she saw that her friends had managed to edge their way in at one of the larger tables towards the back of the room. She moved through the crowd carefully, trying not to get her tray of drinks jostled, and was relieved to put it down on the slightly sticky table and take her seat, though she was sitting uncomfortably close to Charles and was at the same time in danger of elbowing Daphne in the ribs.

'Gosh, I've never seen it like this in here before, it's like Piccadilly Circus,' she remarked, looking round.

'I hope it's not people revving themselves up about the vigil later on,' said Charles under his breath. 'If this many are in the crowd, goodness knows what could happen.'

'With any luck Jennie Moffat has spread the word about Josh Whittsall. But it won't hurt if we say he's left town too, that should calm things down,' said Sarah.

'Excuse me, were you talking about Josh Whittsall?' said a grumpy-looking man wearing a tight polo shirt, looming up beside Sarah.

Sarah drew back a little, but then squared her shoulders. 'Yes. We were just all saying that it's a shame he's left Merstairs, he's gone to London for... for a job,' she said firmly, looking round at her companions for confirmation.

'That's right, he's becoming a, a, fireman,' said Daphne.

'A fireman? But he works at the Wittes Hotel, doesn't he?'

'I think he's decided on a bit of a career change,' said Sarah, hoping fervently that that would be the last of the questions. But the man opened his mouth to ask more – just as a familiar figure tottered over.

'Pat! What are you doing here?' said Daphne, as Charles got up and offered the old lady a seat. Pat was Daphne's friend from her book group, and someone Sarah had rather got off on the wrong foot with.

'Just here for the Stitch and Bitch,' Pat said with one of her trademark cackles. She must have been a ferocious smoker at some point in her long past, Sarah decided.

'Stitch and... what in the world is that?' said Charles, raising an eyebrow.

'Oh, it's just a nickname we give ourselves, the handicrafts group – that table of gels by the window,' Pat said. She pointed to a group that seemed more like women of a certain age than girls, but as Pat was probably eighty if she was a day, these things were all relative.

The group was laughing and gossiping rather than doing any sewing, as far as Sarah could see. There was an elegant elderly lady in a flowery dress at the centre of the table, who looked familiar. Oh yes, there was the curly-haired man she'd seen her with before. There was also a woman with a pleasant, open face sitting next to her, wearing little round glasses and a bright red dress. As Sarah watched, she picked up a complicated piece of crochet that seemed to be on a long round hook and worked away at it effortlessly while chatting away to the elegant matron.

'Packed for a lunchtime, isn't it? Looks like it's going to be really busy later on with the vigil, and everything,' Pat commented, with a gleam in her eye that suggested she rather relished the idea of a rambunctious evening.

'Crafts, I see,' said Sarah. 'That's one club you're not in,' she remarked mischievously to Daphne.

'What do you mean? Of course I'm a member. I've got great friends in the craft club. Oh, here comes Mabel, you'll love her. Her father was the local GP for years.'

The middle-aged lady in red with the Harry Potter-style glasses was approaching, but she didn't seem to have time for medical reminiscences. 'Daphne, can I ask you a favour? I need your Mariella's number,' she said with a rather harassed air. 'I've got something I ought to... well...'

'Oh, of course, I'll text it to you,' said Daphne. 'This is Sarah, by the way,' she added.

Sarah stuck out a hand and Mabel shook it absent-mindedly, looking over her shoulder. 'So sorry, I must get back to the table. Regina needs me,' she said with an apologetic smile.

'Shame she's a bit distracted today,' said Daphne. 'Her

crochet is really extraordinary. I do love the craft group. I'm always there, aren't I, Pat?'

'Well, at least as often as you get to the book group,' Pat cackled, with the suspicion of a wink. But Daphne appeared highly satisfied with the answer.

'There you are, you see, Sarah. This is why I'm always so busy,' Daphne said with a martyred air.

'Anyway, what did I miss about young Josh Whittsall? Was someone saying he was becoming a milkman?' Pat husked, patting her chest.

'Not a milkman, Pat, um, a fireman,' said Daphne, looking nervously over at the cross-looking man, who still seemed to be listening in on their conversation.

'That's a bit of a turn-up, I always thought working on hotel reception suited him down to the ground. Can't see him shinning up ladders and rescuing people from burning buildings,' Pat mused wheezily.

'It's better than what he has been doing,' said the grumpy man, breaking in on their conversation.

'What's that, then, pet?' Pat said.

'Well, word has it he's been stalking that Abi Moffat... might even have bumped her off.'

'Nah,' said Pat, with a playful swipe at the man's arm. 'You're having me on! That boy wasn't interested in young Abi... and he wouldn't hurt a fly.'

Sarah listened anxiously. While she was keen to get the message across that Josh was innocent, she didn't want things to go too far towards suggesting exactly why he had no motive.

'That's not what Jennie's been saying. Her own mum,' said the man, gritting his jaw pugnaciously.

'Have you spoken to her today, though? I know she had her suspicions, but I think she's changed her mind,' Sarah said brightly.

'What do you know about it, then?' he said, turning on her.

Charles put himself between the man and Sarah. 'Rather than asking my friend here, maybe you should get over to Jennie's place and have a chat with her?'

'All right, but the vigil's outside the shop, and we're starting tonight at seven, just like we planned,' the man said, his face flushing even more. 'Are you telling me there's been a change to all that?'

'Best to check,' Charles shrugged.

With that, the man banged his pint down on the bar, called to a few similarly restless-looking chums, and they all strode out. Once the pub door had shut on them, the place seemed a lot calmer.

'I feel as though I can breathe now,' said Daphne, filling her lungs exuberantly. 'Where would we be without you, Charles?'

'Do you think that's going to be enough to stop them, though?' said Sarah anxiously.

'I'm not sure anyone was really going to do anything so awful tonight, you know, Sarah,' said Charles reassuringly. 'Not really. Not in Merstairs.'

Sarah took a deep breath and turned to Pat. 'It didn't seem to be news to you that Josh wasn't involved with Abi. Do you know who her real boyfriend was?'

Pat gave Sarah a ferocious wink. 'Now that would be telling, wouldn't it?' she cackled, finishing with a hacking cough.

Really, Sarah thought. The woman needed to get to her GP for a lung function test, as soon as possible. Then Daphne broke in.

'Nonsense, Pat, if you'd have known, you'd have told me, I know you would. I do think it's odd Abi said nothing.'

'Maybe he was unsuitable. A granddad or summat,' said Pat with relish, rather revealing that Daphne had been right. 'I had a man when I was twenty-one, ooh he was sixty if he was a day...'

'Yes, well,' said Charles quickly. 'But I hardly think Abi was that sort of girl.'

'You don't want to think of your grandchildren's teacher getting up to anything, do you, Charles?' said Sarah, not unsympathetically. 'But she was an attractive girl. I bet half the boys in Merstairs were after her. Let's think about why people keep relationships secret. Because they fear other people won't understand or will get hurt – or because they are not free in some way.' Sarah carefully didn't look at Charles when saying this. 'Anyway, I think we should all keep our ears to the ground. You never know when you'll hear something that'll lead us in the right direction.'

She finished up her tonic water and put the glass down. 'I was going to suggest getting a sandwich, but it's still pretty crowded. What do you say we meet up again here this evening instead? If people are planning to gather before this vigil thing, whatever it turns out to be, we can keep a weather eye on it all,' she said.

'Sounds good. Time in the pub is never wasted,' said Charles, waving his glass in her direction. Daphne, too, looked pleased at the idea.

Sarah got up to go, looping Hamish's lead round her wrist. 'Not coming now, Daphne?'

'I'll just finish my drink and have a chat with Pat. See you later,' her friend said warmly.

She was quite glad to have a bit of time to herself, Sarah decided, as she edged past the crafting table, where the flowery lady was in the centre of things, and the young man with the curly hair was buying everyone a round of drinks. There was quite a family resemblance, now that she studied them. Both had blue eyes and the lady's hair, though a fetching white, had a natural wave. Perhaps sensing her scrutiny, the woman looked up and Sarah hurried out.

At least she was pretty sure they had headed off whatever

confrontation had been planned for the vigil. Nevertheless, she felt a prick of anxiety and she looked back over her shoulder at the pub door as she and Hamish walked home along the coastal path. And she made a resolution. Just in case, she was going to keep Mariella's number on speed dial tonight.

NINETEEN

The air felt a little chilly as Sarah retraced her steps for her rendezvous that evening. She had changed into a simple black top and slacks and carried a light baby pink silk shawl over her arm for later, but she was quite tempted to put it on right now.

Her shivers weren't all temperature related. There was already a knot of people forming over by Daphne's Tarot and Tealeaves shop, now even more festooned than ever with wilting bouquets. Unfortunately, many looked as though they'd been purchased at the large garage on the Whitstable road, where all the flowers were well known to be dead on arrival. There was a crowd milling around, and there was a hum of talk, gruff male voices the loudest.

Just then, two girls strolled past to join the group, arm in arm and clutching damp tissues. On the spur of the moment, Sarah shot out a hand to touch the nearest girl's sleeve. 'I'm sorry, you look like you were close to Abi. Could I have a word?'

At times like this, Sarah blessed her years in medicine. They had given her a usefully authoritative manner, and now that she was over sixty, few found her threatening.

'Yeah? What's up?' said one of the girls, blotting her eyes and inadvertently smearing her mascara.

'It's just... this is going to sound odd, but I was hoping to speak to Abi's boyfriend.'

Immediately, the girls looked at each other and the taller of the pair gave a humourless laugh. 'Yeah, you and me both.'

'You mean... you don't know who he was, either?'

''Fraid not. Wish we did. We've been to the police about it, and all,' her friend added.

'Do you know how long they'd been together, even?'

'Only a couple of months. "Like a bolt from the blue," Abi said. She was crazy about him.'

'What reason did she give, for not confiding in you? Presumably you three were close?'

'Best friends since school,' they both nodded proudly, then the slighter girl gulped and shielded her eyes again. 'She said he wasn't ready.' They both turned up their noses at that. 'Not ready? He should have been proud. His loss,' she said.

'No, it's our loss,' said her friend, and they both dissolved in tears again. Sarah did what she could to comfort them, then they walked away to join the group. She turned back to see Daphne and Charles standing outside by the pub door.

'I'm beginning to think it's going to be hard to track down Abi's boyfriend. We're going to have to keep our eyes peeled for anyone who looks like a possible contender. What do you think of this lot, for instance?' Sarah said, her back turned to the fiery orange skies as the sun disappeared into the sea.

'Hmm, what?' said Daphne, who was drinking in the glories of the view. Charles was more thoughtful.

'I think I can see that bad-tempered chap from the pub earlier... and his friends. Surely none of them are likely candidates. There's no sign of Jennie Moffat either, is there? I don't think they can really get up to any violence without her appearing to endorse it,' he said in relieved tones. Sarah, who hadn't thought of it this way round, felt a weight lifting from her shoulders. Charles was right, this crowd wouldn't want to look like a band of thugs, she was sure.

But, just then, a man strolled past them in the gathering twilight. Suddenly the onlookers at the shop were electrified.

'That's him!'

'It's only Abi's stalker!'

Within a few seconds there was a movement, like a wave, and the mourners had surged forward, crossed the street and were almost surrounding the passer-by.

'Here! What're you playing at?' Sarah heard him say.

'It's that Whittsall geezer! The one who made Abi's life a misery!' came a voice in the crowd. All of a sudden there were rowdy cries and, in the dim light, Sarah saw people jostling to get at the man.

'Hang on! Wait just a minute,' Sarah found herself shouting, to her own astonishment. 'That's not Josh Whittsall. And Josh wasn't with Abi anyway. What do you people think you're doing? You won't accomplish anything with this.'

Charles stepped forward, just as a few of the crowd whipped their heads round to stare at Sarah. 'She's right, you know. This chap has nothing to do with Abi, do you, sir?'

The man, by now surrounded by hostile faces, stammered his answer. 'W-who? I'm just trying to find my way back to my B&B.' He held up a carrier bag. 'Just popped out to get chips for the wife and kiddies. Things look different here at night, don't they?' he added, nervously.

At that, the mood of the crowd seemed to turn. Whether it was the desire to put their best foot forward in front of a tourist, or whether they'd realised this man had nothing whatsoever to do with the slaying of a favourite teacher, they were suddenly patting him on the back, offering directions, and generally doing their best to be helpful citizens.

'Phew,' said Sarah in a low voice. 'For a minute there I thought we'd have a riot on our hands.'

'Oh, no,' said Daphne, waving an arm dismissively. 'Just a bit of high spirits. People round here are the salt of the earth,' she said.

To Sarah's relief, Daphne seemed to be right, and the crowd started melting away. As the last stragglers wandered home, Sarah saw the girls she'd spoken to previously. One of them made a beeline for her.

'Just thought you should know. I've remembered something,' the girl said, the mascara still giving her panda eyes.

'Oh yes?' Sarah said, trying not to get her hopes up too much.

'Abi was pretty cagey about this boyfriend, but she did say she was finally going to introduce us to him soon.'

'She did? That's amazing,' said Sarah. 'Did she say where, or when? Any detail would help.'

The girl frowned. 'She just said the fair would be the right time.'

'The fair?'

'Yeah, there's one every year. We always went. With our mums and dads, when we were little. And then on our own, from when we were about sixteen. It's great,' the girl said, with a last sad smile. 'Better be off.'

'Thank you so much,' said Sarah, staring after her.

So Abi had been planning a big reveal of her secret love, at some local fair. Sarah felt as though she was on a solid footing at last. Surely the man wouldn't be able to resist the temptation to go along, even if Abi no longer could? One thing was for sure, Sarah Vane was going to be there too.

TWENTY

Sarah was up early the next morning, thanks to Hamish pulling off her duvet well before 7 a.m. again. Normally she would have been a little cross, but she realised he probably felt rather neglected. Although he'd been along for the ride over the past few days, while Sarah and her friends had done their best to get closer to Abi Moffat's killer, he hadn't really had any quality one-on-one doggy time with his mistress.

'All right, boy, we're going to have a lovely beach walk soon, but first I need to speak to Daphne,' said Sarah, fending off his good-natured attempts to wash her face for her. 'Do you mind? I'm just going to have a quick shower and we'll pop round.'

True to her word, twenty minutes later she and Hamish followed the path up to Daphne's purple door, past her epic collection of garden gnomes. Sarah wasn't about to tell her friend, but despite her best efforts, Hamish stopped to spend a penny on each of them.

It took Daphne a while to answer the bell, and when the door finally swung open, Sarah saw why. Her friend was still in her sweeping emerald silk dressing gown, the belt trailing along the floor as she made her way into the kitchen and shoved a tottering pile of plates on the table a millimetre to the left, presumably so that her visitors could make themselves at home.

'I've only just woken up,' Daphne explained, with a yawn that reminded Sarah strongly of a fact she'd learnt when studying jawbones – hippos can open their mouths to a full one-hundred-and-fifty-degree angle, whereas humans, with a few notable exceptions, cannot. 'I didn't sleep, thinking about all this Abi stuff. Mari's beside herself, and the kids are so upset. Well, you can imagine.'

Sarah was sorry to hear this – but glad Daphne had been discussing the situation with her daughter. She moved the crockery off the table into the sink, piled up a few old newspapers and bits of junk mail, and sat down at the table while Hamish did a quick sniff around the base of all the kitchen units. He was doing his due diligence, making sure that Daphne's ginger cat, Mephisto, was not currently in residence. Once he was satisfied the coast was clear, the Scottie clambered cheekily into Mephisto's basket, curled himself up, closed his eyes in rapture and wriggled fulsomely, enjoying the sweet, sweet taste of forbidden fruit. It was a perfect fit, ideal for a very large cat... or a rather small dog.

Daphne fussed around with the kettle, then plonked an enormous brown earthenware teapot down on the table. Next she wrestled it into a multicoloured woollen cosy, as though putting a tight jumper on an unwilling toddler. Finally she got out two mugs and the milk bottle and sat herself down with a sigh like a navvy after a hard day's graft.

'Don't you feel some days are a terrible effort?' she said, her eyes troubled.

Sarah looked at Daphne worriedly. She wondered whether her friend might be a bit depressed. The death of Abi, who'd been such a popular figure in the community, must have hit the Roux family extra hard. Not only was a wonderful teacher gone, but Abi's sister was Mariella's great friend, and Mariella also had a lot of expectations riding on her as a member of the police force. She needed to find the killer, and quickly, to allay public concern and ensure her promotion out of the uniform department. That was quite a burden for Daphne, too.

'I know this is really hard on you, but we need to keep our spirits up, Daph. Has Mariella been able to tell you anything about the investigation so far?'

Daphne sat up a bit straighter. 'Is that why you've come round? And you're the one who's always telling me she should be more discreet. Well, maybe I should follow your advice and keep everything under my hat.'

Sarah's eyes went involuntarily to Daphne's hair. It was usually covered up by her elaborate scarf arrangement, but at this hour in the morning her bright red locks were trailing this way and that. Daphne patted her head self-consciously, then flapped her hands in annoyance.

'Oh, what does anything matter, compared to finding whoever did this evil thing to Abi?'

'I totally agree,' said Sarah earnestly. 'Listen, I guarantee you'll feel a whole lot better after breakfast.'

Daphne glared at Sarah for a second and then subsided. 'Oh, you're right. I'm starving. But I just can't be bothered...' she said listlessly.

'Let me,' said Sarah, getting up and finding a loaf of bread on the draining board. By the time the toast was done to a turn, she had assembled a jar of raspberry jam and a dish of lovely yellow butter from the local dairy, and had poured cups of hot, strong tea for them both.

Daphne was soon a different woman, sitting back in her chair with her hands lovingly cupped over a full tummy.

'So,' said Sarah carefully. 'What did Mariella have to say last night on the phone?'

'It wasn't what she said, it was the way she said it,' Daphne replied automatically, then she put a hand to her mouth. 'I suppose I've given the game away now,' she mumbled. 'You always were too clever for me.'

The deeply competitive side of Sarah would normally have given a tiny smirk at this admission – which Daphne would surely never have made if she hadn't been feeling at such a low ebb. But Sarah valiantly suppressed it. The common good was what mattered, after all.

'We're on the same side, Daph. We both want this killer caught and brought to justice for what they did to poor Abi.'

Daphne considered it all for a minute. 'You're right, of course you are. OK then, I suppose I'll spill the beans.'

TWENTY-ONE

But the beans, when they came, were neither as lavish nor as piping hot as Sarah had been hoping. In fact, they were more like the sort of congealed mess you might get on your plate at the worst kind of greasy spoon café.

'The truth is, Mari feels completely stuck, just like we do. That's why I feel so low,' said Daphne, now eating a spoonful of jam right out of the jar. Sarah edged forward, trying to get the lid back on before her friend polished off the lot and felt sick, but Daphne batted her hand away. 'I need the calories, like you said.'

That wasn't what she had said at all, Sarah thought, feeling a pang of disappointment. It seemed Mariella had got no further than they had.

'Didn't she have any leads? Did she say anything about what they are looking into? What about Abi's secret boyfriend, did she have any news on him?'

Without even realising it, Sarah found herself nibbling at the toast crusts. She forced herself to put them down and listen carefully.

'No, nothing. And you know how she is when she's fed up.

She just gets into an awful mood and you can't get a sensible word out of her,' said Daphne, hunkering down at the table with a downturned mouth and drooping shoulders. 'I just don't know where she gets it from.'

'I can't think,' Sarah smiled wryly, and patted her friend's hand. 'Maybe just go through everything she *did* say. You never know, something may spark an idea. We need all the help we can get at this point.'

'Just because we solved that business at the Jolly Roger so easily last time,' Daphne said. 'We really got above ourselves, and thought the answers would always jump out at us...'

'Well, I don't think it was as simple as all that,' said Sarah. She'd had to put in a lot of good old-fashioned thinking time before anything had 'jumped out', as Daphne put it.

But Daphne was on a roll. 'We convinced ourselves that we were somehow gifted at all this detective malarkey whereas the plain fact is we're two retired ladies with a second-hand clothes salesman in tow... What on earth can we do if the police themselves are stumped? Mari says if we don't find out anything by the Whitsun holiday then the whole case is going to be handed over to the Canterbury force, and then she'll never get her promotion. That only gives us a couple of days! She's beside herself. It's all a disaster, whichever way you look at it, Sarah. Sarah! *Sarah?* Are you even listening to me?'

But Sarah was sitting bolt upright, with an arrested expression on her face.

'Oh my God, Sarah, are you all right? Are you having a stroke?' Daphne lurched forward in her seat and grabbed Sarah's arm.

Sarah shook her off. 'I'm fine, but what was that you just said?'

'I said, "Are. You. Having. A. Stroke?"' Daphne repeated loudly, enunciating every word.

'Before that,' Sarah said impatiently. 'Something about a holiday?'

'The Whitsun break? Half term. It starts on Monday. What about it?' Daphne frowned.

'Whitsun,' said Sarah, now with a big smile on her face. 'Don't you see?'

'See what?' Daphne said, turning wildly towards the small window over her wilderness of a garden. 'Is it Mephisto?'

At that, Hamish leapt up from his comfortable bed and bristled, looking towards the cat flap with bared teeth.

'No, of course it's not your cat,' said Sarah, growing exasperated. 'It's the word *Whitsun!*'

'You mean, Whitsunday is still a day away, and we're bound to have made a breakthrough by then?' said Daphne.

'No!' said Sarah, putting her hands to her forehead now. 'Whitsun... *wits*... Abi's dying words. She was trying to say Whitsun!'

Daphne's frown cleared. 'Oh! Oh I see! Whitsun, of course. That's brilliant, Sarah.' For a second, she was all smiles. 'Well done, that's so clever of you.' Sarah beamed. But, almost immediately, Daphne's face fell. 'But what does it actually mean?'

TWENTY-TWO

'What even *is* Whitsun?' said Charles, an hour later at a hastily convened summit meeting at the Beach Café. The sun was burning brightly now and he looked dapper in a straw hat and Ray-Ban sunglasses. Sarah decided not to mention the fact that Daphne had described him as a second-hand clothes salesman.

'We always had it drummed into us at school, didn't we, Sarah? I bet you remember chapter and verse about it – so to speak,' Daphne chuckled. Sarah and Charles looked at her, bemused. 'The Bible, you two. Do try to keep up,' she explained.

Sarah thought back to those years of dreary assemblies. She certainly remembered sitting, cross-legged and fidgety, on a cold parquet floor, but she wasn't at all sure she could remember the true meaning of Whitsun. 'I think we'd better google it.'

A few minutes later, after Hannah had brought restorative mugs of tea and a selection of cakes to nibble on, they were all poring over Sarah's iPhone.

'OK, there's a ton of information here,' she said. 'Like this, for instance: *Whitsun is the seventh Sunday after Easter, when the Holy Spirit descended on the disciples.*'

'Well, that's something,' said Daphne, in tones which suggested it was almost nothing, but she was too polite to say so. 'I only know that Mari was hoping to take the kids away for the Whitsun break. If there's no progress with Abi's murder then she'll be stuck here,' she added gloomily.

'All the more reason for us to get our thinking caps on,' said Charles, draining his mug of tea. 'The three of us should be able to find the connection between Abi and Whitsun easily. Come on now, ladies. Let's concentrate.'

It was one thing telling them to try harder, thought Sarah, as she did her best to focus. But it just wasn't that easy. There were so many distractions on the beach here, for a start. There was an enthusiastic game of volleyball going on to their left, while a young lovey-dovey couple had stopped for a snog right in front of them. Sarah saw Charles glancing their way and she rapidly turned her eyes towards the sea wall which separated the beach from the road. Then she sat up a bit straighter and looked again.

'Do either of you see that?' she asked the others excitedly. Daphne, who'd just gathered up the last of the cake crumbs and was popping them into her mouth, shook her head wordlessly. Charles, looking through his sunglasses and then peering over them, suddenly looked almost as animated as Sarah.

'Oh my gosh,' he said. 'That could be it. Well done, Sarah.' He smiled her way.

Sarah, feeling rather flustered all of a sudden, lowered her eyes modestly. Meanwhile Daphne, after chewing furiously, burst into speech.

'Well, I don't know what on earth you two are talking about. I can't see a thing!' She was now squinting ferociously but was obviously not locking onto the poster which had drawn Sarah and Charles's attention.

'What's up with your eyesight, Daphne?' Sarah asked worriedly.

'Oh, nothing,' said Daphne, waving her hand and accidentally dislodging a shower of crumbs from her lap, which Hamish pounced on gratefully. 'I just rely on my third eye, you know, the spiritual one.'

'Right. Well, useful though that must be, if you can't see what we're talking about in the here and now, let's get up and have a proper look,' Sarah said, as Charles took a couple of notes out of his wallet and anchored them under the empty teapot for the waitress.

They all got to their feet, Hamish shaking sand out of his fur as they went. It wasn't far to the line of posters on the wall, but this area of the beach, furthest from the sea, was dry and powdery and difficult not to sink into. They were all mimicking astronauts doing a moonwalk by the time they'd got close enough for Daphne to make sense of it.

It was a row of large, multicoloured posters pasted to the wall, shouting about the delights of a funfair coming to Merstairs. 'Whitsun Family Fete!' they trumpeted, with a frenetic fairground scene peeping out from behind hectic dayglo lettering.

'Oh,' said Daphne, clearly feeling let down. 'It's just the usual. They come every year and set up on the village green outside the school.'

'But don't you see? This must be the fair Abi's friends were talking about!'

Sarah couldn't help sounding excited. It seemed like a solid connection at last between Abi and the word 'wits' or Whitsun, not to mention the mysterious boyfriend and the school itself – but Daphne was looking unimpressed, and even Charles now seemed less sure than he had been.

He sighed. 'As it says on the poster, it's "the most popular fair for all the family". It will be rammed with young men, enjoying the rides, drinking too much, making fools of themselves. That doesn't mean they killed Abi.'

'OK, OK, I agree,' said Sarah, holding her hands up. 'But Abi's friends said she was going there to show off her boyfriend, and she must have meant something when she said that word "wits". She was trying to give me a clue. We need to be at the Whitsun fair, you two,' she said, pleading. 'We can't simply ignore a dying girl's last words.'

TWENTY-THREE

Whitsunday morning dawned bright and clear and, as soon as Sarah opened the curtains, she could tell it was going to be another beautiful day in Merstairs. There wasn't a cloud to be seen, and even the seagulls were being nice and quiet for the occasion, confining themselves to making perfect arcs in the sky with their pristine white wings.

Hamish, catching sight of them as he stood up on his hind legs to assess the weather situation, gave an excited bark. Who knew, today he might finally catch one of those blighters. Both he and Sarah pattered downstairs, eager to begin the day.

The first unwelcome discovery was that Sarah had run out of milk. She'd noticed before that the more time she gave to these murderous enquiries, the less efficient she was at keeping her house running smoothly. For a moment, she tossed up between a quick walk to the nearest shop or nipping next door to cadge some from Daphne. It wasn't the sort of thing she would normally do – heavens, she would never normally run out in the first place – but with a friend as old as Daphne she felt she could take this liberty. Hamish would certainly be keen for an early morning stroll, and maybe it would be best if she touched base with Daphne anyway, to make sure her friend was ready for the evening's funfair stakeout.

'Come on, then, boy. Let's see if Daphne's up yet,' said Sarah encouragingly as she clipped the lead onto the little Scottie's collar.

Hamish was rather circumspect as they set off down their own well-weeded path and then up through the chaotic wilderness that led to Daphne's front door. The little dog had once strolled here with his guard down, only to be pounced upon by Mephisto. The massive ginger puss was apt to conceal himself in Daphne's tufty shrubs, giving a most unfair height advantage. He then dropped down, like an enormous furry parachute, right onto any unsuspecting Scotties beneath him.

Thankfully, this morning the ten-second journey passed without incident and Daphne even answered the door quite fast – it turned out she had just been passing with her morning toast in hand, intending to take it back upstairs with her to munch in bed. Sarah shuddered inwardly at the thought of crumbs in the sheets, and then made her request.

'Of course, of course,' said Daphne, opening her arms wide to both visitors, inadvertently splattering some marmalade on the wall. She scooped it up absent-mindedly with a finger and then licked it off. 'Yum. Come along with you. Not like you to run out of milk, Sarah.' She smiled over her shoulder as she preceded them into the kitchen, today's silken robe, patterned with peonies and roses, billowing behind her like the sail of a ship.

Once in the kitchen, Sarah itched to start on the washing-up, which was now threatening to encroach on the hob, while the table was covered in the usual mix of newspaper articles, magazines, spoons, teacups and biros. Daphne sensed Sarah's slight reluctance to sit down and swept a pile of old copies of the local paper off a chair and onto the floor.

'Make yourself at home. You'll have your tea here now, won't you, and I'll give you a jug of milk to take back with you.'

'That would be lovely,' Sarah said. She started idly tidying the stack of papers on the floor – then stopped as a torn page floated free. She picked it up just before Hamish snuffled over importantly to have a look. She knew to her cost that sometimes papers didn't survive Hamish's viewing process.

She put the page down on the table and smoothed it out. The headline was gone, but the photo seemed to have been taken in the Jolly Roger, showing a group of women.

'What's this, Daphne?' she asked.

Her friend turned round from the sink, where she'd been scraping some singed toast, bits flying everywhere. 'What? Oh, that. It's just that crafting group I'm in. We saw them in the pub the other day,' she said. 'You remember. With Pat and Regina Stanforth. That's Mabel in the centre, with the little round glasses. You met her, didn't you? Goodness, that reminds me, I haven't texted her Mari's number yet.'

'Oh, yes of course, the afternoon before the vigil,' Sarah said. 'It's coming back to me.' She'd thought the women seemed more intent on chatting than on their handiwork. But in the paper, the emphasis was very much on crafting. She looked along the line of smiling faces, some holding up quilting squares and others displaying intricate pieces of crochet. 'I do love this lady's dress, it looks a bit like my bedroom curtains,' Sarah said, pointing to the gracious-looking lady in the centre. 'Oops, don't tell her I said that, she might take it the wrong way.'

Daphne snorted with laughter. 'If you mean Regina Stanforth, she'd most definitely take umbrage. She's very proper.'

'It looks like a fun group though,' Sarah said idly, then stopped. 'Wait a minute. Who's this on the end? Her head's turned away but I could swear...' her voice tailed off.

Daphne came over to join her. 'Oh. Oh, I think you're right. That's Abi. She didn't come to the group that often, just now and again. Gosh, Mari's kiddies miss her so much. They don't understand what's happened at all.'

'Has the school tried to explain things?' Sarah asked.

'They had an assembly. One of the teachers said it was like when your hamster dies. But half the children have been told their pets "go to live on a farm", so they think Abi's just tilling the fields somewhere and will be back soon.'

'It's difficult talking to children about this stuff, but avoiding it can store up problems for later,' said Sarah sadly. 'They do say honesty is the best policy.'

Then Daphne came over to the table, moved a pile of napkins out of the way, and held up a misshapen, lumpy piece of fabric, shot through with holes as though it had been gnawed by rodents. It was in a deep burnt orange colour.

'What do you think of my crochet project?' she asked, the pride in her voice apparent.

Sarah thought for a moment, and her strictures about the truth went out of the window. 'Looks like it's coming along really nicely,' she said with a broad smile.

Hamish, in Mephisto's basket again by the window, gave his mistress a look and buried his tufty head in his paws. That was his least favourite colour, reminding him strongly of his feline nemesis. Good job they wouldn't be asking him for his view, he decided.

TWENTY-FOUR

Once they'd finished breakfast – and after Sarah had insisted on helping with the washing-up, and left Daphne's kitchen as ship-shape as it would ever be – the two women tried to decide on their plan of action for the day. The fair wouldn't start until the evening, which left them plenty of time to fill.

'I vote we take a day off the investigation and just enjoy ourselves a bit. After all, that's what retirement's for,' said Daphne. 'And look at the weather. It's a glorious day.'

All Sarah's instincts shrieked that they should carry on digging. Time was of the essence, when there was a murderer loose in Merstairs. But, on the other hand, Daphne was right. They were retired. They were going to crack on this evening. Perhaps they'd earned a few hours of leisure first.

'You're right, Daphne. Let's have a good walk along the shore. Maybe we could go and visit that ruined castle along the coast?'

'Yes, or perhaps we could pop in at the Beach Café. Hannah did say she was baking a new batch of brownies,' said Daphne in innocent tones.

Immediately, Sarah knew what had prompted her friend's

uncharacteristic desire for healthy outdoor exercise. But she had to admit she did love a brownie. And, of course, they could actually chew over the Abi case while they sampled Hannah's treats. Hamish, too, was happy to hear the jingle of his lead as Sarah got their stuff together and picked up Daphne's donated jug of milk to take next door. He enjoyed his stolen moments in Mephisto's basket enormously, but there was an element of jeopardy that he perhaps didn't want to push too far. Not to mention a whole world of smells out there, with only one small Scottie to test them.

They were soon bowling along the coastal road, a soft breeze toying with Sarah's cap of silvery blonde hair and playing merry havoc with Daphne's red tresses. As it was a Sunday, the beach was relatively quiet, and there were few holidaymakers around.

'I expect everyone's sleeping in. It's always quite hectic on a Saturday night in Merstairs,' said Daphne.

'At least the Beach Café is open,' Sarah said.

'And one other place,' Daphne said rather archly.

Sarah followed her friend's pointing finger, and saw she meant Charles Diggory's antiques emporium and second-hand gentlemen's outfitters, next to Marlene's Plaice. The lavender-painted fish and chip shop was firmly shuttered but there seemed to be a light on in Charles's windows.

'Let's go over and see what he's up to,' said Sarah.

'Haha, I knew it! You like him,' said Daphne with a chuckle.

Sarah stopped in her tracks. 'What do you mean by that?'

'Oh, don't take it the wrong way. I think it's great,' said Daphne. 'As soon as you two met, I could see a bright future ahead,' she added, with that infuriating 'mystic' look on her face.

Sarah stopped and wheeled round to face her friend, aware that a bright pink blush was sweeping her cheeks. 'Daphne, Charles and I are just friends. It's not that long since...'

Immediately, Daphne put a hand on Sarah's arm. 'I know, you still feel terrible about Peter. And I respect that, he was a lovely man. But you've got your whole life ahead of you, Sarah.'

'Hardly,' Sarah broke in drily. Sometimes Daphne seemed to have convinced herself that the natural lifespan of a human was about two hundred years, meaning she was still very much in her prime. 'And anyway, it's just not that sort of relationship.'

'Relationship! See! You admit it,' Daphne pounced exuberantly.

Sarah shook her head. 'Did you want a brownie, or not?' she said.

'Ooh, don't mind if I do.' Daphne grinned and the pair strolled on, with plenty of thoughts churning round in both their heads.

By the time they had found a table, Sarah had regained her usual equilibrium. It was pointless being angry with Daphne. She might be way off beam about Charles Diggory but she was an unstoppable force of nature, and always would be – until her two hundredth year and beyond, if she had her way.

TWENTY-FIVE

The Beach Café really was the best place to watch the mesmerising sea, which today was a calm flat blue straight out of a child's paintbox. You could also keep a beady eye on the citizens of Merstairs from these comfy chairs, and that was how Sarah and Daphne were able to spot Mariella instantly as she made her way up the beach. She was off duty, wearing jeans and a cheerful top.

Daphne waved her arms above her head and called out, 'Coo-ee' very loudly, but there was little necessity, Sarah thought fondly. As usual, her friend had dressed as though she wanted to be identifiable in thick fog, in a variety of shades of chartreuse.

'Mum, Aunty Sarah, how are you,' said Mariella, leaning in and kissing both ladies on the cheek.

'Join us, darling, do,' said Daphne, sweeping her bag off the table and almost onto long-suffering Hamish. He'd learnt to dodge such projectiles, though, and regrouped a little closer to Sarah's feet.

'Can't stop too long, I've got to pick the kids up from their playdate in a couple of minutes, then I'm on shift this afternoon, got to take everything over to the handwriting expert, then I've got to get ready for the Whitsun fair tonight – oh, and in between all that, I've got to pop in at the supermarket, then cook the tea and get the kids' bags ready for the child minder tomorrow.' Mariella was ticking the items off on her fingers, running through a tally that made Sarah feel tired just listening to it. She well remembered the days when she'd had to-do lists a mile long... Hang on a minute, what was that about a handwriting expert?

'Did you say you had some samples to drop off at a graphologist?' Sarah said casually, as everyone helped Hannah Betts unload Daphne and Sarah's orders – a delicious early lunch of cheese and ham toasties, with coleslaw and a salad garnish. And, of course, brownies to follow.

'I'm going to order you a toastie too, Mari,' said Daphne. 'No, don't argue. You need to keep your strength up with a day like that ahead.' She asked Hannah to bring a cup of tea as well, and then turned to Sarah. 'Now, what was that you were saying about cardiologists? Is someone ill?'

'Handwriting experts, Daphne. Mariella mentioned she was taking something over to one?' Sarah said, with a beady look at the young policewoman.

'You've got sharp ears, Aunty Sarah,' said Mariella ruefully. 'I shouldn't have said anything. It just came out because I've got such a lot on my mind.'

'I quite understand, I know exactly what it's like. When I was your age, well, I was finding out that juggling is all very well at fairs, like tonight's – but not nearly so much fun when you have to do it at home.'

Mariella laughed and took a cheeky sip of her mother's tea. 'Just till mine gets here,' she said, patting Daphne's arm. 'I needed that. Well, I suppose it won't do too much harm to tell you,' she continued, as Sarah sat forward and gave her every mite of her attention. 'You'll hear it on the

Merstairs grapevine soon enough. Everyone's going to know because one of Jennie Moffat's colleagues was sounding off about it yesterday down at the Seagull Bakery,' Mariella said.

'The bakery! It's a hotbed of gossip,' Daphne said, disapproval written over her face. 'That's what I tell everyone.'

'Well, yes,' said Mariella. 'It seems poor Abi wasn't quite as popular as we all imagined. I honestly wouldn't have thought anyone had a bad word to say about her. She was a lovely girl growing up, and she was so brilliant with the kids at the school, the teachers loved her too... but before she died, she'd started getting these horrible notes.'

'Notes? What kind of notes?' said Sarah, agog now.

'Really mean things. You know, it does sometimes happen in a little place like this. No one wants to criticise people to their faces, so they get all twisted up inside. There's a mental health element to it, I'm sure.'

'Bound to be,' said Sarah, wishing she could ask again what on earth the notes said. A poison pen aspect to Abi's death might provide a new lead. 'Anonymous letters are usually a woman's weapon, aren't they?' she added, aiming for a light tone. 'That's what people say.'

'Funny you should mention that. There's something feminine about the way these notes are put together. The letters are all cut out from the *Merstairs Marketeer*. Anyone might read that, you'd think, but I've worked out that they come from a specific section of the paper – the women's pages.'

'That's really interesting,' Sarah said. 'So you're already thinking it's a woman.'

'Unless it's a man pretending to be a woman,' said Mariella, tucking into the toastie which Hannah had just put in front of her. 'Mmm, this is delicious.'

Sarah, who'd almost finished hers already, nodded her agreement absently. Something was bothering her. 'If the messages are made up of letters cut from the newspaper, what can a graphologist tell you?'

Mariella laughed. 'I can't get a thing past you, Aunty Sarah. You're right, the graphologist isn't looking at the notes. They'll be studying the envelopes, which were handwritten.'

Sarah chewed thoughtfully for a moment. 'That seems very odd. Why go through the bother of cutting out all those letters – a fiddly task, I'm sure – and then write the address on the front? It makes no sense.'

'Well, perhaps the person was tired after all that cutting and sticking,' said Daphne, slurping her tea. 'Or maybe the whole thing was just a bit of a joke. I can't think anyone would be mean enough to send poison pen letters, and to Abi of all people! It has to be some kind of hoax.'

Both Sarah and Mariella confined themselves to chewing.

'I'd love to see one of these notes,' Sarah said, raising her eyebrows at Mariella in what she hoped was winsome appeal.

'I bet,' said the girl drily and, as Sarah had feared, she got up immediately, swigging the last of her tea as she did so. 'Right, well, I've got to get on. So I'll see you both later. I'm assuming you're coming to the fair? Just remember, I don't want any trouble,' Mariella said firmly, looking at them both as though she was the parent, and they were the naughty children.

'Go on with you, cheeky thing,' Daphne giggled, but Sarah nodded.

'We'll be good,' she said reassuringly.

'Why did you say that?' asked Daphne, as Mariella hurried off to get to grips with her busy afternoon. 'You know you'll be dying to poke your nose into everything.'

'As will you,' Sarah countered. 'Well, you know what they say. If you can't be good, be careful,' and they both laughed. Sarah, though, still had the vestiges of a frown between her brows as they ate their delicious brownies. She really didn't like the sound of these notes one little bit.

TWENTY-SIX

As they had time to kill before the fair that evening, Sarah decided to go back to her cottage to give Hamish a bit of a rest, and also give her home a quick spruce-up. Her daughters Becca and Hattie had promised to pay a visit the weekend after next, and Sarah needed to be sure she had plenty of cot sheets for both her little grandchildren, Amelia and Evelyn. It was rather lovely that the two tiny cousins, born just a couple of months apart, had each other to play with. Sarah wasn't sure whether either of her daughters were planning on enlarging their families – motherhood had come as a bit of a shock to both, as it had to Sarah herself back in the day – but she certainly had her fingers crossed.

Daphne also claimed to be very busy, but when Sarah enquired more deeply, it turned out she was planning a long meditation 'to guide Abi's spirit upwards'. Sarah rather winced at that. It reminded her of the moment when Abi had lost her fight and the light had died from her eyes. Still, it kept her focused on thinking the whole case through, as she sorted out the linen cupboard and worried where the little ones were going to sleep. The house was a squeeze with four guests, even if two of them were only a tad larger than Hamish, but she was looking forward to a marvellous time.

It made her all the more conscious of how much had been snatched away from Abi. She'd had everything ahead of her. Life could be so unfair. Sarah sighed and looked up from her task.

Time was ticking on. Though the sky outside the spare bedroom window was still blue, the clock on the mantlepiece showed it was now past five o'clock. She hadn't made any firm plans for supper with Daphne, but it might be fun if they grabbed hot dogs or something at the fair. She hadn't eaten anything like that for years. When Peter had been alive, she'd focused on keeping his cholesterol down, his blood pressure stable and his vitamin intake up. Not that it had mattered a jot in the end. It turned out cancer was happy to prey on even the best fed retired professors. She still cared about nutrition, of course – but she was happy to go off-piste now and again.

Taking a last look around the spare room and checking that the bed was neatly made, the travel cot was at the ready and the linen for the sofabed downstairs was to hand, Sarah permitted herself a smile. The room was very welcoming, with its duvet cover in stripes of pink and yellow, matching curtains and the rocking chair in the corner which was just the thing if either of her lovely grandchildren had a sleepless night – which she was hoping would not be the case, because in theory at least they should both be knocked out by all the wonderful sea air they'd be getting.

She chose a light cardigan from her wardrobe, and pulled out a gauzy scarf that could double as a wrap when the sun set and the evening got cooler. Then she turned and trotted down the stairs, Hamish at her heels. She clipped on the dog's lead and headed out, securing the door carefully behind her. Had Abi had any of these rituals? Had she locked up before meeting her killer? Could something she'd done that fateful morning have led to her death?

Sarah's brows were still furrowed when Daphne came out of her house a few moments later.

'What's up with you, Sarah? You look like you've got the troubles of the world on your shoulders,' her friend said, giving her a hug.

Just then, a streak of ginger fur flashed past them like a bolt from the blue. Immediately, Hamish took off, barking fit to burst, and Sarah, on the end of his lead, was yanked along in his wake.

Daphne burst into an epic gale of laughter, while Sarah hung on like a water-skier dragged behind a speedboat.

'Don't just laugh, do something!' Sarah yelled.

'Mephisto! Come here, boy,' Daphne urged through her giggles, but it was to no avail. The cat raced across the road and was soon weaving through the tourists' ankles, on a mission.

Sarah, who eventually managed to pull up a thoroughly disgruntled Hamish, was quite out of puff. She wasn't sure who she was crosser with, her own dog, the cat – or Daphne. Once she'd got her breath back, though, she was beginning to see the funny side.

'He'll be off to Tarot and Tealeaves,' said Daphne, catching up with her. 'Likes to pop in of an evening.'

'Well, we mustn't do anything to disturb Mephisto's busy schedule,' said Sarah drily, a hand to her side where all that unexpected running seemed to have pulled a muscle. 'I hope he won't have any trouble getting past the candles and cards. Anyway, let's go and see what's happening at this fair.'

'I hope it's not going to be another damp squib, like Whitstable,' said Daphne.

'We just need to keep our eyes peeled for Abi's boyfriend,' said Sarah encouragingly.

'OK,' said Daphne, looking apprehensive. Then her face

cleared. 'Well, the question now is, do we go straight there, or do you want to get something to eat first?'

'I was thinking we could maybe have a hot dog there? But only when we've had a good look round the stalls.'

'I don't want to seem like a doubter,' said Daphne, screwing up her face. 'But I'm not sure anyone's going to stand there shouting, "Hello, I was Abi Moffat's boyfriend."'

'I know,' said Sarah with a shrug. 'But her friend was very clear. Abi was going to come clean about him tonight, so it really seems like the best place to track him down. But if you've got any better suggestions, I'd love to hear them.'

'Well, I do have one thought,' said Daphne, with a mischievous look in her eye.

'What's that?' asked Sarah, eager for any kind of a pointer.

'Well, it's just that we ought to get into the hot dog queue straight away. What if they sell out?'

* * *

Ten minutes later, with a hot dog in one hand and a fizzy drink in the other, Daphne was looking a lot happier. Sarah, who was holding out until she had worked up a proper appetite, and Hamish, who had been most unfairly excluded from the snack purchasing, were reacting in entirely characteristic fashion. Sarah averted her gaze as Daphne chomped away enthusiastically, while Hamish glued his eyes to Daphne's and did his utmost to communicate his yearnings telepathically. Strangely, for one so in tune with the vibrations of the universe, Daphne seemed quite oblivious.

There was a lot for Sarah to fix her own attention on. All around were the sights, sounds and smells of a fairground – the distinctive hot vanilla scent of the candyfloss machine, the mouthwateringly buttery aroma of the popcorn cart, the blare of the merry-go-round with its flashing lights and parade of ponies bobbing up and down with the youngsters of Merstairs hanging onto shiny dappled necks. Everywhere there were whizzes and bangs as hopeful daddies took their shots at the coconut shy or the hoopla, trying their best to win giant plush teddies.

'This is a needle in a haystack,' sighed Sarah, looking around and realising her chances of spotting the dead teacher's boyfriend in the lively fairground were probably nil squared.

Just then, she caught sight of Charles Diggory. He was holding onto two huge sticks of candyfloss, and the tiny hands of a pair of cherubic and beautifully dressed children. Aged about five, they were clearly twins, a boy and a girl. The girl was in a blue smocked frock and little Mary Jane shoes, with frilly white socks, and the boy was wearing a sailor suit – something Sarah had last seen in a costume drama and had never actually witnessed being worn by a contemporary child. Bringing up the rear was Tinkerbell the Chihuahua, today also wearing a little sailor outfit, though she had left the hat at home.

At once, Hamish sat up straight and tried to look as though he hadn't been salivating over Daphne's hot dog for the last ten minutes.

'Ah, um, there you are,' said Charles, looking slightly furtive. Sarah soon divined the reason why, when Francesca Diggory stepped out from behind the Wurlitzer, where she'd been having a word with a group of townsfolk. As usual, she was dressed in full-on Princess Anne mode, with a headscarf clamped under her long chin and a shiny patent handbag on her arm, her horseshoe-patterned silk shirt looking absurdly formal for an evening at the fair.

'If it isn't Sally and Daffy,' Francesca said, in a voice so loud and posh it could have been heard in Whitstable. 'I really ought to invoice you. Thanks to you I've lost a gardener.'

Sarah goggled. 'Would you really want a murderer working for you?' she said, realising Francesca was referring to the person who'd shoved their victim into a trunk just after she'd arrived in Merstairs. 'Lovely to meet your grandchildren,' she said with a smile at the twins, who'd come forward to say hello to Hamish. He had his head on one side and was looking at his most tuftily adorable.

'Please may we stroke him?' said the little girl politely.

'Of course,' said Sarah. One thing you could say for Francesca was that her grandchildren were impeccably behaved. But perhaps they got that from their grandpa.

'Max and Calista, this is Sarah and Daphne. And Hamish,' said Charles, bending down to pat the little Scottie too, who licked him lavishly for his pains. This was a step too far for Tinkerbell, who seemed outraged at the amount of attention the unkempt interloper was getting. She shot Hamish a contemptuous glance, and bolted into the gathering crowds, trailing her bright pink lead behind her.

'Drat!' said Charles, straightening up abruptly. The twins immediately took off after the little dog and, with an apologetic look, Charles hared away on their trail, looking tall and gangly as he sped along.

'Well, well,' said Francesca, confronting Sarah and Daphne. 'I see you two haven't lost your talent for creating chaos wherever you go,' she sneered.

Daphne preened and looked thrilled. 'So nice of you to say so, Francesca. I wouldn't have thought this was your type of thing, though?'

Francesca took a contemptuous look around her, at the happy families traipsing between stalls, eating toffee apples and enjoying the buzzy fairground atmosphere. Francesca's voice carried well at the best of times. Tonight, to compete with the funfair noises, the mayor raised her voice just that little bit too loud.

'Of course not, I hate this sort of thing,' she boomed. A couple of families took a step backwards, but Francesca was oblivious. 'I'm here in an official capacity, of course. I wouldn't be seen dead here otherwise,' she finished.

'Well, that's nice to know,' said Sarah, much more conscious than Francesca of the crowd gathering around them.

'It's a lovely Merstairs tradition,' said Daphne, in shocked tones. 'What a shame you don't enjoy it. Your grandchildren seem to be loving it.'

'Well, they're only five years old,' Francesca said haughtily. 'They don't know any better yet. Now, I must get on, I need to make my announcement.'

She turned to go, only to find a press of people behind her, all looking mightily disgruntled. Among them was Jennie Moffat. Now she stepped to the front.

'Sorry to hear you'd rather be dead than enjoying this evening with the town,' she said, her eyes still red-raw from weeping. 'My daughter *is* dead. You don't know how much I wish she was here instead of you.'

There was a loud murmuring from the crowd. Sarah recognised faces from the abortive disturbance at the vigil. She really hoped things weren't going to turn nasty.

TWENTY-SEVEN

Just when it looked as though Francesca might get her comeuppance, Tinkerbell saved the day. She rushed out of the crowd, hotly pursued by Max and Calista, with Charles bringing up the rear. Confused and distressed by the noise, the little dog ran right over to the mayor and nipped her on the ankle.

As Francesca hopped from foot to foot, rubbing the sore place, red in the face with anger and humiliation, the large crowd laughed gustily – and Sarah and Daphne couldn't help joining in. There was more than an element of relief for Sarah – she'd been really worried things might turn ugly for a minute. And she never failed to get the giggles when Daphne did. Then she caught sight of Charles's face, and abruptly stifled her mirth. Admittedly, his own mouth was quivering, as though he was suppressing a guffaw or two, but he was also looking rather worriedly at Francesca. After all, she was the mother of his child, and granny to his grandchildren. And, like many difficult people, she was probably even more of a nightmare to deal with when she was riled.

Sarah stepped forward. 'Let me have a quick look at that.

Dog bites can be quite toxic... I'll just see if Tinkerbell's broken the skin.'

Francesca drew herself up to her full height. 'You'll do no such thing. I'm about to make my speech.' With that, she swept off, slightly ruining the impression by having to limp. A couple of minutes later there was a microphone screech over by the big carousel and Francesca stepped out fearlessly in front of a crowd that had, not so very long ago, looked as though it might turn on her. You had to admire her bravery, thought Sarah – if nothing much else. Charles, at her elbow, clapped enthusiastically, but the sound petered out as he realised he was in a minority of one. Nevertheless, once Francesca had started on her spiel, she soon managed to win round her audience, with lavish thanks to all for attending. She pointed out the fundraising buckets on the gates to raise money for a memorial for Abi and for extra books for the school library to be bought in her name.

It was a masterclass in public speaking, and by the time she handed the microphone back to a fairground worker, she had the crowd eating out of her hand.

'Phew, that really looked like a close one for a minute, I thought she might get lynched,' said Sarah.

'Lunched? Well, a bit late for that, but maybe one of those burgers might be good,' said Daphne, locking onto the refreshments stand like a heat-seeking missile despite her recent hot dog, and striding off. Sarah shook her head but realised she was now feeling pretty peckish herself.

They were soon in the long queue for snacks, and Sarah realised it was quite a good vantage point to scope out what was going on at the fair. Who knew, someone here might provide the vital clue to unlocking the Abi mystery. There were plenty of men around, but would any of them be Abi's type? Her eyes were out on stalks as they slowly shuffled closer to the front of the line. She watched the little clumps of people here and there, throwing balls at the coconut shy and taking aim at the rifle range. Hang on a minute…

'Daphne, see that stall over there? The shooting gallery? Who is that they're aiming at? Do you know, it looks a bit like… no, it can't be.'

Sarah squinted hard. It looked as though the shape was wearing a headscarf. Well, she had to admire the cheek of whoever was running that stall. She grabbed Daphne's arm and, a second later, they were hurrying towards it.

'Here,' said Daphne, outraged. 'We were nearly at the front of that queue! I want my burger.'

'Shh!' said Sarah urgently. 'Do stop making a fuss. We need to get a proper look at that stand. Killing women, even in pretence? Doesn't it make you think?'

'Quite honestly, it's hard to think when you're literally starving to death,' Daphne grumbled. 'I don't know what's got into you, Sarah. I had my order all ready, double cheeseburger with ketchup, mayo and a large helping of fries, no salt though because I'm really careful with my blood pressure. All this scurrying about will be doing it no good.'

Sarah scarcely had time to frown in wonder at Daphne's priorities. They were nearly at the rifle range. Again, there was a queue, so the two women joined it, with Daphne still muttering crossly. Even Hamish was a bit disgruntled; all those nice smells were now far away and he wasn't sure he liked the ominous popping sound of the guns as they fired projectiles at the target.

They were the only women in the queue, Sarah realised, as they started to move forward. There really was a lot that was questionable about this attraction; she thought she might have a word with whoever organised the fair when this was over. For the moment, though, she was concentrating on getting a look at the staff loading the guns and handing them to the patient fairgoers when they got to the head of the queue. And if anyone proved a particularly good shot, well, that could be interesting too.

'I don't see what's so fun about this stall. I'd much rather have a go on the hoopla, if we must chuck our pensions away on this sort of thing,' said Daphne crossly. 'My aim really isn't terribly good.'

'But don't you see, Daph, this is about assessing who might want to hurt a woman.'

'That's a bit of a leap, Sarah. This is all make-believe, you know. The target isn't a real person.'

'It looks like one, though, doesn't it?' Sarah pressed her friend.

Daphne couldn't deny the resemblance to Francesca. 'But it's not the mayor who got killed, is it?' she hissed at Sarah.

Sarah thought for a moment. Perhaps she'd got carried away. There was no real comparison between a bit of target practice and the stab that had cost Abi her life. Suddenly she felt a bit silly. And a hunger pang reminded her that they could have been tucking into, well, not exactly a gourmet supper, but a very tasty one at least.

She turned to her friend. 'I'm sorry, Daphne, you're ri—' she started, when Daphne made a very strange gurgling sound.

'Don't look now,' she said. 'But I think I've just seen our killer.'

TWENTY-EIGHT

It was an extraordinary statement, not least because it showed Daphne acknowledging for the first time that murder had been committed on the streets of Merstairs. She usually shied away from the idea like an extremely nervous horse.

Sarah looked at her in astonishment, and then the temptation to turn and gawp at whatever had arrested her friend's attention became too great. She wheeled round, only to have a strange and sinister sight meet her eyes.

Standing sideways on to the target, and with the fairground rifle clamped into his shoulder just like a sniper, was a dark man Sarah had never seen before. He had a shock of inky hair that fell over his brow, and was tall and thin, garbed from head to toe in black. His long black coat almost swept the floor, and she could see the dull gleam of elaborate silver buckles on his chunky black boots. He looked a little like the stereotypical baddie in a Western, the sort who would shortly trick the sheriff with a heart of gold into a ruthless, fatal showdown.

'Who on earth *is* that?' asked Sarah, as the man finally loosened his finger on the trigger. The plastic pellet flew straight at the cut-out, thudding into it with a satisfying thunk. With a little shiver, Sarah realised he'd got the outline right in the chest – exactly where Abi's wound had been.

'That's the deputy head of the primary school,' said Daphne, with a sort of sigh. 'He fancied Abi, I forgot till I saw him just now. He's rather sexy, isn't he?'

Sarah didn't dignify this with a reply. In her view, being a potential killer instantly reduced anyone's attractiveness to zero. The fact that this young man was so charismatic was neither here nor there.

'Does he hate Francesca, or something? I think this whole business of the stallholder using her as a cut-out is appalling, by the way.'

'Don't tell me you're her biggest fan all of a sudden,' scoffed Daphne.

'I'm not – but I don't think that's an excuse for rampant misogyny. It's such bad taste, pretending to shoot at a woman in a place where a girl has just been stabbed.'

'You're reading too much into it,' said Daphne. 'It's a Merstairs tradition. The serving mayor, whoever that is, is always the cut-out, and the money goes to charity. It's a joke.'

'Hilarious,' murmured Sarah. 'But I suppose that does put a different complexion on it. So what did you mean about that man being the killer?'

'It's only just struck me,' said Daphne, looking quite smug. 'But everyone knew about his crush on Abi. Of course, she was pretending to go out with poor Josh. But she could have put that aside to date Johnny Bartlett – that's his name. I mean, wouldn't you?' Daphne had her head on one side, dreamily contemplating the young man as he raised his gun again, aimed carefully, and this time hit the cardboard version of Francesca neatly between the eyes.

'That's irrelevant,' said Sarah, though her gaze did linger on the young chap's impressive physique. 'Anyway, he's young enough to be either of our grandsons.'

Daphne spent a moment trying to tot things up on her fingers. 'Maybe a son. But I take your point. Well, if you've quite finished gawping at him, shall we go and get our burgers?'

Sarah didn't bother to point out that she hadn't been the one mesmerised by Johnny Bartlett's dark good looks. Well, not really, anyway.

'Hang on a minute, Daphne. You've just provided quite a good reason for him to bump off Abi, don't you think? We need to look into it. I'd like to talk to him, at least.'

Just then, Johnny Bartlett turned away from the stall, having finished his go. Sarah immediately nipped after him.

'Oh, honestly, Sarah, we're going to miss our turn at this now as well. I don't think you understand how queuing works,' wailed Daphne, trotting after her friend.

Johnny Bartlett loped off quickly. By the time Sarah managed to put a hand on his arm, she was quite breathless. Daphne, bringing up the rear, bent over double and panted unashamedly as soon as they all came to a halt.

'I'm sorry, Mr, er, Bartlett,' gasped Sarah. 'But, um, well, Daphne here wanted to have a word.'

'I did?' said Daphne, red in the face and unamused.

'Yes, erm, it was about your grandchildren,' said Sarah, giving Daphne a meaningful look.

'Oh, ah, yes,' Daphne puffed a little wildly. 'Um, have you given any thought to the Nativity play yet? Because Louis would be absolutely perfect as Joseph.'

Johnny Bartlett looked from one woman to the other. 'Well, that's a first. I don't think I've been asked about the Christmas play this early in the year before. You're keen, I'll give you that, Mrs Roux.'

'Oh, you remembered my name,' squeaked Daphne, looking as though she might faint from excitement. 'Well, I know Sarah's got a couple of things she wants to ask you as well, so I'll just leave you to it,' she said, and beetled off, leaving Sarah looking after her in surprise. But then she saw her friend was heading in the direction of Madame Grimaldi's tent, and guessed she was going to check out the competition.

Sarah racked her brain for a way to get the man talking. 'You're so good at shooting things,' she said, inwardly wincing but thinking it might at least butter him up.

'Oh, that's from a misspent youth, playing darts in the Jolly Roger,' said Bartlett with a laugh. 'I'm long-sighted, so I have a bit of an advantage. I'd be absolutely hopeless if the target was any nearer,' he shrugged. Sarah tried not to look disappointed.

'So, what exactly is on your mind? And what year is your grandchild in?' Johnny Bartlett fixed her with those mesmerising brown eyes.

'Oh, er, no, it's not for me, I was just wondering... people have been connecting your name with Abi Moffat's, I just wondered—'

Bartlett took a step back. 'Are you kidding? Do you seriously think I had something to do with what happened to Abi...?' he was saying indignantly, when a woman's scream suddenly pierced the night air. More chillingly still, Sarah recognised that voice instantly. It was Daphne.

TWENTY-NINE

'Excuse me,' Sarah gasped to Bartlett, before picking Hamish up and running with him to the source of the terrible sound. A crowd was already gathering around Madame Grimaldi's tent, but people were standing back, hesitating whether to open the tent flaps. Inside, Sarah could hear Daphne keening. She pushed the thick red curtain out of the way and walked into the dimly lit interior.

It was, to say the least, rather spooky inside, with silvery stars and planets drawn on black velvet drapes hung all around, and a creepy dummy in the corner dressed up like the genie that came out of Aladdin's lamp. At its feet was a neat pile of handbags. There was also a strong smell of cheap incense. Sarah tried to control her anxiety. It was a fortune teller's tent, for goodness' sake, it was bound to be a bit unusual. Once her eyes got used to the gloom, she saw Daphne, standing huddled by the table. She was snuffling and seemed to be in a bit of a trance. Sitting in front of her, opposite the elaborate but empty chair which must usually be Madame Grimaldi's, was a woman. She was completely motionless, her body slumped over the desk, her head flat against it and her arms dangling limply over its sides.

'Daphne, what's going on?' Sarah rushed over to her friend.

Daphne collapsed into her arms. 'Oh Sarah, it's so terrible... I just popped in, to say hello really, and there she was – lying like that.'

'Who on earth is it? Is she breathing?' Sarah said, stepping round to the other side of the table. She put a finger on the woman's neck, to feel for a pulse. Nothing. She was gone.

It was curious, the body wasn't yet cold, and there was no obvious indication as to what the cause of death had been. Not like Abi, for instance. There was no sign of a disturbance, either. The tent's interior was quiet and orderly, and there was a pack of cards in front of the lady that hadn't been disarranged in any way. It was as though she had just keeled over.

There was another sob from Daphne and Sarah shook herself, realising her first priority had to be to the living, not the dead. She put her arm round her friend and helped her slowly out of the tent.

'Have you called Mari?' she asked her. Daphne shook her head mutely.

'Right.' Sarah fished her phone out of her pocket and quickly told Mariella the terrible news. Thankfully the police-woman was already en route for the fair and was only a few minutes away.

Although Sarah kept her voice down, the tidings that something awful had happened seemed to spread throughout the fair like smoke on a summer's night, sucking all the joy out of the atmosphere. By the time the police cars had parked near the little green, all the rides had been shut down and the stall-holders were waiting nervously to see what would happen next.

'Mum, I can't believe this,' said Mariella, who had the pathologist, Dr Pamela Strutton, in tow.

'I'm going to have to up my rates if we keep having these block bookings,' Dr Strutton said wryly to Sarah as she passed her and disappeared into the tent. Sarah couldn't help a tiny smile at the typical medical gallows humour, but Daphne at her side started sobbing noisily again.

Once Mariella had efficiently supervised the positioning of police tape, and then got the SOCOs started, she left Dumbarton and Deeside in charge, waiting for DI Brice to arrive.

She turned back to Daphne and Sarah. 'Right. I'll take you back to the station and you can tell me what's what. But before that, answer me this. Who is that woman?'

Sarah looked at Daphne. This is exactly what she wanted to know herself.

Daphne sniffed into a sodden tissue. 'Don't you know?' she wailed.

'I wouldn't be asking if I did, now, would I, Mum? Come on now,' Mariella said more gently.

Daphne looked from one to the other, and finally quavered out the name. 'It's M-Mabel. Mabel Moorhead.'

THIRTY

Sarah was glad they weren't in the official interview room, with its grim nailed-down chairs and two-way mirror. But, although this office was a lot less intimidating, she would have a thousand times preferred to be tucked up in her cosy cottage with a mug of cocoa. Why, oh why had she arrogantly assumed she could sort everything out at the funfair? All that had happened was that Daphne had been severely traumatised. Her poor friend was now too tired even to sniff any more, and as for Hamish, he'd given up on the day and subsided into a fitful sleep under the desk a long time ago.

'One more time for me, please, Mum. Just tell me what you were doing in a fortune teller's tent with a dead body.'

'It wasn't like that, Mari,' Daphne said, shifting restlessly on the tiny sofa that was trying to accommodate both her and Sarah. 'I just nipped in to see what Madame Grimaldi was up to. You know I have to keep abreast of paranormal developments, I have a duty as Merstairs' leading clairvoyant. And also... I wanted to see how she was cheating.'

'So you had no idea anyone would be in there? Apart from Madame Grimaldi, that is.'

'Absolutely. And of course Madame Grimaldi *wasn't* there. I never dreamt she'd actually attract a client. I mean, who would go to her when they could come to me? I wouldn't have gone in there for a second if I'd have known... Poor Mabel. I don't want to speak ill of the dead, she was a wonderful woman, but what on earth was she thinking of? It's just too awful,' she said, subsiding into sobs again.

'She's the one from your stitching classes, isn't she?' Sarah asked gently.

Daphne nodded silently.

'It is rather surprising she'd be having her fortune told,' said Sarah. 'Her father was a GP, you said.'

'What do you mean by that?' Daphne asked, quick as a flash. 'You're a GP, and you fully support my gift.'

Sarah coughed. 'Well, yes. I was just, um... assembling a few facts about her. Um, to help Mariella.'

'Thanks, Aunty Sarah,' said Mariella drily. 'Any information is useful, Mum. For instance, do you know where Madame Grimaldi might be?'

'No.' Daphne looked up quickly. 'There was no sign of her in the tent. But surely you've found her by now?'

'We've got people out looking,' said Mariella shortly. 'Any reason you can think of that would make her take off like that? Anything... odd in the tent, for example?'

Sarah looked at Mariella. 'Apart from the dead body, you mean?' She tried to think back to that weird interior, with all its strange signs and symbols. The genie model alone was enough to give anyone the heebie-jeebies, but that probably wasn't what the policewoman meant. It had been so dark... something had definitely seemed out of place, but for the life of her Sarah couldn't remember what it was now. Mabel's body made everything else seem unimportant. She shook her head. 'Do you think Madame Grimaldi could be another victim? Or is she a suspect?'

'Madame Grimaldi? Oh, I hope she's safe! She can't have had anything to do with all this,' said Daphne, startled. 'You don't think so, do you, Mari?'

'We just want to eliminate her from our enquiries,' said Mariella. 'Right. Well. How about telling me if anyone had a grudge against Mabel? Had she annoyed anyone recently? Maybe you saw a row... I don't know, did she steal anyone's wool?' she asked her mother rather desperately. 'Pat can be quite, erm, challenging sometimes, did they fall out over patterns, have a dispute about where to sit in the pub, even?'

'Of course not,' said Daphne with dignity. 'Mabel wasn't like that. She was a real peacemaker, she couldn't bear people arguing. She was a wonderful person. In fact, she was always *giving* people wool. Regina is going to be absolutely devastated, they were so close. And Mabel was fit and well too, always going for healthy walks. The last person I'd have thought would die of a heart attack.'

Mariella and Sarah's eyes met over Daphne's bent head. There was a short silence. Then Daphne looked up.

'Oh no! Don't tell me... Don't tell me it's another murder!' Her shoulders shook as she started crying again. Sarah patted her back and handed over another tissue.

'Mum, we just don't know,' Mariella said. 'We'll need to do a lot of tests. All I can say at the moment is that we're looking at it as a suspicious death.'

At that, Daphne let out a wail. It was going to be a long night, thought Sarah. To take her mind off the horrors of the evening, she let her gaze roam round the room. It was at least twice the size of the previous interview cubby-hole they'd been questioned in, and looked like the station's incident room, right down to a whiteboard at the front with pictures of Abi Moffat on it, and what Sarah could only assume was a maze of potential leads. There was no sign of a murder weapon, but she could see photocopies of the poison pen letters with their cut-outs from the *Merstairs Marketeer*. There was also a blurry picture of an elderly woman, who must be Mabel Moorhead, which looked as though it had just been hastily tacked up with tape, and a scrawl underneath that Sarah, with her years of deciphering other doctors' handwriting, read as saying, 'possible heart attack?' She tried not to gawp too much and resisted the temptation to sit as close to the board as possible. Mariella had brought them in there without thinking things through, and if Sarah made a wrong move, they would be hustled out to somewhere much less revealing.

Daphne shifted restlessly on the uncomfortable sofa and started playing idly with the cord of a landline telephone on the table next to her. 'All this has been such a shock – Mabel Moorhead was such a nice person. Why on earth would anyone want to kill her? It's just so peculiar. And Abi, too. She was so kind, so much loved.'

'It's like someone is targeting some of the most popular people in Merstairs,' Sarah said, her head on one side.

Mariella looked from one to the other. 'Are you expecting me to tell you everything I know? Because of some misguided idea that you can help me out? Well, I'm sorry, but that won't wash. There's such a thing as confidentiality, you know,' she said, compressing her lips firmly.

'We completely understand, Mariella, we do,' Sarah said, trying her best not to let her gaze stray to the fascinating whiteboard. 'It's just that, well, we did manage to help you out a bit before...'

'That was sheer fluke, Aunty Sarah. And Mum, I can't believe you want to get involved again,' Mariella snapped this time.

'Believe me, I don't,' said Daphne, wringing her hands. 'It's the last thing I want. I want all this to go away, for Merstairs to go back to the way it was before. But you do see, don't you, Mari?'

'See what, Mum?' Mariella said tiredly. Sarah looked at her sympathetically, diagnosing sleep loss – so common in parents of young children – plus stress, of which there must be a plentiful supply in Merstairs police station at the moment.

'Well, if someone's killing off the popular people – how long can it really be before they come for me?'

Sarah and Mariella stared at Daphne, who shrugged back at them with round, terrified eyes. At one level, Sarah thought, it was actually funny that Daphne saw herself as a potential target – but it was also dreadful that anyone in a sleepy seaside town felt they were in mortal danger.

'Don't worry, Mum, I don't think you're at risk, but of course I'm going to take all this very seriously. I tell you what, I'll have a word with DI Brice. Maybe he can get Tweedledum and Tweedledee, I mean Dumbarton and Deeside, to do a patrol past your cottages every day. How's that?' said Mariella, squeezing her mother's hand.

Just then, the phone on the desk shrilled – which was as well, judging by the look on Daphne's face. It didn't take a lot of decoding for Sarah to get the message that her friend did not consider the odd stroll by that plodding duo to be adequate protection at all.

As soon as she picked the phone up, Mariella seemed to realise the mistake she had made by inviting Sarah and Daphne into the incident room, and then taking a call while they were there. She glanced suspiciously at Sarah, who whipped her mobile out and started looking at it as though it was the most fascinating object she'd ever seen in her life. Daphne, meanwhile, seemed distinctly sleepy, clearly tired out by her emotional outburst. While Mariella was peering at her mother in concern, Sarah quickly turned her phone and took a few quick surreptitious snaps of the whiteboard, making sure she got it in focus. Mariella's gaze shifted as she put down the receiver, and Sarah looked down again and scrolled through her messages.

'Oh, just heard from Hattie, little Amelia's started sleeping through the night, isn't that marvellous,' trilled Sarah, hoping her daughter would forgive her for the fib. She'd had this message from her, that much was true – but it had been much earlier that day.

'Terrific,' said Mariella, her mind clearly on more pressing matters. 'That was DI Brice on the phone. I've got to get on. Now, Mum, if you're feeling better – Sarah, perhaps you could take Mum home, and keep an eye on her for me?'

Sarah nodded quickly. 'Of course I will, Mariella. Always.' With that, she got to her feet and opened the door. In the corridor, it was pandemonium, with loads of other potential witnesses from the fair being questioned. Sarah hesitated with her hand on the doorknob. 'You'll still be wanting to interview us in depth, I imagine? About the fair and so on?' she reminded Mariella.

'What? Oh yes, we'll get to it. But if you want to go home now, that's fine,' said Mariella vaguely, already bending her head over her very full notebook.

'Shouldn't we just get it over with now?' Daphne said querulously. 'I'm not sure I want to come back later.'

'Mariella's busy with other things,' said Sarah gently. 'We have to let her get to work. The first few hours after, um, something like this, are so important, you know.'

Daphne shook her head and looked close to tears again. 'Poor Mabel. I still can't believe it.'

'Best get some sleep, Mum. Things will look brighter in the morning. You've always told me that,' said Mariella.

Sarah smiled sadly at the girl. The entire Merstairs police force was going to have its work cut out, that was for sure. She took Hamish under one arm and linked the other with Daphne, then steered her friend down the corridor towards the double doors leading to the outside world.

THIRTY-ONE

Sarah woke with a heavy heart that Monday morning. Even though Daphne had been exhausted by her horrific discovery last night, it had taken ages for her to be calm enough to sleep. Eventually, after making her a hot water bottle, giving her a big mug of warm milk with cinnamon, and settling her with a night-light on in the corner of her room, Sarah had tiptoed away to her own house next door. Hamish had leapt into his little tartan bed gratefully and both had slept like logs. But the realisation had hit her as soon as she opened her eyes. It hadn't been a dream. Mabel Moorhead had died last night, and they were still no closer to solving Abi's death, either.

Nevertheless, Sarah knew she had to get herself up and dressed as quickly as she could. Daphne would be in terrible pain at the loss of her friend. She was willing to bet her inclination would be to spend the morning in bed with the duvet over her head, but Sarah knew that getting her out and about would do a huge amount to perk her up after the shocks of the previous evening.

Sarah decided to leave Hamish guarding the house while she nipped over to Daphne's with her spare keys. As she'd expected,

Daphne was still in bed when she called up the stairs, and when she went into her room, there were tears streaming anew from her eyes.

'It's real, isn't it? I can't bear this,' Daphne said, her shoulders quivering under her mound of eiderdowns.

'I know, it's very hard. Poor Mabel. But you know, she wouldn't want you to give up,' Sarah said earnestly.

'Give up? Of course I'm not going to,' said Daphne through her sniffs. 'But at the same time, I... I feel so awful. I never did give Mabel Mari's number, like I promised. And now we won't ever know what she wanted to talk to her about,' she confessed, subsiding again with a deep sigh.

'Well, there's nothing we can do about that,' said Sarah briskly. 'So let's not dwell on it. I really think the best thing for you now is a bit of fresh air and exercise. Even if you just poke your nose out of the front door for a moment or two. Come on, let's be having you. A hot shower will do you loads of good and then we'll see about the rest.'

Half an hour later, Sarah had chivvied her friend into her clothes and out into the spring sunshine, picking up Hamish on the way. Though her eyes were still very pink, Daphne couldn't help turning her gaze up to admire the blue skies.

'Tell you what, Daphne,' Sarah said, watching Hamish frisking about on the coastal path in front of them. 'How about I treat you to the biggest breakfast you've ever seen?'

'Honestly, I don't know how you can think of food at a time like this,' said Daphne, but Sarah couldn't help noticing that her friend abruptly changed direction and made a beeline for the Beach Café.

Sarah sat Daphne and Hamish down at a table with a magnificent view of the golden sands and frolicking sea. Over at the counter, Hannah Betts was looking sombre and had heard all about the latest calamity to befall Merstairs.

'You couldn't wish to meet a nicer lady than Mabel.' She

shook her head. 'I remember her sitting where Daphne is, just doing her lovely crochet, and chatting to that friend of hers, Regina is it?'

'Regina Stanforth, that's right,' said Sarah. 'A full English for Daphne. Better make that two. And some crumpets,' she said.

'Funny, really. Regina seemed a little out of sorts last time I saw them. Someone had seen something they shouldn't have,' said Hannah.

'Oh really?' Sarah pricked up her ears but was careful to keep spooning sugar into Daphne's tea casually.

'Some stick or other, I don't know. I think it was probably one of their crafting things. Crochet stick, would it be?'

'I think that's a hook, and for knitting it's needles,' said Sarah thoughtfully. 'But thanks, Hannah. I'll take these teas over, save you the bother.'

Back at the table, Sarah handed Daphne her cup. Had she been watching, she would have smiled at the way her friend winced at the sweetness of the brew. But Sarah was gazing into the middle distance, thinking hard.

'Everything OK?' Daphne asked as a waitress arrived and doled out the scrumptious-looking breakfasts and crumpets.

Sarah turned back to her. 'Of course. Just... mulling something over. But never mind about all that. How are you feeling?' she asked, realising it was best to avoid any discussion of murder, suspects, alibis, motives and cases with Daphne for the foreseeable future. How hard could that be?

Then she saw a familiar figure and her hand shot up to wave, almost of its own volition. The woman waved back and came over to sit with them.

'How are you doing, Daphne?' said Jennie Moffat, looking her over. Everything about Daphne was off-kilter today, from her grey tunic to the fact that her hair was scarf-free for once.

Jennie herself had brushed her hair, though there were still purple shadows under her eyes.

'Oh, you know. I feel things deeply, being in touch with the universe does that to you,' Daphne said. 'But your loss is so much greater. Have a crumpet.'

Jennie slid one off the plate and munched thoughtfully.

'I feel so guilty about Mabel, I suppose that's the worst thing,' said Daphne. 'I-I wasn't very nice to her last time we crafted in the pub. She offered me some wool and I turned her down. It was a navy blue angora mix, lovely quality, you know. But it just wasn't my style. Well, me and navy blue, I mean to say. How dull. But I-I hurt her feelings.'

'Oh Daphne, I'm sure Mabel would have been fine about that,' Sarah said, proffering a tissue. She tried not to look down at her own navy blue silky top and make her friend feel even worse, though the comment stung a little. 'Mabel doesn't sound like the kind of person who'd take umbrage. Besides, people always feel guilty when someone dies, it's quite natural.'

'Yeah, that's true,' said Jennie, shaking her head.

'Surely you don't have anything to feel bad about?' Sarah asked. 'You and Abi were very close, I believe.'

'But we did argue.'

'Mothers and daughters always do. I've had my moments with both my girls. They were experts in boundary-testing, from a young age.' Sarah smiled.

'Not the same, is it? You've still got your daughters. But I had a fight with Abi right before she died. I can never take back those words now.'

'Was it Josh? Because you know...'

'No, not him,' said Jennie quickly. 'Although it smarts, that she didn't trust me with that. This was about, well, a work situation. Something that didn't sit right.'

'Oh. Johnny Bartlett, maybe?'

Jennie stared at her. 'How on earth did you know that?'

'We met him last night at the fair,' Sarah explained. 'He's a good-looking chap, and I'd say he knows it. Though he's a bit older than Abi, he was right there at the school, so it's not such a stretch. Abi was a very pretty girl. Did he try it on with her?'

'Yeah, he did,' Jennie sighed. 'He was a right pest.'

'He seems... arrogant,' said Sarah. 'That strange outfit he was wearing, it was almost theatrical.'

'Black with silver accents,' said Daphne. 'He certainly has a bit of swagger about him.'

Sarah gave Daphne a sharp glance.

'What?' she responded. 'I'm only human, you know.'

Sarah turned to Jennie, asking gently, 'What happened, with him and Abi?'

Jennie sighed, getting a tissue out of her bag. 'It was cheeky comments every time Abi passed him in the corridor, you know, looking her up and down, winking, stuff like that. He always got into school really early, like she did. Sounds like nothing, but it gets wearing, when it goes on day after day. Abi didn't do a single thing to encourage him, not at all.'

Daphne looked horrified. 'Goodness! To think I actually considered him quite sexy.'

Sarah tutted. 'He sounds like a total pest.'

'Yeah, that's what he was,' said Jennie, sniffing. 'A nuisance. I was always saying to Abi, just have it out with him. Tell him you're not interested. But she'd say, "He knows I'm not. He just enjoys it. Calls it banter." God, that word. I think it should be outlawed. Gives people like him licence to keep on nagging away. But in the last few weeks, she seemed to get better at ignoring him. She stopped mentioning it so much, anyway. Perhaps she just had other things on her mind.'

'That's interesting,' said Sarah. Maybe Abi's real romance was taking her mind off Johnny Bartlett's behaviour. She wondered if that had irked the man. Embarrassing a young girl and making her squirm, day after day, might have satisfied his ego – at least he'd been getting a reaction. But if she suddenly stopped registering his efforts to intrude on her space, could that have angered Johnny Bartlett? And was he the sort to take that out on her in a final, deliberate, act of physical revenge for her perceived slight?

It didn't seem completely in keeping with the man she'd encountered. True, it had only been a matter of minutes. But he had seemed at ease, possessing a charm that surely garnered him a lot of female attention. Daphne had been virtually swooning, and Sarah couldn't deny he had a certain brutish something. He was probably the sort who could convince himself everyone liked his suggestive comments, even those who played 'hard to get'. But that was a long way from having murderous thoughts, and further still from carrying those out. Then there was the issue of his long-sightedness. Abi had been killed at close quarters, with a single targeted wound. Could he even have killed Abi, if his eyesight was as bad as he said? Surely she would have been a blur to him, so close to? Then something struck her.

'What sort of time did he tend to arrive in the morning, do you know?' Sarah asked.

Jennie thought for a moment. 'Abi always said he'd be there waiting for her when she got there before seven,' she said.

'Hmm.' That meant he'd probably been at the school, tapping his foot, while Abi was quietly dying outside Tarot and Tealeaves. There was no doubt about it, Johnny Bartlett was slipping down Sarah's list of possibles.

Just then, a rather elegant elderly lady in a flowing floral dress knocked into their table – the café was becoming crowded, as the day wore on and tourists and locals alike started going about their business, either enjoying the beautiful beach or making a living out of it. The jolt shook all their cups and Daphne, who'd just been about to take a sip, spilt tea all down her front.

'Blast,' she said loudly, but the woman responsible swept

past without seeming to feel the impact, and certainly without a word of apology. Sarah realised she recognised her – she'd seen her a couple of times, in the pub and at the Wittes Hotel.

'Oh no! That's so annoying for you, Daphne,' said Sarah, handing her friend some tissues to swab down her top.

'It's nothing really, it's just Regina,' Daphne said, laughing it off. Sarah turned to watch the woman waft past unperturbed, threading through several groups of people before making her way over to a large table. Seated around it were some of the women Sarah recognised from the photo in the paper. It was the crafting group. Their mood was sombre, which wasn't at all surprising given Mabel's death last night.

Jennie nodded sagely. 'Too big for her boots, that one, for sure.' Her lips were compressed into a thin line.

'Oh, she's just... well, she's just Regina,' said Daphne. 'Let's let it go.'

Sarah watched as the woman hesitated for a second in front of the table. All the other crafters immediately squashed up to make room for her, and a few patted spaces next to them. She was obviously popular. She slotted herself gracefully onto a chair and said a few words. The crafters sat up and listened carefully, almost as though they were making notes.

'Looks like she's giving a speech, I wonder if it's about, well, Mabel. Is Regina the chairperson of the group, or something?' Sarah asked.

'Chair.' Daphne guffawed. 'As if! Merstairs was a democracy, when I last looked. No one's in charge of the crafting group, it's a really relaxed, pop-along-if-you-like vibe.'

'Hmm, are you sure?' Sarah said. 'Regina seems to be taking a register now.'

'Oh drat, is she? Excuse me one second,' said Daphne, shooting out of her seat and beetling over to the other table, elbowing her way in and sitting herself down like a hen settling into a nesting box. When Regina turned to her, Sarah could see rather than hear Daphne forming the word, 'Present,' and even putting up her hand meekly.

Well, wonders would never cease. Daphne was actually at one of her classes, for a change – even if it was rather an unusual meeting. They must have decided to get together to honour their fallen comrade. Presumably they'd been summoned by Regina. She looked delicate, even rather fey in her floaty florals, but the elderly lady really must have quite a compelling personality, Sarah decided.

'Do you know much about, um, Regina, wasn't it?' she asked Jennie.

'You do have a way of asking questions. Didn't they tell you what happened to the cat?' she replied with a cryptic smile.

For a second, Sarah wondered if some ill had befallen the mighty Mephisto. Then she twigged what Jennie meant. But in Sarah's view curiosity wasn't a killer – ignorance was.

'The trouble is, when you've only just arrived somewhere, like I have, you have to ask questions. Otherwise you don't know what on earth is going on.' Sarah said it with one of her most charming smiles, and Jennie seemed to concede.

'It's hard, settling in somewhere new, I'll give you that. Well, Regina Stanforth is one of those Marmite people. You either love her or hate her. I wouldn't call her a bossy-boots, but people do what she says all the same, right enough.'

'Oh, I can see that from here. It seems to be all about the boots with her – she's too big for them, and they're bossy too. Does she get on with Francesca Diggory?'

Jennie snorted a little. 'Hit the nail on the head there, Sarah. No, they are not best pals. Regina's a bit of a different genera-tion. She doesn't worry about making her mark, the way the mayor does. Regina just expects people to fall into line, and they do. It's like a magic trick with her. Now Francesca, well, she can be a bit shrill, if you know what I mean. People don't respect her the same way. No, Regina's problem is that she's broke. Her family were much richer than Francesca's back in the day. Then Regina's dad, or granddad even, lost the lot – duff investments or something, I've never understood money... which is lucky as I've never had any.'

Sarah smiled at that. 'You seem to be doing fine.' Then she could have kicked herself. Luckily Jennie didn't seem to take it amiss.

'I was. Nice little place, and we were happy – well. Until all this.' Jennie's face fell as the memory of her terrible loss flooded in. To distract her, Sarah piped up again.

'So were Francesca's family and Regina's on a par, then? The same sort of status?'

'What? Oh, no,' said Jennie, dragging her thoughts back to the here and now. 'The Stanforths are "old money", as people say. One branch of the family is really, really posh, titles and all. But the lot down here just owned the Grange. You know, the big house that's been turned into a hotel.'

'Not the Wittes?' Sarah was electrified. Yet another connection with the place, after finding that Josh Whittsall had worked there. 'But I thought that was owned by someone called Rollo Wentworth,' she said, remembering Charles's horrible friend who'd called her a 'little lady'.

'Yeah, the Stanforths sold it, oh, must be a hundred years ago at least, and that Wentworth geezer eventually bought it. Next the family moved to the house that the mayor lives in now, then they had to sell up there too. I told you, Regina's on her uppers now. Well, as much on her uppers as that sort ever gets, anyway. To the likes of me, she still seems to be sitting pretty.'

It was a good description of the lady, Sarah decided. Whenever she'd seen her, she had, indeed, been sitting pretty, bedecked in flowers, smiling graciously and yet somehow more in charge than anyone else.

Sarah's rush of euphoria at a potential connection fizzled out as fast as it had come. She could also see Jennie was beginning to tire of the subject, and she remembered how exhausting grief could be. Either thinking about your loss, or trying to block it out, were both equally taxing options. She felt so much sympathy for the woman in front of her. 'Can I get you another cup of tea?' she asked gently.

Jennie hesitated for a second. Clearly, the idea of whiling away the day was appealing. There wasn't much waiting for her at home; not like when her girl had been alive. But Jennie resisted the temptation. 'No. Better be on my way. This is my life now. I've got to get used to it.'

'Can I walk back home with you? See you to your door?'

'That's kind of you,' said Jennie with a small smile. 'But what good would that do? It's broad daylight, nothing bad can happen. Not when the worst already has.' She gathered up her bag and stood, saying goodbye to Hamish with a nice pat and saying a quiet 'Thank you' to Sarah.

'What for?' Sarah asked.

'Oh, just for treating me as an ordinary person. No one knows what to say to me any more,' Jennie added sadly. 'You know what it's like.' A moment later, she was gone.

Sarah sat and thought. Jennie Moffat was absolutely right, one of the awful things about losing someone dear was that people struggled to treat you normally afterwards, even your closest friends seemingly at a loss. Some wouldn't leave the subject alone, bringing up their own relatives who'd died horrible deaths, sometimes in solidarity with your loved one's struggle but often as if to say they'd had it worse. Others simply never mentioned them again, leaving conversations full of awkward pauses and difficult silences. And some just avoided you, as though death itself was catching.

THIRTY-TWO

Sarah was contemplating the dregs of her tea with a rather sombre expression on her face when a voice broke into her musings.

'I was going to ask you if you wanted another cup, but if it makes you feel as gloomy as you look, maybe you shouldn't,' Charles Diggory said with a chuckle.

'Oh, it's nothing. Just... thinking.'

'You don't want to do too much of that. Vastly overrated,' he said with one of his twinkling smiles. 'I'm surprised to find you on your tod. I never thought I'd manage to get you on your own.'

Sarah looked up into his blue eyes, a little taken aback. 'I came with Daphne. She's over there.' She gestured in the direction of the crafters. Her friend had somehow got her hands on a ball of dayglo lime wool and was now wielding a crochet hook as though it was a cricket bat. 'She's been very upset, you can imagine. She was the one who found Mabel, and she's taken it very hard. She was really fond of her. Hopefully a bit of crochet with the group will help her. Poor Jennie was here too, she's just left. She's at that stage... well, let's just say it's very difficult.'

Charles looked at Sarah sympathetically, and for a second

his large warm hand came down on hers and pressed gently. 'You're so concerned with everyone else's troubles. Maybe it's time to spend some time thinking of yourself and what would be best for you?'

Sarah was silent for a moment. 'Um. Well, I suppose that's an idea.'

'So... I was wondering.' Charles cleared his throat. 'Um, if you might like to—'

Then there was a kerfuffle at the café entrance and Charles whipped his hand away as though it had been scorched by the fires of hell. A familiar figure was bearing down on them, her scarf knotted firmly under her chin.

'I thought I'd find you here,' Francesca Diggory said through gritted teeth. 'Got shot of the grandchildren, did you, so you could carry on your dalliance?'

'I surely don't need to remind you that they're with their mother today, enjoying the Whitsun break,' Charles said, his voice weary.

'Do sit down, Francesca. Would you like a tea? I could order one,' said Sarah, at her most polite. The mayor raked her with laser beam eyes, totally ignored her offer, and carried on berating Charles.

'Honestly, at such an important time for me, with the town reeling from these tragedies, the least you could do is stick by my side.'

'Look, I'm sorry, Frankie,' said Charles, his palms wide. 'We really aren't together any more and you know that. You didn't want me anywhere near you, remember? I'm not sure what you expect of me at this point.'

'Just ordinary, common human decency,' Francesca hissed, and took a deep breath, to fuel her next diatribe. But then Daphne arrived back at the table, completely ignoring the looming mayor, and sat herself down with a flump. She still looked a little woebegone but was significantly less sniffly than she had been earlier. And she was totally impervious to the atmosphere at the table. Sarah had rarely been so glad to see her.

'We've decided to make something as a group, the crafters, as a tribute to Mabel. Such a beautiful idea. I've made this fantastic square already, isn't it just lovely?' Daphne said, holding up a misshapen object that was nearer to a parallelogram than a square, in the blinding lime yarn. Sarah couldn't quite look directly at it.

'Well that is... truly amazing,' Sarah said. 'And so nice that you've gone for cheerful colours, instead of something more sombre. That will be a wonderful memento.'

Charles nodded like a rabbit caught in the headlights and Francesca sneered so hard that her upper lip curled and made her look like a shoddy Elvis impersonator.

Daphne seemed to take this as wholehearted approval. 'I knew everyone would love it,' she said smugly, tucking the square away carefully in her capacious handbag, perfectly satisfied it had been duly admired. 'Play your cards right and I'll make another just for you, Sarah. Your cottage could really do with a bit of livening up.'

Sarah coughed. As far as she was concerned, her little home was beautifully restful, and full of the restrained yet pretty patterns that she loved and found so relaxing to live with. 'Um. That's very generous, Daph, but I do like it the way it is, you know. You should probably concentrate on Mabel's special memorial blanket for now. Anyway, I was just asking if people would like more tea,' she said.

Thank goodness Daphne never seemed to take rebuffs too badly. 'I'm OK for the moment,' she said. 'But I could have sworn you promised me chips.'

'At this hour?' Francesca shuddered and finally turned on her heel and left them. The trio exchanged a relieved smile.

'I don't think it's too early for chips, do you, Sarah?'

Daphne said wistfully, and it immediately seemed to Sarah that it was the perfect moment for them, even though she was pretty sure she'd only promised her friend a full English breakfast – which she'd already eaten. Poor Daphne had been so fond of Mabel.

'I wish you could have got to know her, Sarah. She just was the nicest person, so calm and sensible.'

'She sounds lovely, Daph. What was her job, before she retired?'

'Oh, she was a teacher,' Daphne said idly.

'Just like Abi, then?' Charles remarked.

'Yes, I think that's why they always got on.' Daphne was staring out to sea, a million miles away.

Sarah thought for a moment too. Then she spoke quietly. 'I wonder if that could be a link, then? Both of them were teachers, Abi and Mabel.'

'Yes, but so many years apart,' said Charles. 'I can't see for the life of me what the connection could be.'

Sarah sighed. 'Me neither. Did they spend much time together, just the two of them?'

'Not really,' Daphne said when she'd thought for a while. 'I'd say they were friendly – both of them got on with everybody – but they didn't have a lot in common. Abi was so busy with the children, and with her secret man, I suppose, she was always rushing everywhere. Whereas Mabel was more at our time of life. She'd done her years at the school, now she was just enjoying her leisure, sharing her love of crochet with us all. She and Regina were really close, of course.'

'Were they?' said Sarah, the sun's rays now gently stroking her arms and making it more difficult for her to concentrate on hard sleuthing.

'Oh yes, they spent a lot of time together. Mabel had a lovely little house on the seafront – not far from ours, Sarah. Those two were in and out of each other's houses all the time.

They were pretty much inseparable. No secrets, that kind of a relationship, though they did have the odd spat, of course.'

'Sounds familiar,' drawled Charles, tipping his hat over his eyes and rolling up his sleeves a centimetre. 'I must say, this is a lovely spot.'

'I hope Hannah won't get cross with us, hogging her best seats,' Sarah said.

'Nonsense, she'll be thrilled to have us. Especially if we order a big lunch,' said Daphne.

In the end, not only lunch – three towering club sandwiches with the chips Daphne had been yearning for – but also tea – featuring Hannah Betts's delicious strawberry shortcake – slipped down before Sarah and Hamish finally made their way back home. Every now and then, she had brought the subject back to the matter in hand – the two tragedies she was dying to solve. But, though they had all worried away at the knotty problems like Hamish with a tasty bone, Sarah still had the maddening sense that a vital piece of information was eluding her.

The feeling persisted, right through Hamish's supper time, and her own plate of scrambled eggs, which was all she fancied after so much food at the Beach Café during the day. She forked it down while alternating between finishing the crossword and dragging her mind back to the two murders. She also couldn't help her mind straying to that deliciously tantalising moment when Charles had been on the brink of saying something. Had he been about to ask her out?

It was absurd, really. They were constantly going out to eat or bumping into each other and grabbing a bite. It was something that happened so frequently it was pretty mundane. But at the same time, she remembered his nervousness and hesitancy – and the plain fact that eating out by appointment was totally different to sharing a meal after an accidental encounter. Francesca had popped up like a jack-in-the-box, however, and the moment had gone. Would Charles ever try again? And would Sarah say yes if he did? She didn't know the answer to the last question and indeed, it made her so uncomfortable that she turned back almost with relief to her tussles to make sense of the murders.

But it was no good. Even later on, when she was sipping her mug of cocoa with Hamish lying across her toes in the sitting room, Sarah couldn't concentrate on her book, a thriller by her favourite author. Nor could she make any progress at all with the real life mystery on her hands. It was very frustrating.

Just as she was turning off the light, and Hamish was settling into his snug little bed, she had a sudden thought. Who, or what, did people consult when they were stuck in their own lives, and badly needed guidance? A smile spread across her face. At last, she had a plan for tomorrow.

THIRTY-THREE

The next morning, Hamish was up and about early, ready for the beach walk he now expected as his due. But Sarah had other ideas. Once his lead was on, she took him straight round to Daphne's cottage. He wouldn't have minded so much, as Daphne did feed him the odd snack when his mistress wasn't looking, but for once Mephisto was still in situ as the purple door opened wide and they were ushered in.

The first sign of the cat's presence was a bloodcurdling hissing sound that had Hamish pressing against Sarah's leg. Just to get the lie of the land of course, not because he was scared. The fact that the hideous marmalade cat was about twice his size and four times as savage was neither here nor there.

Hamish wouldn't say he was relieved when his mistress picked him up and tucked him under her arm – but he did give her a quick lick on the nose, just the way she liked.

'Do stop that or I'll put you down,' Sarah remonstrated. 'Sorry to drop round so early, Daphne, but I, um, just wanted to see how you are doing, after – well, everything, really.'

'Mabel, you mean,' said Daphne, whose own nose was distinctly pink after all the crying yesterday. Luckily it toned well with today's magenta tunic. She led her visitors into the kitchen. 'As well as can be expected, I suppose. She wasn't family – but she was a lovely person and I really enjoyed spending time with her. Help yourself to tea and toast.'

Mephisto, after one last glare at the dog so rudely invading his domain, stalked over to his cat flap and with great dignity (and a little difficulty) wiggled through it and out into the garden beyond.

This morning, the kitchen was not only festooned with the array of old newspapers and chewed biros that Daphne seemed to collect, but also had misshapen bits of crochet dotted all over the table.

'I was just planning out my project, it's a cushion cover,' Daphne said. 'Mabel would have wanted me to make something with it. We're doing the group tribute blanket, of course, but I owe it to her to finish this work, too. She was such a help, so encouraging. She loved all the colours, she told me they were really unusual and bold. It's coming on, isn't it?'

'It most definitely is,' Sarah said, as enthusiastically as she dared while she buttered her toast. Unusual and bold were excellent words, much better than garish and clashing. But it was a fine line. If she seemed too keen, Daphne might try to give this project to her as a present, thanks to her lovely generous nature and her erroneous view that Sarah's tasteful cottage needed a bit more oomph. Yet if Sarah didn't say anything, her friend would be hurt. 'It's really, really... large, isn't it?' she said finally.

'I'm glad you said that,' Daphne beamed. 'It's going to be by far my biggest cushion yet. But you probably didn't come round to discuss this,' she said, stroking a square fondly.

'No. I've been thinking about the case again. After all, I know more about it than anyone, having been there right at the start.'

Daphne turned away from Sarah at that and busied herself

at the kitchen sink. As Sarah knew washing-up was very far down on her friend's list of favourite pastimes, she was aware something was amiss.

'What's up, Daph? Are you OK?'

'Fine,' Daphne mumbled. 'Just keeping everything spick and span. You know it's my way,' she mumbled.

Sarah goggled. 'Are you sure about that, Daph? Is something the matter?'

Daphne turned round, waving her hands in their yellow rubber gloves. 'It's just that you've got this obsession, now, with death. It's not healthy. You seem to think you're at the centre of everything, the only one who can sort out all these questions – but you're not. And it's not all about you. I don't like being dragged into it all the time, especially, well. Especially after what I found in that tent. It was the most horrible thing that's ever happened to me, finding Mabel like that. Even worse than when we found Gus in that trunk in my beach hut. I'm beginning to think Mariella's right. We should leave all this to the professionals.'

Sarah sat down, Hamish on her lap. 'I'm surprised, Daphne. You're saying you think I should take a step back, because I've got the impression this is all about me?'

'Well,' said Daphne, pulling at the gloves unhappily. 'I wouldn't go that far, but...'

'OK. I see,' said Sarah, feeling very hurt but trying not to show it. She got to her feet again and popped Hamish back on the ground. 'Well, if it's like that, I'll just get on with it on my own.'

Sarah couldn't deny that Daphne's little speech smarted – particularly the notion that she was somehow trying to put herself centre stage for personal glory – but she'd often thought she might get things done faster alone. Perhaps this was all to the good.

'Now you're upset,' said Daphne, wringing the gloves in her hands, before dropping them into the washing-up water.

'And you've ruined your Marigolds,' said Sarah – and immediately they were both laughing.

'Oh, honestly, how ridiculous is this? We really don't need to fall out, not with all this going on,' said Daphne when their giggles had died down a little.

'You mean, with a killer on the loose,' said Sarah, and suddenly neither of them was laughing any more.

'Look, I could do with your help on this bit, Daph,' Sarah said carefully. 'I'd really like to try and get a word with Madame Grimaldi. Do you have any idea where she might be?' This was the revelation that had flashed up in her mind last night before she'd fallen asleep – the person those in trouble went to when they were seeking enlightenment.

'That charlatan!' Daphne was instantly up in arms again. 'I don't know how you dare mention that woman's name in my house. She's a complete fake and everyone says so. Not that I'd ever hear a word against her, because there is such a thing as professional solidarity, you know.'

'I don't want to consult her,' Sarah said quickly, without adding that she'd never consult anyone on clairvoyant matters – not even her oldest friend. 'I just wondered if she knows anything about what happened. You know, in her tent.'

'The murders again,' said Daphne glumly.

'Like it or not, Daph, they are a big deal,' Sarah pointed out. 'And I don't know Madame Grimaldi. She'd be much more likely to talk to you.'

'That's true,' Daphne said, considering the matter.

'Of course, you probably don't even have to speak. You can just communicate on the astral plane.' Sarah raised her eyebrows.

'Now I know you're joking,' Daphne said, shaking her finger at Sarah. 'Because old Grimbo can't, being a fraud. I *could*, but

I've got very few people I can talk to on that level. It does hold me back,' she added in martyred tones.

'Of course,' said Sarah patiently. 'So, where do you suggest we look for her? I know the police have an eye out, but maybe you can help Mariella here. Are there any clues in the Beyond?'

Daphne gave Sarah a searching glance, but obligingly pressed her fingers to her temples and then closed her eyes tightly. 'Ah, I see it. She's set her tent up on the beach again. Not far from the Beach Café, which might make a nice spot for an early lunch.' She opened her eyes a slit to see how Sarah was taking this and seemed delighted to spot a big smile.

* * *

Sarah wasn't enormously surprised, a few minutes later, to be out on the beach with Daphne and Hamish, with absolutely no sign of a fortune teller's tent anywhere to be seen.

'Um, excuse me,' she said to a passing family. 'Have you seen Madame Grimaldi here today? You know, she reads palms and so on.'

'Oh yeah, I know who you mean. She usually sets up her booth round here, on a sunny day, selling her wares,' said the dad, tapping the side of his nose. 'Haven't seen her today, though,' he added.

'Thanks,' said Sarah, puzzling slightly over what he meant.

'That's odd,' Daphne said, turning around as though Madame Grimaldi's tent might be hiding right behind her. 'I distinctly saw it in my mind's eye, right about here...'

'Hmm, I wonder,' said Sarah.

There must have been something ominous in her tone, because Daphne looked at her, panic in her eyes. 'No, not someone else... please don't say so,' she clutched Sarah's arm. 'It doesn't mean anything that she's not here! She doesn't set up every day. She could have gone on holiday, or have visitors staying...'

But with two murders already committed, there was an unspoken question, fraught with anxiety, hanging in the air. The family was also gazing up and down the beach now.

'Oh goodness,' said Daphne, clutching her headscarf. 'I'm starting to get a message from the Beyond. Everyone shush now... it's not looking good.'

Just then, there was a kerfuffle a little further along the sands and a woman in comfortable middle age with jet black, lustrous curly hair pushed past the family. 'Looking for me, Daphne?'

'Madame! Madame Grimaldi,' said Daphne at the top of her voice.

Immediately the woman's head whipped round, to see if anyone had noticed. Needless to say, people were looking up from their sandcastles and ice creams like autograph hunters spying a member of the royal family. 'Shh! I'm not on shift yet. You should know better to bandy my professional name about when I'm in mufti, Daph. That's breaking the code.'

'I'm so sorry, I meant *Mrs Grimble*,' said Daphne, clutching a hand to her bosom. 'I was just pleased to see you. Everyone's been worried about you. You're usually here much earlier than this. Then there was what happened, you know. *The other night*,' she added in a loud whisper.

'I want a word with someone about that. I got back to my tent and it was covered with that crime scene tape. Madness, what a waste of taxpayer's money. Just because I needed to go and spend a penny. My bladder's not been the same since the menopause, you know,' said Mrs Grimble. Almost immediately the little knot of onlookers started to drift away.

'Didn't you hear what happened?' asked Sarah, astonished that the palm reader seemed not to know about the tragedy on the night of the fair. 'Surely the police have been in touch?'

'To be honest, I saw the tape and I just thought better of the whole affair,' Mrs Grimble said in a confiding tone. 'Well, I haven't had much custom lately so I've been... doing a little extra business on the side. Know what I mean,' she said, directing a colossal wink to Daphne.

'I haven't a clue,' said Daphne, somewhat primly. 'Are you casting runes as well as doing Tarot? Because if so...'

Meanwhile, Sarah was thinking quickly back to the tent and everything she'd noticed before the discovery of Mabel. The silver stars and moon, the velvet drapes, the incense, the weird genie model – and the little mound at its feet. 'No. You were selling bags, weren't you?'

The fortune teller gave a start, then mustered a jaunty smile. 'Nothing wrong with that, is there?'

'No,' said Sarah slowly, her mind ticking over. Mrs Grimble had kept the bags tucked away in her tent, then she'd run off when she'd seen the police tape. It was all adding up to something on the shady side of the law. 'But they were designer handbags, weren't they? Or should I say, *fakes*.'

'That's a strong word. I prefer to call them lookalikes myself,' Mrs Grimble said loftily. 'Very nice they are too – Armani style, Aldi price, I always tell people. I can just see you with a little quilted cross-body in a nice fresh beige, just say the word,' she said, squinting at Sarah with a speculative look in her eye. 'A girl's got to make a living. When I saw the police sniffing around, it seemed like a very good time to pop and see my daughter down in Ramsgate. I'd had a very odd feeling about that fair right from the start, anyway. Daphne, you must have felt the same.'

'What? Oh yes, totally,' said Daphne, nodding with so much emphasis that Sarah was worried her earrings would go flying.

'You were getting a bad feeling about Mrs Grimble herself a minute ago, Daph,' Sarah couldn't resist putting in.

'Well of course, and you can see why now, can't you? I was

picking up on her bad vibrations from the night of the fair,' said Daphne, highly satisfied with herself. 'Do you have anything in purple suede?' she asked Mrs Grimble, who shook her head regretfully.

Sarah, who was pretty sure Daphne had been divining something much more fatal than misaligned vibrations for her main competitor on the clairvoyant front in Merstairs, decided to say nothing. Then there was a crackle of static and the sound of large, stumbling boots and Tweedledum and Tweedledee plodded onto the sand.

'Mrs Grimaldi? Clari... clear... erm, palm reading act?' The larger of the two came up to them and confronted Daphne.

'Certainly not!' Daphne said. 'I'd have thought you'd know by now that I'm your colleague Mariella's mum,' she added with dignity.

'And my palmistry is no act,' said Mrs Grimaldi equally crossly. 'Also, I'll thank you to remember that I'm Madame to you,' she added.

'Right then, Mrs Madame, this way. Let's be having you,' the constable said. 'We need you down at the station for questioning.'

Mrs Grimble sighed and adjusted her shiny black hairdo a little – it had slid down slightly on one side. 'Well, I'll be seeing you, ladies. Something tells me this could take a while.'

'I worry about Mari working with those people,' said Daphne in a very audible whisper as the fortune teller went off with the two constables.

Tweedledee turned his head and Sarah tried to cover up her friend's faux pas. 'Oh, I'm sure they're highly competent officers,' she said quickly.

'That's not what you said the other day,' Daphne said at top volume, and Sarah gave up.

THIRTY-FOUR

'Right, the Mermaid Café now then, I think,' said Daphne, and Sarah didn't disagree. It would be good to regroup and think about whether Mrs Grimble's illicit handbag trade had anything to do with the investigation, apart from clearing up two little mysteries – why she had skipped town after the murder, and also why she got more customers than Daphne.

The police had certainly taken their time to run the fortune teller to ground, which didn't augur well as far as catching the killer went. If Sarah had been running things, the owner of the tent where the murder had taken place would have been much higher up on the list of people to be questioned. As they turned to go, they collided with someone striding the other way at top speed. It was Regina Stanforth.

A little winded, Sarah gasped out, 'Oh, you're the lady from the crafting club.'

Regina, brushing down her floral dress, looked up. Her eyes were large and blue. Quite elderly, she was very attractive, with an appealing smile. 'Yes, that's right. And we're always eager for new members, as Daphne here will tell you. Are you thinking of signing up?'

'Oh, I'm sorry, no. I have two left thumbs when it comes to anything like that. But, um, I suppose you do have a space to fill, don't you?' Sarah tried to look innocent as she said this, but she heard Daphne's sharp intake of breath.

'I suppose you mean poor Mabel Moorhead,' said Regina, narrowing her eyes at Sarah. 'You're Daphne's doctor friend, are you?' Her voice was very clipped, and extremely self-assured, most definitely the product of an old-fashioned private education.

Not for the first time, Sarah wondered why her own time at boarding school had not equipped her with the same patina of privilege and entitlement. Her poor parents should have asked for their money back, though it was a bit late now. She nodded in reply to Regina's question, a little mesmerised.

Regina carried on staring hard at her, then she seemed to relax. 'Daphne's told us all a lot about you.' Inwardly, Sarah sighed. This was just what she didn't need. Regina carried on. 'I think Daphne would be the first to say she didn't know one end of a crochet hook from the other when she joined our group – and look at her now.'

Regina put her head on one side and Daphne glowed at the praise. It was the first time Sarah had really seen her wilful and wayward friend fall under the spell of another person, and she found it very interesting.

'Yes, Daphne's crochet is... truly extraordinary,' Sarah said politely. 'I'm sure you've taught her a lot.'

It was Regina's turn to smile. 'Well, you'll forgive me, but I have to get on. I'm putting together a tribute for Mabel, Daphne may have told you.'

'Yes, it sounds like a lovely idea,' Sarah said. The woman reached out a hand and patted Daphne's shoulder as she passed, and Daphne preened, a little like Hamish whenever Tinkerbell the Chihuahua deigned to give him the time of day.

'She certainly makes an impression,' Sarah said under her breath to Daphne when Regina was safely out of earshot.

'Oh, she's amazing,' Daphne said, a rapt expression on her face.

Sarah made a mental note to get to grips with this case of hero worship when she had a proper chance. But the thought flew right out of her head when she spotted a familiar plume of red hair up ahead.

'Look, it's Mariella,' she said to Daphne. 'Let's see how she's getting on.'

Daphne didn't need asking twice, charging through the sand as quickly as she could. As they came up to the girl, Sarah saw she was on the phone.

'Better not disturb her,' she whispered to Daphne – while edging as close as she could.

'Right, sir,' Mariella was saying, after listening to the caller intently. Sarah hoped it was her boss, DI Brice. 'Of course I'll check it out. Her own writing, you say? That's very odd... Yes, I know poisoning is traditionally a female... Did Dr Strutton agree with you on that? That it was definitely insulin? I see... OK, well yes, I'll get back to you as soon as I've done my quota of interviews. Yes, sir. Yes, sir,' Mariella carried on, waving Daphne and Sarah away in no uncertain terms.

Sarah was dying to say to Mariella that she knew the police were swamped and would be only too happy to help them out with any bits of investigation they couldn't manage themselves – but she could just imagine how well that would go down.

Instead, she turned to Daphne. 'The first thing we need to do,' she said as they pounded the pavement on the way back to their cottages, 'is find out why Abi Moffat was sending herself poison pen letters.'

THIRTY-FIVE

'What?' Daphne said to Sarah in consternation. 'How did you work that out?'

'Mariella just said the writing on the envelopes was Abi's,' said Sarah patiently.

'Did she? Oh, oh, I see, while she was on the phone... Honestly, Sarah, you are clever. But that's so odd...'

'Yes, why on earth would she do that?' Sarah puzzled.

'Unless...' said Daphne. 'She did always write envelopes for the parents, when they had to send letters back into the class. Just her name. She said it made it that little bit easier for people when they wanted to send all those slips into school about school trips and so on. People couldn't find an envelope at home, and permission forms and money and whatnot would go missing all the time before she started it,' said Daphne. 'So it could be that.'

'Drat,' said Sarah. Abi sounded like such a thoughtful teacher – but she had handed the poison pen writer a gift there. 'Back to the drawing board on that, then. Next question, were either Abi Moffat or Mabel Moorhead diabetic, do you happen to know?'

'Why on earth should I know that?' said Daphne breath-lessly as she tried to keep up with Sarah's hectic pace. 'And why is it important?'

Sarah glanced at Daphne carefully. 'The thing is, an insulin overdose, whether accidental or not, could mimic the symptoms of a fatal heart attack.'

Daphne shuddered. 'You're talking about poor Mabel. Why do I always wish I hadn't asked? That's the kind of information that only people's doctors would have, surely. It must be confidential.'

'Technically, yes,' said Sarah, without breaking her stride. 'But you'd be surprised at how much people love to talk about their medical problems. For some, their complaints almost become a part of their personality, they're defined by them. Did either Abi or Mabel chat about not being able to eat certain foods for instance, or did they worry about sugar levels?'

'Well, I only saw Abi occasionally, just while I was taking Mariella's little ones to school. When we talked, it was about how well Leila and Louis were doing, and what a love Leila is, sometimes Abi did have a quiet word about Louis being a bit of a pickle, though I'm glad to say that's straightened out now, he's doing so—'

'Well, that's great,' said Sarah. She didn't like to cut Daphne off, but on the other hand now was not the time for another paean of praise to her wonderful grandchildren. Besides, the competitive part of her brain reminded her, if anyone was a lucky grandmother, it was of course Sarah herself. 'So you never heard her mention not eating snacks at school, for instance, or turning down boxes of chocolates from parents?'

Daphne looked horrified at the very idea. 'No. I'd certainly have remembered that.'

'Then how about Mabel? When you were sitting round the table in the Jolly Roger, did she ever say she had to watch what she ate? Or did you see her checking her sugar levels?'

'What, with a test tube? No, I would have noticed,' Daphne shook her head.

'Well, you can monitor your glucose on a smart phone app these days, people have a little implant in their arms. Or some can measure it via their earlobes.'

'Gosh, science is wonderful, isn't it?' Daphne marvelled. 'But no, I never saw Mabel fiddling with her ears. Poor lady, I can't bear to think of it...'

'Then you mustn't,' said Sarah, patting Daphne's hand. Much though she felt her friend's pain, she really didn't think it would help to dwell on it. 'So if neither of them was diabetic, then maybe our killer is. That's a lead,' she added excitedly.

'But Sarah, I don't know anyone who's diabetic.'

'Some people don't like to talk about their health issues,' Sarah said.

'But that completely contradicts what you were just telling me,' Daphne said.

Sarah brought herself up short. Her friend was right. She couldn't have it both ways – and she also couldn't make a link between anyone who'd ever been in the frame for Abi's murder and insulin, or diabetes itself. Her face fell.

'Look, Sarah,' said Daphne kindly. 'We said we'd have an early lunch, didn't we? You know you always feel better after a meal.'

Sarah nodded, though this applied much more aptly to Daphne. But still, a little something and a sit-down at one of Merstairs' lovely cafés would hopefully be just the thing to get her brain cells firing again. At the moment, she felt as though there was nothing between her ears but wet sawdust.

* * *

'There we are, best seats in the house,' said Daphne happily as she snuggled into a nice comfy chair at the Beach Café. 'And just look at that view! It's hard to have a care in the world when you can see something as beautiful as that.'

Sarah looked out, following the direction of Daphne's gaze. It was, indeed, a magnificent sight. The day was so clear and bright that the coastline of Reculver, further round the bay, looked as though it had been precision-cut, and the castle perched atop the rocks was as beautiful a ruin as ever graced a tin of biscuits.

'We really must go round that one day,' said Sarah.

'There are some lovely cottages up there, too,' said Daphne. 'Regina has one. You can see for miles, though the place is teetering right on the edge of the cliff. I'd hate it, with my head for heights, but she adores the place.'

The rattle of teacups signalled Hannah Betts weaving through the tables towards them. Though it was by no means her usual choice for lunch, Sarah had cracked and ordered cake – nowhere in Kent could rival the Victoria sponge made by Hannah's own fair hand. Today's specimen, placed before her by the smiling Hannah, looked particularly good. The layers of sponge were as golden as the sun, and beautifully risen, while between them oozed a goodly amount of cream. Strawberry jam peeked out shyly and the top of the slice was dusted with icing sugar. A cup of strong tea accompanied this treat and, once her plate bore nothing but crumbs, she did feel a whole lot better, as Daphne had promised.

'I needed that,' Sarah said, pushing her empty cup and plate away. Daphne was still diligently tracking down all escaped snippets of cake and transferring them to her mouth with a moistened finger. It was a practice which had been strongly discouraged at their boarding school, on pain of detention after lessons, but which Sarah now smiled on kindly.

'Do you remember what Peter used to say when you did that?' Sarah asked her friend idly.

They spoke in unison. 'You'll take the pattern off that plate.'

They laughed, and then Sarah sighed. 'It's over a year now.'

'I know,' Daphne said, patting her arm. 'You're doing so well.'

'Am I? I feel quite lost, really,' Sarah said, remembering Charles's abortive suggestion the other day. Would he have asked her out to dinner, if Francesca hadn't put the kybosh on it? And would she have said yes? She pushed the thought away. 'It doesn't help that we're getting nowhere fast with this Abi thing.'

'I know. And don't forget Mabel,' said Daphne. 'If we really are sure it's connected. All right, all right, don't say it,' she carried on, before Sarah could break in. 'I know there must be something linking them. I just can't think what it could be.'

'Abi wasn't in any of the same clubs or groups as Mabel, was she?' Sarah asked. Joining like-minded people in activities seemed a huge thing in Merstairs, and not just for the retired population.

'I don't remember seeing her at anything,' said Daphne thoughtfully. 'Apart from the crafting, of course. But she scarcely ever came to meetings.'

'What about in the summer? She must have had time then, during those long holidays. I wonder what she got up to.'

'Yes, and who she met. Do you think that could be important?'

'Definitely, Daphne. Although I suppose it's quite a long time ago now, last summer. If she'd been killed in September, when the school year had just restarted, that would have made a stronger link. But we should definitely check it out with Jennie.'

'Poor Jennie. Won't she be sick to death of us by now?' Daphne scrunched up her face.

'Well, she probably is, but she wants to find out who did it more than anyone, surely. So I think she'll forgive us.'

'Do we have to go back and ask her now? I was really enjoying sitting here,' said Daphne a little querulously.

'You know what, let's stay here for a while longer.' Sarah was relieved to see her friend looking a little perkier after the dreadful shock of finding Mabel Moorhead's body. 'Hamish is having a snooze and we're happy too, aren't we? I'll go and get us another tea and we'll just relax,' she added, digging out her purse and wandering over to the Beach Café till.

She was lucky, the queue wasn't too long, and she was idly scanning the horizon, tracking the seabirds racing across the sky, when she overheard something that changed the course of the investigation.

Two middle-aged women were ahead of her in the queue, waiting to catch Hannah's eye with their orders. 'Such a shame about Abi, isn't it?' one said.

'Her poor boyfriend. That's who I feel sorry for,' said her companion.

Sarah pricked up her ears. At this stage, she almost thought of Abi's true boyfriend as a mythical beast, like a unicorn, and after all the business of Mabel's death, she had nearly lost sight of him as a potential lead. But someone, somewhere must know who he was. Could it be these ladies? She bent closer, pretending to be examining the sausage rolls behind the glass counter. The first woman spoke again.

'I suppose he'll be going to the funeral,' she said in a matter-of-fact way.

'I'd have thought so. After all, they do say he was actually her fiancé.'

'You mean they were engaged?' her friend said, agog at this juicy morsel of gossip.

'What?' said Sarah out loud. At that, the women wheeled round. 'What...what's that bird called, up there?' she said a little desperately, trying to cover her tracks, pointing into the sky. It was just too mortifying to admit she'd been eavesdropping.

The women looked at her as though she was mad. 'It's a seagull,' said one, giving her companion a significant look. Sarah had just been diagnosed as a feather or two short of the full plumage. It was their turn to order next and they quickly gave their choices to Hannah, then went back to their table to wait, giving Sarah worried little glances as they passed.

Hannah looked at her expectantly.

'Two more teas, please, Hannah. The sponge was gorgeous, by the way.' Hannah beamed at her, which emboldened her to continue. 'I've just heard Abi actually had a fiancé, did you know about that? I feel terribly out of the loop.'

Hannah gave her a sideways look. 'Not still up to all that poking around, are you? No reason you should know about Abi's private life anyway, is there?'

'Oh, no, of course not. I suppose they meant Josh Whittsall anyway.'

'I don't think so. She was a softie, was Abi,' sighed Hannah. 'She was helping Josh out, you know, his family are strict. But yeah, people say she was sweet on someone else.'

'Any idea what his name is?'

Hannah eyed Sarah. 'None at all. And I'm not sure why that would be anyone's business?'

'I... I agree. It's just so sad for him. His bride-to-be dying, I mean.'

Hannah seemed to relax. 'Yes. Yes, it's so awful. One young life, but the effects spread out, like ripples in the sea.'

Sarah was a little taken aback, she hadn't realised Hannah had such a lyrical mindset. But then she remembered her light-as-air cakes. The woman was an artist, so it should be no surprise she had a poet's soul.

'You're so right. It's a calamity. And now poor Mabel too.'

'Awful,' said Hannah a bit more abruptly. Behind Sarah, the queue was building up. 'You're sitting in the same place as earlier? Oh, but you'll need another cup.'

'What? Why?' said Sarah, and turned round, to see that Charles had appeared and was now sitting with Daphne,

Hamish perched jauntily on his knee. She swung back, a little pink in the face. 'Oh, you're right,' she added, all fingers and thumbs as she put her purse away.

Sarah was still a little flustered when she regained her seat a minute or two later. She took a couple of breaths before saying, 'Well, hello, Charles, how are you?'

Charles, on the other hand, merely twinkled his blue eyes at her and seemed supremely at ease, despite their broken-off conversation the other day. 'Sarah. Lovely to see you,' he said in that well-modulated voice that sometimes almost sounded like a purr. Infuriatingly, Hamish cocked his tufty black head at her enquiringly from his vantage point on Charles's knee, as if to ask her what the problem was.

Sarah tutted under her breath. 'Anyway, have either of you heard anything about a fiancé?'

'A fiancé? In general, Sarah, or for anyone in particular?' Daphne said with a suppressed chuckle, looking from her friend to Charles and back again.

'For Abi,' Sarah said in a voice that was suddenly rather high-pitched. 'Hannah was saying she was engaged all this time. Well, there was Josh, but as we know that was just a blind. But her real boyfriend was more than serious – he was about to become permanent. We need to know who she was involved with.'

'But that's easy,' said Charles. 'It was Teddy Stanforth.'

Both Sarah and Daphne goggled at him.

'Teddy Stanforth? Are you sure?' said Daphne. 'That's funny.'

'Why's it funny?' Sarah asked, starting to hand out the cups of tea the waitress just delivered to their table. When the girl had gone, she turned back to Charles. 'Unless you mean odd – and yes, it's definitely strange you didn't tell us this before.'

'Francesca only mentioned it yesterday,' Charles said, his

eyes wide and innocent. 'I don't know where she got it from. Why the hoo-ha, anyway?'

'Well, because this Teddy has got to be a suspect, of course,' said Sarah. 'That surname sounds very familiar, by the way.'

'Yes, that's because he's Regina's boy – Regina from the crafting group. She's never once said a thing about it,' Daphne said, spooning sugar into her cup. 'That's odd, too, particularly since Abi's, well, since her horrible death. You'd have thought Regina would be devastated. If Abi was going to be one of the family, after all.'

'Could it be that she didn't like her?' Sarah asked, although she was almost sure of the answer she was going to get.

'How could anyone not like Abi? No, it couldn't have been that. Maybe she didn't know how serious things were. Maybe it was a secret engagement,' said Daphne, frowning hard.

'And would Regina discuss her son's private life? If you're all busy knitting or whatever,' Charles added in languid tones.

'We do have far-ranging discussions, you know, it's not some kind of mothers' meeting you can just dismiss as silly women's issues,' said Daphne with a trace of acerbity. 'I know Francesca doesn't like Regina but I thought you were above all that sort of thing,' she added.

'I'm sure I don't know what you mean,' Charles shrugged. 'Francesca can have her prickly moments—' here, Sarah almost choked as her tea went down the wrong way '—but she and Regina have known each other for years. They went to the same school, just like you two.'

'Not at the same time, surely? And that doesn't always create lasting friendships, anyway,' said Sarah sagely. 'Daphne and I have been lucky that we always got on.'

'Yes, Regina must be a good few years older than Francesca,' Daphne agreed. 'And Francesca does sometimes get, well, what one might call a bee in her bonnet about people, doesn't she, Charles?' she said, fixing him with her clear-eyed gaze.

Sarah looked at Daphne fondly. She wouldn't have dreamt of putting Charles on the spot herself, but it was great watching her friend do it. Charles seemed to have tired of the subject, though. He shrugged with one of his graceful movements.

'Maybe so, but analysing Francesca's character won't get us any closer to finding out about Abi's relationships, will it?' Though he said it lightly, it was clear that he wasn't happy to discuss his wife, or ex-wife's, shortcomings. Sarah realised she rather admired him for this, although she still hadn't got to the bottom of his comment in Whitstable about Francesca delaying the divorce. His wife was happy enough to blacken his character, to others and to his face, but he had never bad-mouthed her and this loyalty was a pleasing characteristic, she thought with a little smile.

'I don't see what you're smirking about,' said Daphne. 'We're no closer to finding out what's going on with Teddy.'

'Well, I suppose you could ask Regina, whenever the crafting group next meets?' Sarah suggested. 'That could be the easiest way to get on with things.'

'But we're not due to meet for ages,' said Daphne. 'Surely you'll have died of curiosity by then,' she teased her friend.

'Ideally, I'd like to know now, this minute. But I do see it could be hard to find out. Unless...'

'What are you thinking of?' asked Charles, scratching behind Hamish's ears, to his intense delight.

'Could we just pop round and see him? Where does he live?'

'You mean, foist ourselves on a grieving man?' said Daphne disapprovingly.

'Well, when you think about it, we should either do that, or tell Mariella to, right away,' said Sarah. 'You know it's almost always people's loved ones who turn out to be the murderer in cases like this.'

Daphne shuddered. 'Sarah, that's so grim. Teddy Stanforth

seems like a very nice boy, and his mother is wonderful. How can you?'

'Me? I haven't done a thing,' said Sarah. 'Now, are you going to ring Mariella and ask her to meet us, or should I? Someone should get on and question this chap as soon as humanly possible.'

THIRTY-SIX

To say that Mariella wasn't thrilled to receive a call from her mother and Sarah promising choice new information would be a bit of an understatement. But she turned up, looking weary and rather harassed, and slid into a seat at the table. Sarah and Daphne had ordered a few of the Beach Café's famous chocolate chip cookies to keep them all going while they waited for her. Unfortunately these large, soft biscuits, well-studded with chunks of delicious milk chocolate, were but a distant memory by the time Mariella made it.

She pushed her mane of red hair out of her eyes, undid her ponytail and rearranged it to her satisfaction before looking at each member of the group very seriously, including Hamish whom she tickled under the chin.

'Hello Aunty Sarah, hello Charles. So. What's so urgent that you had to drag me here in the middle of the afternoon, Mum? I've been rushed off my feet since this morning,' Mariella said.

'Have you got anywhere with all the interviews of people who were at the fair?' Sarah asked before Daphne could speak.

Mariella just shook her head at her. 'Do you seriously

expect me to answer that, Aunty Sarah? Come on. What's this about, now?'

'I thought you could do with a break. Isn't this lovely, with the sea looking so pretty?' said Daphne, while Mariella looked crosser and crosser.

'Actually, Mariella, we do have something we thought we ought to raise with you,' Sarah put in before the young police-woman could get to her feet and stomp off. 'And we've ordered you a cuppa, too. We thought you might need one.'

The waitress arrived on cue and put the cup down in front of Mariella, saving the day. She took a sip, and visibly relaxed. 'All right. I'm not going to lie, it's nice to have a break. But you really can't drag me out for no reason, Mum. You'll get me the sack.'

'Well in fact, Mari, we've got some information you'll really love. Well, not love, because what's to love during a murder investigation. But you'll like it. Probably. Oh, you know what I mean. The thing is—'

Sarah, rather impatient with Daphne's delivery, broke in. 'We've discovered that Abi had a secret fiancé. And we think you ought to question him as quickly as possible, in case he was the one. The one who killed her.'

Mariella looked from Sarah to Daphne and back again, and let out a long, low whistle.

For a second, Daphne and Sarah looked at each other with rather a self-satisfied glow. They'd pulled it off again, the plucky crime-solving duo—

But then Mariella spoke and broke rudely into their fantasy. 'I've told you two before about getting involved in things that don't concern you! When will you learn, Mum? And Aunty Sarah! I'm relying on you to keep Mum out of trou-ble, and honestly you're doing a terrible job. As for you, Charles...'

Charles just tipped his hat over his eyes and gave every

appearance of drifting off to sleep in the lovely sunshine, much to the women's annoyance.

'Oh Mari!' said Daphne, even her earrings looking crushed and colourless at this onslaught. 'We're only trying to solve the case to help you out. I just don't want you to be in danger.'

'How many times!' Mariella thundered at Daphne again. Then she turned to face Sarah. 'It's not one of the crossword puzzles you love so much, Aunty Sarah. This is real life, it's serious – and it could be very dangerous.'

Sarah held her hands up. 'OK, OK, believe me, I have no desire to put myself in harm's way. We just came across information we thought you should have. There's a little phrase, "Don't shoot the messenger." You might have heard it.'

For a second, Mariella glared at Sarah anew, then she subsided. 'I'm sorry. I shouldn't have let rip like that. It's just... this case is so frustrating. Yes, of course we had heard about Teddy Stanforth. If you knew how many people we saw this morning alone, you'd realise how impossible it is to keep a secret here. Did you really think no one apart from you would get to hear about this "clandestine" relationship, and mention it to us? We're all over it, and I must admit it was quite exciting when we first got on the case, checking it out, but it looks like it's another dead end.'

'You mean he's definitely not responsible?'

Mariella shook her head. 'I shouldn't say a word to you, I know that, but I'm so tired, and it's not like you don't have your ears to the ground night and day, so you'll hear soon enough anyway. Teddy Stanforth has the perfect alibi.'

'Does he indeed? Well, you know what they say about these watertight explanations,' said Charles, waking up to give everyone a significant look.

Mariella gave him an exasperated tut, and laid her palms face up on the table. 'It's like this, guys. Abi and Teddy had to keep their relationship secret, because she was helping Josh with his, um, tricky situation. But she and Teddy were the real deal. They were madly in love, Teddy says – and he looks like a broken man.'

'That's no proof,' scoffed Charles. 'Anyone can put on an act.'

Sarah was suddenly reminded of a moment, not so long ago, when it had seemed as though Charles himself had been giving an Oscar-winning performance, which abruptly fell apart. But as it happened, he hadn't been the culprit after all, and someone else was now safely locked up for the crimes that had been committed. Still, it had been an anxious time and she remembered how convincing he'd been when he'd pulled the wool over her eyes.

'Don't look at me like that,' Charles said to Sarah, his expression amused but wary.

'Just agreeing with you,' she said. 'Sometimes things aren't the way they seem.'

Daphne, who was looking from one to the other with interest, shrugged at this point. 'Well I have no idea what you two are tussling about, but I think we should focus on what Mari is kindly going to tell us,' she said, smiling encouragingly at her daughter.

Mariella shifted in her seat. 'Well, as I said, I don't feel comfortable coming across with this information, but as you're going to weasel it out of someone anyway, and it's now pretty much in the public domain... Teddy, it turns out, was playing his first match of the cricket season. He's in the Merstairs Men's first team,' she said, with just a tinge of awe in her voice.

'The Merstairs Men – is that the same as the Men of Merstairs?' Sarah wrinkled her brow, thinking of the less-than-impressive specimens she'd encountered not so long ago in the area's male consciousness raising group.

Mariella shook her head emphatically. 'Couldn't be more different. The Merstairs Men are a top-class cricket team – last year they beat Ramsgate, Margate and Broadstairs,' she said. 'They're really taking off. Anyway, they won this time as well – of course – and as it was their maiden game of the season, they went out to celebrate... Long story short, Teddy got completely incapacitated and had to stay the night in his teammate's Airbnb. We've spoken to the guy, who corroborates the story. And he also said Teddy was too drunk to get his cricket boots off unaided, let alone drive back to Merstairs and stab his fiancée.'

Sarah, Charles and Daphne stared at each other for a long moment. Then Daphne broke the silence. 'What? Why are you staring at me like that?'

'I'm not looking at you,' Sarah explained. 'I'm just at a loss. Again. Every time we turn up something that might be useful, it turns to dust. Teddy Stanforth seemed like a really solid lead. I mean, he could be a lovely boy, I've never met him so I don't know, but on the face of it he's really promising. A sporty young man, who might not know his own strength, who drinks to excess – he's an absolute copybook accidental murderer.'

'Except that killings like that tend to be via strangling, or maybe blows from a blunt instrument. It's not that common for a man to stab a woman during a heated domestic row,' mused Mariella.

'Oh goodness, Sarah's got you at it now,' sighed Daphne. 'She can't go two minutes without saying something really grisly about death these days.'

'It's not just these days, Daph,' said Sarah gently. 'It's been my job for quite a while now.'

'Oh, silly me,' said Daphne crossly. 'And there was I, thinking a GP's job was to keep people alive.'

Charles broke in before things could get too prickly. 'Unfortunately, people will persist in dying, Daphne, despite Sarah's best efforts. Now, let's not get away from the matter in hand. If this young Teddy is off the hook, who on earth are we left with?'

Sarah sighed. 'That's just the problem, Charles. We seem to

have run out of road. Abi gave me that marvellous clue, "wits".
That ought to have solved everything in a flash. But we've
turned up nothing at all. Whitstable was a washout, the Wittes
Hotel was worse. That poor Josh boy was a red herring and now
even Abi's real fiancé hasn't done it. There was nothing doing at
the Whitsun fair either – except for another, apparently unre-
lated, murder. Then there's Johnny Bartlett, who looks like such
an ideal villain. He always went into school early to badger Abi,
so he'd have been waiting for her there while she was being
stabbed on the seafront. Plus he was too long-sighted anyway –
you've checked all that, haven't you, Mariella?'

Here Mariella gave a tired nod.

'As for the poison pen letters,' Sarah continued. 'Abi wrote
the envelopes themselves for the parents in her class to use, so
that's not going to help.'

'I'm not sure you should sound so disappointed that all
these people are being proved innocent, Aunty Sarah. Being
found not guilty is generally thought to be a good thing,' said
Mariella ruefully. 'And as for the notes, it turns out they were
actually from, well, you'll never believe it... but they were from
Jennie.'

'*Jennie*? Jennie Moffat? No,' said Daphne, her jaw sagging.
'They can't have been! Why on earth would she do such a
thing, to her own lovely daughter? It's obvious she adored the
girl – quite rightly so, of course.'

Sarah shook her head in disbelief. 'That's extraordinary.
Are you absolutely sure, Mariella?'

'I'm afraid so. Jennie's admitted she was so fed up with the
Josh situation that she decided to have a go at her daughter via
some nasty notes. She thought it might make Abi see sense,
after she'd failed to get through by talking to her. She was fed
up with their constant arguments. She thought if Abi felt she
was being watched and judged, she might think better of
persisting with the relationship. But of course it wasn't a real

love affair at all, and Abi didn't want to leave Josh in the lurch. It was just an unpleasant extra stress for the girl, right before she died.'

'I never would have thought Jennie could be the culprit,' Sarah said. 'But I can see that sometimes, as a parent, you can feel you've tried all the options, and still not got through. Perhaps she felt it was somehow worth a go because all her reasoning – and arguing – had failed.'

'I guess so,' said Mari. 'And she had access to those envelopes Abi wrote for the parents, they were easily available, lying around at their house. Everyone gets the *Merstairs Marketeer* and Abi had plenty of glue and scissors and whatnot from her school supplies that Jennie could dip into.'

'I just don't get it,' Daphne said. 'How did she think that was going to change poor Abi's mind?'

'Jennie somehow thought Abi might take more notice of her views if she made out half of Merstairs thought the same way, and expressed it in horrible terms,' Mariella said with a shrug. 'She's really ashamed of what she did now.'

No wonder Jennie had seemed to have so much on her conscience when they'd spoken at the café.

'I knew there was something she was hiding,' said Sarah. 'I suppose she was at the end of her tether about Josh, and as a result of all that tension, Abi then didn't tell her about Teddy. What a terrible shame, I'm sure Jennie would have been thrilled to hear all about that. It would have been good news about her daughter's love life at last.'

She sat back and stirred her tea for a second. 'It sounds awful to say it, but that's another promising lead gone. The poison pen writer seemed like a solid suspect for Abi's murder, if not Mabel's. But Jennie has no motive for killing Mabel that we know of. I'm sure you've already checked out what she was doing at the time of both deaths.'

Mariella nodded. 'Jennie was at the bakery when Abi died,

and home with her sister and her family right the way through the Whitsun fair.'

'Well, that's something,' said Sarah. 'And I'd agree with you, normally, Mariella, that being proved innocent is a good thing,' she added. 'But you see, there's another victim here, apart from Abi and Mabel.'

'Oh my goodness, not another one!' shrieked Daphne. 'Who on earth is it?'

THIRTY-SEVEN

'Calm down, Daphne,' Sarah said frantically. 'I didn't mean it like that. I just wanted to say, the whole of Merstairs is suffering while everyone's under this cloud of suspicion. There can't be a person here who hasn't turned round and wondered if a friend or a neighbour, or even a total stranger, has just gone loopy and started killing. And the thing is, that has a really negative effect on Merstairs itself.'

'You're right,' said Daphne thoughtfully. 'I've had hardly any appointments at Tarot and Tealeaves recently, that must be why.'

Sarah and Charles immediately looked very interested in the contents of their teacups, and Mariella moved the conversation swiftly on. 'It's true, we really need to sort this awful business out, before Merstairs is ruined as a destination. We're not that far off high season now, and already I'm hearing that bed and breakfast bookings are down. Who wants to go and stay at a resort where you might end up dead?'

It was sobering thought, and the little group sipped their tea in silence for a minute. While Sarah's pockets were not going to be adversely affected by the situation, she hated the thought that shops and restaurants might have to close if this went on for long. She'd already come to know many of the local shopkeepers and had a serious addiction to Hannah Betts's cakes and the delicious fish and chips at Marlene's Plaice. Hamish loved meeting and greeting his favourite business owners, too, as they went for their walks along the promenade and high street. He'd be really sad if he got less than his usual quota of pats and strokes as they made their rounds. Not to mention the whole living-in-fear with a killer in their midst thing. Nobody wanted that.

'Look, I know you won't necessarily love this idea straight away, Mariella, but please hear me out,' said Sarah, putting her cup down decisively. 'I think we should pool all our information. We know a certain amount about Abi by now – beloved teacher, kind daughter, much-missed fiancée. These are all things we can use to build up a picture of someone who might want to snuff her life out. But Mabel, now. I really feel I still don't know an awful lot about her, except that she was a teacher too before she retired, and great at crochet.'

Mariella thought for a moment. 'I had a bad feeling back there that you were actually going to ask me for access to our case notes, or even worse, our whiteboard,' she smiled.

Sarah laughed a little too loudly at this and got a sharp glance from Daphne. Thank goodness Mariella couldn't see the contents of the photo file on her phone. She'd spent a lot of time studying the facts and pictures the police had already built up about the young girl's movements. But, as they'd only had access to the room shortly after Mabel's murder, her part of the board was a blank, apart from her name, that blurry mugshot and the diagnosis of heart attack which had now been proved wrong anyway.

'We're still piecing things together on Mabel,' Mariella continued. 'On the face of it, it's hard to develop any connections there may have been between the two women. Mabel was single, she had no children or grandchildren. That means it's unlikely she ever came across Abi much at all, apart from occasionally at the craft group. A mother or grandmother would have a solid link with the school, it's where most children in Merstairs go and that's why so many of us knew Abi. She was a fixture. But Mabel was a quiet lady, who kept herself to herself.'

'Usually, when the police use that phrase, it's about a serial killer,' said Sarah. She was trying to lighten the tone, but her attempt fell flat.

'What a dreadful thought. There's no way Mabel was a maniac. She was absolutely brilliant with Tunisian crochet. Most people don't even attempt it,' said Daphne.

'Well, I'm not sure if that automatically clears her name – but I don't think there's any suggestion that Mabel killed Abi and then herself, am I right, Mariella?'

Mariella shook her head, then said, 'Well, of course I can't confirm or deny. But the site of the insulin injection mark would certainly suggest it wasn't self-inflicted.'

'In her back, then?' Sarah said meditatively.

Again, Mariella's instinctive reaction was to nod – then she tutted. 'You know I really can't say,' she remonstrated with Sarah.

'Don't worry, I'm not asking,' said Sarah, who now didn't need to. 'So, both of them were killed, it wasn't a murder-suicide situation. It could have been different perpetrators – but why? I really think there has to be a link, if we think hard enough about it.'

Then Charles chipped in. 'I wonder... obviously they both knew Regina. But apart from that, maybe crafting? Abi often did activities with the kids, cutting and sticking dried leaves, making pasta necklaces, things like that. Do you think it's possible that she consulted Mabel about a special craft project she had in mind?'

Sarah and Mariella stared at Charles, while Daphne

drained the last drops of tea from her cup, then looked up too. 'My gosh! That could be a possibility.'

Mariella turned excitedly to her mother. 'We'll look into this officially, of course, but could you give me the number for your group? I'll need to talk to DI Brice but it could be a promising line of enquiry.'

'Ooh, yes of course, darling,' said Daphne, turning to her huge velvet handbag and rooting around in its depths. In a surprisingly short amount of time, she'd located her mobile and was pressing buttons. 'I'll give you Regina's number. I mean, she's not exactly in charge, we're more of a collective, but she's probably the one you want,' she said. 'She's lovely, I'm sure she'll be super-helpful. She was in the police station this morning, but maybe she saw one of your colleagues,' Daphne said, texting something across to Mariella's phone. Then she seemed to think a little. 'Well, sometimes Regina is a bit stern, but I know you'll get on the right side of her. Just be really, really polite. I know you'll manage it,' she said, patting her daughter's hand.

'Mum, honestly,' said Mariella, in the cry of exasperation that daughters have used throughout the ages. 'I am capable of talking to someone without your input. And in fact, Regina has no choice but to tell me everything she knows, no matter how I approach her. I'm the police and this is a murder investigation.'

And with those trenchant words, Mariella smoothed down her hair, got up and said her goodbyes. 'Better get back to it. I'll give you a ring later, Mum,' she said in more conciliatory tones.

'Well, that's wonderful,' Daphne said, as Mariella strode away, purpose in her every move. 'Maybe the police will finally get somewhere at last, thanks to us!'

'Never mind that,' said Sarah impatiently. 'Give me that phone number, quickly.'

'What do you mean, Sarah?' Daphne asked as she delved into her bag again. 'The number for Regina Stanforth? But I'm not sure what you want it for. We can leave that to Mari, can't we?'

'Come on, Daph, you heard what she said. She's got to run it past DI Brice first, and you know what will happen when she does,' Sarah said, motioning with her hand for Daphne to hurry up and find her phone.

'Well, I've no idea,' Daphne shrugged.

'He'll just give the job to those two lummoxes, Tweedledum and Tweedledee. Then they'll mess it up.'

'Hang on, Sarah,' drawled Charles. 'Perhaps we should just let them get on with things. They do have the training, you know.'

'Listen, you two,' said Sarah, at her most forthright. 'Don't you want us to get this business sorted out, once and for all? We've spent so much time trying to work out what happened, and following goodness knows how many leads. It's nice to have something solid to go on for a change. Do you just want to meekly hand all that over to the authorities? What if they don't manage to get the right answers?'

'So... you're saying you can sort things out better than the police, then, are you Sarah?' said Daphne, her voice dangerously quiet.

Sarah knew she had to tread carefully; Mariella was Daphne's little girl, and anyone could see that she was shaping up to be a great police officer. But she wouldn't necessarily be able to do what needed to be done – not with DI Brice and his underlings in charge.

'I think,' Sarah said, feeling her way, 'that if we play our cards right, we can actually make her job much easier. Don't you think she'd appreciate that, Daphne?'

Daphne looked at Sarah suspiciously. 'Are you sure it's not your competitive nature talking again? You always want to get to the answer first.'

Sarah sighed. 'I promise you, Daphne, I only want to do this in the interests of Merstairs. The police station will still be chaos, with all those potential witnesses waiting to be interviewed. What if Mariella gets asked to take that over as soon as she gets in, and what if no one is prepared to listen to our brainwave? What if it takes them hours to get round to making the call? *What if someone else gets murdered as a result?*'

This last point was unarguable, and Sarah was mightily relieved when Daphne took up her phone again. Then she hesitated before handing it over to her friend. 'But what on earth are you going to say?'

Sarah looked at Daphne, silenced for a second. Her friend had a good point. 'We need to plan this out carefully. We don't want to get Regina's back up. She won't know who the killer is, or she surely would have spoken to the police herself. But she might have information that could really help us. We can't afford for her to get annoyed and refuse to cooperate.'

At this, Charles gave a dry cough. 'I wonder...' he said, narrowing his blue eyes. Daphne looked over at him blankly, but then Sarah turned back.

'Ah,' she said. 'Are you thinking Regina might be more amenable if you made the call?'

'Well...' said Charles modestly. 'I did know her late husband, Robert. At the old school, you know,' he said in that offhand way.

'Right. You, and that awful Rollo, and Robert as well. And then Robert died, I'm imagining?'

'Good few years back,' Charles confirmed. 'Heart attack. Poor blighter. They say he was dead before he hit the grouse moor. Most unfortunate for the day's shooting.'

Sarah mentally rolled her eyes. Until recently a confirmed city dweller, she had little time for the ravaging of wildlife that some country folk called sport. And Charles's reaction to the man's sudden death seemed at best unsympathetic.

'Didn't you get on with him?'

Charles hesitated. She could almost see the warring factions in his mind – old school tie loyalty, versus giving an honest answer to a question.

'Saw him a fair bit over the years, I suppose. Reunions and what have you. Nice enough as a boy. But he changed over the years. Not like Rollo, who was a tick from the start. Robert didn't play fair with Regina,' he said, with the sort of finality that meant he wouldn't be discussing the man further.

'I see,' said Sarah. Her best guess was that Robert had become a philanderer. 'And I suppose you and Francesca carried on socialising with Regina over the years.'

This time, it was Daphne's turn to break in. 'Oh no. Francesca can't abide Regina. There's that whole new-money thing, I thought I explained?'

Sarah couldn't help a tiny smile peeping out. The idea of Francesca being out-snobbed was quite appealing. It must really sting for a woman who so wanted to be at the top of the pile, to find herself being looked down on instead.

'They never really hit it off. Could never understand why, for the life of me,' said Charles. 'Perfectly nice woman, I always thought.'

Something about his tone suggested to Sarah that the problem might not just be money and status. It could be something worse, an emotion she knew full well that Francesca suffered from terribly – jealousy. Even though her marriage had been over for some time, Sarah suspected the mayor of Merstairs had not given up hope of a reconciliation with her husband. That was presumably why she was trying to stall the divorce. Had Regina been trying to cosy up to Charles? Or had Charles just seemed that bit too sympathetic over Regina's predicament, and therefore aroused Francesca's suspicions? Sarah was well aware of the kind of reception Francesca gave any suggestion of flirtatious behaviour – not that Sarah herself indulged in anything of that description. She'd hardly seen Charles alone for days.

'So it might be a great idea if you rang Regina, then,' Sarah decided. 'Sounds like she's got a soft spot for you – and if she's not keen on Francesca, as Daphne points out,' Sarah nodded towards her friend, 'then she might enjoy the thought that talking to you will make your wife very cross.'

'*Estranged* wife,' Charles murmured. 'Oh, ah, yes, of course. Very smart, Sarah. Well, let's give it a go. Nothing ventured, nothing gained, eh?'

With that, he took his phone out and then unearthed half-moon reading glasses from his breast pocket and perched them on the end of his nose. Daphne gave a little snort.

'What?' Charles said, looking up from his phone screen and eyeing her over his specs. He tutted and went back to studying his phone, keying in Regina's number and pressing speaker-phone mode.

It only took two rings before someone answered.

'Charles!' Regina said with undisguised enthusiasm. 'How are you, dear chap? I was just thinking about you, as it happens,' she said, dropping her voice to a more seductive pitch.

'Oh, er, goodness, were you?' said Charles, fumbling to pick up the phone while Daphne glanced at Sarah with shaking shoulders. Sarah didn't know quite what to think; on the face of it, Charles's alarm was amusing... but it was a little unfair that Regina didn't know Daphne and Sarah had been listening in.

'Well, that's done,' Charles said, having made a hasty arrangement to meet up with Regina. He put down his mobile with the air of St George, after slaying a particularly ferocious dragon. 'I suppose I'll just report back to you both – you know, let you know how it goes.'

'Oh, I don't think so, Charles,' said Sarah slowly. 'I think Daphne and I need to be there too.'

Daphne boggled at Sarah over the debris of their tea while

Charles pottered off to settle their bill. 'Don't tell me you're going all green-eyed like Francesca,' she hissed.

'Of course I'm not jealous,' said Sarah, ignoring the hollow feeling in the pit of her stomach. 'How could I be? I have no right to feel proprietorial about anybody, let alone Charles.'

At this point, Hamish reminded her of his presence with a tiny yap, and she bent down and petted him. 'Well, I've got you, boy, but thank goodness there are no other entanglements holding me back. Surely you know that, Daphne? It would be so wrong. With Peter only just...'

The sentence petered out and Daphne squeezed her hand. 'Of course, of course,' her friend murmured. 'I thought for a second... But I completely understand. Tell me, what's the point of us gate-crashing this meeting between Charles and Regina, then?'

For a moment Sarah was lost for words. 'Isn't it obvious?'

'Not to me,' said Daphne, twirling an earring round one finger. It promptly dropped off and fell into the sand. After a brief tussle for ownership with Hamish, Daphne clipped it back on.

This respite had given Sarah time to get her ducks in a row. 'I just think it could be really important for the investigation, for us to hear what Regina has to say first-hand. After all, she could be the only person who can really provide a link between Abi and Mabel and their killer.'

'Well, maybe – but surely Charles is quite capable of relaying any information he gets to us? Or, more to the point, passing it on to Mari and the police. We don't have to do every-thing as a trio.'

'We don't, we absolutely don't,' Sarah said earnestly. 'But this is one time when I really think it might work better if we did. Regina is obviously expecting one kind of meeting – what if Charles is too, um, gentlemanly, to keep things on track and get on with the questioning? We don't want Regina to take advantage of his better nature,' she said firmly.

'Right,' said Daphne. 'I get you. OK, fine, then.' When Sarah glanced over at her, she could have sworn her friend was hiding the glimmerings of a smile. But it was gone before she could say anything.

Just then, Charles loped back to the table. 'Well, that's all sorted out then, ladies. Um, I suppose I'll see you later, then? If you really want to come along.'

From his stiff back and slightly abstracted manner, Sarah inferred that Charles, too, thought arriving mob-handed at his rendezvous with Regina was a bit much. But she didn't let that worry her; a plan was a plan.

'Yes. All set for this evening. Let's reconvene at the Jolly Roger at seven o'clock.'

With that, the little group all went their separate ways. Daphne bumbled off to Tarot and Tealeaves, muttering about urgent paperwork. Sarah had her suspicions that her friend was just going to join Mephisto in napping in one of the comfy chairs in the shop. Charles told an equally unconvincing tale about a vital shipment to his antiques emporium, though all three of them knew the place had a turnover that would make most cemeteries look lively.

Meanwhile Sarah promised Hamish a lovely walk on the beach, then spent the whole of it with knitted brows, trying to think hard about the Merstairs killings, but actually straying into areas concerning Charles, Francesca and Regina which were almost as difficult to come to grips with.

THIRTY-EIGHT

That evening, at seven on the dot, Sarah turned away from a fine sunset over the sea and pushed at the door of the Jolly Roger bar. In some ways, it seemed a crime not to watch the last washes of crimson and pink drift away as twilight fell on the beach – but tonight, Sarah knew there were more important matters to tackle inside the pub.

The place was busy, but not by any means heaving the way it had been last week, when the vigil for Abi Moffat had looked as though it might overflow into violence. The tinkle of glasses and hum of conversation now seemed soothing. She remembered her first trip to the place, what seemed like years ago, and how strange she'd found the décor. Now she looked quite fondly at the plastic sea urchins and automatically avoided the netting that swung low over the banquette where their little group always met.

She and Hamish were the first to arrive, which didn't surprise her in the least. Daphne's timekeeping was notoriously lackadaisical, and Charles was apt to forget the world when pottering around his antique shop, running his feather duster over his unappreciated treasures.

She wandered to the bar. Claire was busy serving a group of tourists with shandies and Merstairs Monk beers, so Sarah signalled to Jamie, the new barman, that she'd like a round of their usuals – her tonic water, a pint of Monk for Charles and a Dubonnet for Daphne. She wasn't sure what Regina would like, and in any case she wouldn't be arriving for twenty minutes or so. The theory was that Charles, Daphne and Sarah would use this time to get their conversational gambits organised, but as the minutes ticked by and the others didn't appear, Sarah thought crossly she might as well not have bothered to show up either.

A commotion at the door signalled that Daphne at least had finally made it. 'Sorry, sorry, Sarah. It was all go at the shop. You wouldn't believe how busy I've been,' she said, shaking her red locks.

Sarah decided she'd have less trouble swallowing that story if Daphne hadn't borne the imprint of what looked like a stack of filing on one of her cheeks. It was clear she'd fallen asleep on her 'urgent' paperwork, and what was more, judging by the lavish scattering of ginger hairs on her royal blue top and scarlet skirt, Mephisto had snuggled up with her while she'd been in the Land of Nod.

Just then, Charles poked his head round the pub door, also looking a little bleary-eyed. Sarah exchanged a glance with Hamish, whose fur had been shaped into a ridge by the breeze as they'd enjoyed their blowy walk by the shoreline. He looked almost like a miniature, tufty black stegosaurus, while his black button eyes seemed to say, 'Are we the only reliable people in town?'

Sarah didn't answer him out loud, but she was signalling a definite yes, until Charles veered off towards the bar, and then came back with a bowl of water and a couple of treats for the dog. Hamish panted up at him slavishly and wagged his stumpy tail. Sarah, while quietly delighted, told herself to watch out for the man's charm. He always seemed to know how to win people round. Well, at least that might come in handy now, as Regina walked through the door bang on time.

Charles hastily got up and hailed her, and a smile spread across her face – until she saw Sarah and Daphne already ensconced in the banquette. She collected herself, then strolled over, her trademark pretty silk floral dress floating around her shapely legs.

'I see we're having a group session of some sort. Daphne, how's the crochet going? And Daphne's shadow, how are you this fine evening?'

'Aha, my name's Sarah, actually.' Sarah got to her feet to shake Regina's hand. 'We have met before, when we bumped into each other on the beach. And of course I've seen you in the pub and at the Beach Café, too.'

'Oh, silly me,' said Regina, quite unabashed. 'Terrible memory for names and faces. Daph'll tell you. Of course, you're the doctor, aren't you? Anyway, can I get anyone a drink? Charles, we're going to stay with the gang, are we? Or we could always go and sit over there?' she said in an aside, gesturing towards a nice quiet table, out of earshot, on the other side of the bar.

For a second, Charles looked sorely tempted. Then he happened to glance in Sarah's direction. 'I thought it would be great if we could all get to know each other,' he said rather feebly.

'Well, I know you and Daphne already,' Regina said. 'But what a splendid idea,' she said, in a way that stopped just short of suggesting the complete opposite. 'I see you have drinks. I'll just get myself something,' she said.

'Oh, I wouldn't dream of it.' Charles got to his feet and stepped round her to reach the bar. 'Um, a Chardonnay, isn't it?'

'I'll have a gin and tonic, thanks Charles,' Regina said,

sitting down daintily at the banquette, spreading out her frock
and making both Daphne and Sarah squash up. For such a
slender person, she seemed to take up an amazing amount of
space. 'Well, ladies, now that Charles is safely occupied – what
on earth is this about?'

Sarah and Daphne looked at each other. Daphne clearly
had no idea what to say, so Sarah burst into speech. 'The thing
is, Regina, we thought you might be so useful... that is to say, we
thought you could shed some light on what's been going on in
Merstairs over the last few days.'

'What's been going on? In what sense?' Regina looked from
one woman to the other, her eyebrows raised.

'You can't have failed to notice the murders,' Sarah said
mildly.

'Of course I've noticed,' Regina replied, her voice beautifully modulated but somehow containing a rebuke. 'I'm every
bit as stunned as the next person,' she said with a shrug.
'Daphne, you've been here a little while, you know how out of
keeping this is with everything Merstairs stands for.'

Next to her, Sarah felt Daphne bridling, as she considered
herself a local after all this time.

'I'm always telling Sarah this stuff never happens here,'
Daphne said, a tad mulishly.

'Exactly,' Regina leapt on her words. 'It's sure to be the
work of an escaped criminal from a city, somewhere where this
sort of behaviour runs unchecked, like London, where you came
from, I believe, Sarah. Or even Canterbury,' she continued.

Sarah, who'd always associated Canterbury with its cathe-
dral and knew the place to be extremely sedate, said nothing.
Daphne piped up, though.

'That's exactly what I think,' she said, though she had never
once mentioned this to Sarah.

'Oh, here's Charles,' Sarah said, as he slid a tall glass in front
of Regina. She took a sip. 'We think there may be some sort of

connection between Abi, Mabel and crafting, you see, Regina,' Sarah continued.

Regina went red in the face and gasped for breath. 'Goodness, that went down the wrong way,' she choked out. After a cough or two, she recovered. 'A connection, you say?'

Daphne piped up. 'Well, Abi was always doing lovely creative projects with the kids at the primary, and then Mabel was so good at crochet – she was really gifted. So we thought, maybe they knew each other, collaborated on ideas for the classroom, something like that, you know?'

'I see,' said Regina slowly. 'But even if that were the case, what would it prove?' she added thoughtfully. 'There must be loads of teachers at the school who are good with their hands. And excellent crocheters are two a penny, as you know, Daphne.'

Daphne seemed surprised at this. 'Oh, come on, Regina. Mabel wasn't just excellent. She was really gifted. Wool seemed to come alive in her hands, she could make it do absolutely anything. She was like a sculptor with her four-ply.'

Regina laughed. 'Well, I wouldn't go that far. I did help her a lot, you know.'

Immediately, Daphne deferred to Regina. 'Oh, of course. No one's a patch on you. But Mabel—'

'Well, precisely. Such a sad loss,' Regina broke in. 'Lovely G&T, Charles. How's things? I heard a rumour you've got some new paintings in your shop.'

Charles perked up. All this talk of crochet seemed to have been washing over him, but he could hold forth about his own wares until the cows came home. 'Ah yes, just got in quite a catch, actually. Set of terrific nineteenth-century seascapes. Really capture the drama of the coast. A little after the school of Turner. He painted just along the bay, I don't know if you knew?' Here, even Hamish sighed. You could hardly walk a hundred yards in Merstairs without someone broadcasting this.

'Every now and then one strikes lucky and finds an unattributed masterpiece.'

Sarah, who'd seen the canvases, and dismissed them as the works of someone suffering from chronic myopia, and probably astigmatism too, took a quiet sip of her drink.

The talk moved on to everyone's hopes for the high season. Sarah suddenly realised she didn't know what Regina did for a living. 'Are you retired, Regina, or do you have a shop too?' she asked.

Regina didn't say a word for a moment, but Sarah was somehow conscious that she had transgressed. 'You couldn't possibly know, Sarah, as you're so new to the area, but I do have, well, quite a history here.'

'Oh,' said Sarah. 'Forgive me if I've said something out of turn.'

Regina waved her apology away. 'No, no, it was silly of me. I suppose I always assume... it's just we have lived here for over five hundred years, after all,' she smiled gently.

Sarah smiled politely. 'Well, somehow I must have missed the section on you in the guidebook,' she said, with an attempt at levity.

It went down surprisingly well. Regina stared at her for a moment, then collapsed into a trill of laughter. 'Guidebook! Oh, that *is* a good one. Daphne, you didn't tell me your friend was a comedian,' she said when she'd got her breath back.

'I didn't know she was,' said Daphne, looking pretty astonished at Regina's reaction. 'That's Sarah, full of surprises.'

'The thing is, Sarah, I suppose I don't do a lot in the traditional sense. I was a stay-at-home mother to my wonderful son, Edward, and I really found that a full-time job. Then, long ago, my family used to appoint the vicars, open the fetes, keep the villages going, well, we pretty much owned the place. And I'm still expected to sort a few things out in that way, people come to me, you know,' she said with a wave of her hand. 'But since we had to sell up our country place – my grandfather was a bit of a fool when it came to stocks and shares, alas – I've taken something of a back seat, officially. Left all that to those with the, er, enthusiasm for it,' she said, with a meaningful glance at Charles. Sarah presumed she meant Francesca, who did indeed seem to have thrown herself into the full 'lady of the manor' schtick that had apparently been Regina's birthright.

Sarah now remembered visiting Francesca's home not so long ago and making the assumption that it had been in her family for generations. But in fact, Daphne had said the other day that it was Regina who should have been presiding over the gracious Georgian manor house.

'So how do you find living in the town?' Sarah asked. She felt she was taking a risk asking another question, as Regina had firmly stamped on her curiosity just now. But she couldn't resist. 'If you're more used to the surrounding countryside.'

'Well,' said Regina with a little laugh. 'I'm still out on a limb, rather. I live in one of the coastguard cottages, you know, on the promontory leading over to Reculver. You can see my place from anywhere in Merstairs,' she said.

'Oh yes, Daphne did say. You don't mind your new circumstances?' Sarah asked, knowing she was pushing her luck.

'I've had quite a while to get used to them,' Regina said crisply. 'And how are you getting on in Merstairs? Next to Daphne, aren't you? Enjoying the view?' she asked, with a bland social smile.

'Just magnificent,' Sarah said. 'But back to the crafting. Abi came to a fair few of your sessions, didn't she?'

Regina blinked, perhaps at the change of subject, or maybe just at being asked all these questions, Sarah wasn't sure.

'Oh. I certainly don't remember her coming much... Daphne, how about you?'

Daphne pleated her forehead obligingly and went through all the motions of thinking hard, but even though she'd shown

Sarah the photo of Abi at the pub with the crafters, she didn't contradict Regina's version of events.

'You know, I really couldn't say, Regina,' she mumbled.

'There, you see,' said Regina. 'Now that's all tickety-boo. Was there anything else you wanted to ask?' she said, directing a rather affronted look at Sarah.

THIRTY-NINE

Sarah was feeling uncharacteristically flustered. Regina wasn't overtly bossy or confrontational, but she certainly had an air about her, and Sarah somehow got the odd feeling that it just wasn't her place to cross-question her. Nevertheless, she thought of Abi, dying in her arms, and Mabel, limp and lifeless in the fortune teller's tent. She owed it to them not to let this opportunity pass her by.

'Regina, this might be a bit of a ticklish subject, so please forgive me, but I understand your son was actually engaged to Abi Moffat. I just wondered how you felt about that?'

For a second, all Sarah could see was Regina's wide eyes staring back at her. Then she felt a sudden cold wetness as a tidal wave of drinks surged in all directions across the table. Jamie was passing with a tray of orders and they had suddenly gone flying everywhere – including all over Regina's lovely silk dress. She stood up, revealing that the silk, now almost transparent, was clinging to her legs. Charles, his eyebrows raised, seemed glued to the spot.

'I'm so sorry, ladies, I-I must go home and change,' Regina

said, making straight for the exit, and brushing off Jamie's stream of apologies.

'Let me get you a round on the house,' said the woebegone Jamie. 'I'm so sorry, I have no idea how that happened.'

'That's very kind,' said Daphne. As soon as the boy had collected all the glasses – none broken, thankfully – mopped the spills and replaced their drinks, she picked up her Dubonnet. 'Oh dear, poor Regina,' she said. 'I hope her dress doesn't stain.'

'It won't,' Sarah said, shaking her head briskly. 'She got mostly gin and tonic on it, it's all clear fluid.'

She couldn't help feeling a bit thwarted. They'd been trying to find out who Abi's real boyfriend, or fiancé, was for days. Now they knew, and they hadn't been able to discuss it with one of the few people who was best placed to tell them more about the relationship. 'It's really bad luck Regina dashed off like that.'

'Well, you can hardly blame her. She was showing a bit more leg than she'd bargained for.' Charles couldn't help smiling.

'Yes,' said Sarah. 'Embarrassing for her. But I do wish we'd got a bit further,' she said.

'Well, even if Teddy was engaged to Abi, and Abi was good at crafting, and Regina runs the crafting group, and Mabel was in it too, the whole thing doesn't really add up to anything, does it?' said Daphne reassuringly.

'I suppose you're right,' Sarah said. 'We already know Teddy didn't kill Abi, he's got that great alibi. And why would he murder Mabel? Unless he thought she'd killed Abi?'

'Maybe we could see what he was up to when Mabel died?' Daphne said absently.

'That was the night of the fair,' Sarah said slowly.

'Oh yes. In that case, he's probably OK, isn't he? I don't remember seeing him there,' said Daphne firmly.

'Well, that's not conclusive,' Sarah said. 'Half the town was there that night. It was so crowded, don't you remember? And you wouldn't have registered seeing him anyway, because at that point we didn't know about his connection to Abi.'

'Oh, this is all so confusing,' said Daphne. 'I'm fed up with it all. I know you love sleuthing, and puzzling it all out, but I just want everyone to be happy.'

'Don't you see, though, Daph? We can't really go back to being happy until this is straightened out. We shouldn't just let it go. We can't be too far off now.'

'That's true,' said Daphne, cheering up as she always did. 'In fact, I can feel it in my bones. Something's coming, a resolution from the Beyond. Oh, thank goodness,' she said, looking round at her friends with a big smile.

Sarah, looking at her, felt a shiver down her spine. Things were bad enough as they were. But when Daphne started getting cheery messages from the spirit world, that's when the situation got really alarming.

FORTY

The next morning, Sarah was still feeling disappointed that she hadn't been able to grill Regina about Teddy. She now felt it was almost her duty to get things straight with her. It wouldn't take much, surely, just to pin her down on the matter of Teddy?

Unless... would it be easier to approach Teddy himself? She couldn't quite remember where he worked, or what he did for a living. But she knew someone who'd either have the answers or know where to get them. Not for the first time, she would make the most of her dear friend Daphne's years of experience of all things Merstairs.

Hamish cocked his head at his mistress. She had that determined look on her face again. While that was a lot better than the droopy bloodhound air she'd had back in the big city, he'd found it generally meant that small dogs would be doing a lot of hanging around, while she did plenty of barking at other humans. He much preferred the days when the two of them could just yomp across the sand dunes. Sometimes, he would indulge her by playing that fetch game she liked so much with sticks. Then, when she was nice and tired, he'd bring her back home for a lovely big dinner. He very much hoped today would be one of those days, but something told him different. He put his head on his paws and whined.

Sarah, who was munching determinedly away at a rather tough piece of toast – she really must stop somewhere today and get some fresh bread – heard him and said brightly, 'Don't worry, Hamish, we're heading out as soon as I've finished breakfast. We've got lots of people to chat with today.' She spread a little more blackberry jam on her toast, hoping its richness would help the dry crusts down.

Hamish shook his ears thoroughly, but Sarah just looked at him fondly, as though she was about to bestow an enormous treat on him. 'First stop is next door, to collect Daphne.'

Hamish turned round crossly in his basket. He'd just about had enough of that marmalade monster in the purple house. It would serve his mistress right if he ate that feline up one day, he decided, while acknowledging in one tiny portion of his fluffy head that such a day might not be coming any time soon.

Once the kitchen was set to rights and Sarah's favourite tea towel, covered with cute black and white Scottie dogs, was dangled over the taps to dry, she found her handbag, made sure her phone was charged, and finally got Hamish's lead. Within seconds, he was at her side, a curiously beseeching look in his eyes today.

'That's right, boy, we're just popping over the way first. Come on, now, let's go,' she said, locking the door behind her. The salty breeze immediately started playing with her hair and ruffled Hamish's coat too, while the sun felt promisingly warm. Out at sea, there were several fishing boats bobbing, reminding Sarah that cod would make a lovely dinner tonight. She stepped briskly round to Daphne's rusty gate, and as usual dodged the brightly coloured gnomes dotting her neighbour's path. But when she got up to the lurid front door, it was already swinging open.

'Daphne? Daphne!' she called, stepping gingerly into the

crowded hallway, trying to avoid a tangle of heavy winter coats on the bannisters. As it was getting hotter every day, she wondered why on earth Daphne didn't put these out of the way until the seasons changed. Then she realised she was being ridiculous, her friend simply had no interest at all in such notions. And where on earth was she? Getting more than a little concerned now, she inched forward down the hall, with a curiously reluctant Hamish.

'Don't you want to see if your friend Mephisto is in the kitchen?' Sarah asked him. 'You usually like to play together,' she added.

Hamish looked at her as though she was crazy and continued to sniff his way along slowly and carefully. You never quite knew what might be waiting for you in this house. Turning the corner, there was no sign of the awful cat – but none of its owner either.

'Well, this is very odd,' said Sarah, looking round in consternation. On the table, there were all the signs of a hasty breakfast – but knowing Daphne, they could have been left from the day before. The sink was full, the draining board bore a tottering pile of pans, there was washing haphazardly flung over an airer by the back door. Sarah went over to it and felt a voluminous bright green skirt tentatively. It was still damp, which surely must mean Daphne had only just hung it all up. She stepped to the back door and opened it – and immediately a furry orange hurricane rushed in. Little Hamish took one look and ran out into the back garden with Mephisto quite literally on his tail.

'Hamish! Come back here,' Sarah said worriedly, but it was too late, both he and the cat had disappeared.

She tutted and decided to leave him be. What harm could he come to? Instead, she called out 'Daphne?' a little more loudly,

Sarah was turning round, wondering what on earth to do, with no sign of either her dog or her friend, when there was a call of 'Coo-ee' from the hall and Daphne bustled into the kitchen. 'Thought I heard someone rootling around, Sarah! Where did you spring from? Did you tunnel under the fence or something?'

'No, I came through your front door, which was wide open. Honestly, Daphne, you really need to be more careful. There's a ruthless killer wandering around Merstairs and you're putting yourself at risk.'

'All right, all right, keep your hair on,' said Daphne, holding up a hand to fend off Sarah's onslaught. 'I can see someone got out of the wrong side of the bed this morning. I left the door on the latch for the postie – you know he has the occasional spot of trouble with Mephisto – and then I went up to have my shower and forgot all about it. Simple as that.'

'Well, I'm sorry, but I thought something dreadful might have happened to you,' said Sarah, still feeling ruffled.

'Come along in, sit down and I'll make you a nice tea. Then you'll soon be right as rain,' said Daphne soothingly.

'I don't think we should hang about, though,' said Sarah. 'We really should get on the case and see Regina again, if not Teddy himself. We need to make some progress, otherwise both these two murders might end up being unsolved...'

'Not if my Mari has anything to do with it,' said Daphne briskly, filling the kettle. 'And who hasn't got time for a nice cup of tea? It'll soothe those jangled nerves in no time.'

Sarah swallowed any further objections. She knew Daphne had a point. She'd just had a shock – when she couldn't easily find her friend, all kinds of terrible scenarios had gone through her head, especially in view of Daphne's pet theory that all the most popular people in Merstairs were on the killer's list. Her body was now just catching up with the good news her brain had already processed. A quick sit-down would do no harm.

The tea, when it came, was of course delicious, and Sarah wrapped her hands around the comforting warmth of the jazzy turquoise and purple patterned mug. It looked homemade, and for a second she distracted herself with the notion that it might be the fruit of yet another of Daphne's hobbies, though she hadn't heard a word so far about a pottery club. She couldn't help but smile at the image of Daphne in an apron, covered from head to toe in clay, and the grin made her realise how tight her facial muscles had been. She had definitely been overreacting. These murders were making her feel jumpy – and with good reason. But she needed to calm down.

Right then, there was an ear-splitting combination of screeches, barks and yowls from outside, and Hamish started to yelp in earnest. That didn't sound like the brave little Scottie she knew so well.

Sarah jumped to her feet. 'Hamish? What's the matter?' she shouted, and then felt absurd. The dog couldn't tell her. She rushed for the back door instead, with Daphne hot on her heels.

Outside, Mephisto contrived to look as innocent as the day was long from his vantage point in Sarah's lilac tree, whose bough dipped low over Daphne's fence – and even lower with the enormous cat perched on it. Hamish, meanwhile, looked as woebegone as only a Scottie in pain can, holding up a paw which dangled limply, while he continued to yelp. Sarah immediately rushed to his side, trying to inspect the wound without causing him further distress. She then glared up at the cat in the tree.

'Honestly, Daph, Mephisto is a menace,' she said crossly.

'But he's miles away from Hamish,' Daphne protested. 'And look at him! He wouldn't hurt a fly. You know Mephs, he's all meow and no yeow.'

'You tell that to Hamish. Didn't you hear that bloodcurdling noise Mephisto was making? Look, the poor boy can't put any weight on his leg,' Sarah said in alarm, as Hamish bravely tried to walk a few steps and gave it up as a bad job, subsiding onto

Daphne's scruffy lawn with a whimper. 'Besides, didn't that cat nearly have the postman's arm off last month?'

'That was a mere scratch,' said Daphne quickly. 'The postie was hamming it up. He's one of the Merstairs Players. You know what these amateur dramatics types are like.'

Sarah barely registered the news of yet another Merstairs group, she was so concerned about her little dog. Irrationally, her thoughts flew to Peter, who'd presented her with the Scottie and made her promise faithfully to look after him. She suddenly felt she had let him down. She'd allowed the dog to get injured on her watch. She knew the guilt was ridiculous, but that only added to her anguish. 'This is dreadful. I must get him to a vet.'

'Oh, I'm sure he'll be right as rain in a minute,' Daphne said, to Sarah's quiet fury. 'Surely you can sort him out, you're a doctor after all?'

'A human doctor,' said Sarah crossly. 'Animals are quite a different matter. I'm sure I could patch him up but he'll probably need a very strong course of antibiotics to stop the wound going septic thanks to your cat's saliva, and strangely I don't have one of those about my person.'

'Well, if you insist,' said Daphne, as though indulging Sarah in a crazy whim. 'We'll be killing two birds with one stone, I suppose,' she added with a light-hearted giggle.

Sarah turned to her. 'How on earth do you make that out?' she said impatiently.

'Well, we can take him to Teddy Stanforth, can't we? You wanted to question him anyway. So it's perfect, really.'

'Why in heaven's name would I drag my poor injured dog to go and interview a suspect? His wound needs urgent medical treatment.'

'Wound? It's just a tiny scratch—' Daphne started, then thought better of it when she saw Sarah's face. 'Yes, anyway, let's get our stuff and go,' Daphne said, heading for the kitchen door. 'And don't worry about Mephisto, I'm sure he'll be fine,' she tacked on kindly.

'I certainly wasn't worried about that... that creature,' said Sarah under her breath. 'But Daphne, I don't understand this. I really need to get Hamish straight to a vet. There's no time to be messing around with anything else.'

'Yes, yes, I know, you keep saying. And I agree, why not pretend there's something really wrong with him? Great idea. Teddy'll put a bandage on him and make him feel a whole lot better. The Placido effect, they call it, don't they? Though I've never quite seen how Placido Domingo comes into it.'

Sarah, who'd been about to open her mouth again and really lay into Daphne, putting her straight on the placebo effect amongst other things, suddenly stopped dead. The penny had dropped.

'You mean... Teddy Stanforth is Merstairs' vet?'

'Of course,' trilled Daphne as she picked up her bag from the kitchen table. 'Didn't I just say that?'

FORTY-ONE

As Sarah slid Hamish onto the back seat of her Volvo, did up his harness and tenderly covered him with a tartan blanket, she realised she hadn't been this cross with Daphne since they'd been in the sixth form together and her friend had 'borrowed' her favourite Mary Quant eyeshadow without asking, and then casually left it behind at a party.

But as she got into the driving seat and put the car in gear, Sarah realised that, this time at least, it wasn't justified. Daphne couldn't be held responsible for the actions of her psychotic feline. Yes, she was its owner, and potentially could have spent more time trying to curb his excesses, but it was well known that cats were laws unto themselves. It was more Daphne's attitude to Hamish's injury which rankled. She'd tried to minimise it, while pretending Mephisto was somehow not the culprit.

At the same time, as Sarah's temper cooled from boiling point to somewhere around the irritation mark, she knew she would feel similarly defensive if, heaven forbid, Hamish were to bite someone. But she also hoped that she would step up and take responsibility – and make sure it never happened again.

There was no hope, at this point, of anyone retraining the

mighty Mephisto. He was, and always would be, a massive ginger menace and she hoped the whole experience had taught Hamish to give the creature a very wide berth from now on.

Taking a breath and feeling a bit less agitated, she finally turned to Daphne. 'Strapped in all right?'

'Yes,' said Daphne meekly. Then she put a hand on Sarah's arm. 'He didn't mean it, you know.'

Sarah thought for a moment, knowing how much this admission had cost her friend. 'Well, we might have to disagree on that,' she said finally. 'But I suppose Mephisto is Mephisto, after all.'

'Exactly! He's a free spirit, totally at one with nature. He's magnificent, untamed and true to himself,' Daphne continued, then seem to realise this praise might not go down too well just at the moment. 'But he can be a very naughty boy,' she added in a smaller voice. 'I'm always trying to tell him. I did his Tarot cards last week and they said he'd have a difficult encounter.'

Sarah yanked at the handbrake and signalled to move off. She wasn't even going to comment on the absurdity of doing a Tarot reading for a cat. 'I think it was Hamish who had the difficult encounter,' she said, remembering the gleam in Mephisto's eyes as he had sat at his leisure, surveying them all from the lilac tree. Even though the tree was a beautiful specimen, and about to burst into flower, she currently felt quite like hacking it down, just so the darned cat would lose his comfortable vantage point.

She shook her head. It was no good dwelling on it. 'All right, there, Hamish?' she said, eyeing him in the rear-view mirror. He gamely tried to raise his little tufty head, but gave it up as a bad job, but she distinctly saw his stumpy tail wagging. It looked as though he was going to be fine.

Cheering up a little, Sarah drove on into Merstairs proper. They passed the growing shrine at Tarot and Tealeaves, which now took up most of the pavement, and then a few minutes later saw the tributes and condolence cards fluttering on the railings of the school. It seemed rather sad that there wasn't such a public outpouring for Mabel Moorhead.

'Did Mabel have any relatives? You've said she had no children. I just wondered... someone must be mourning her, too.'

'Absolutely,' said Daphne. 'I'm grieving, for one. Not to mention Regina, she's in bits. Mabel was such a kind and generous soul, Sarah. I truly think she was one of the nicest people I've ever met, always encouraging, always kind. A marvellous teacher. You won't believe it, but before she took me aside and gave me a few pointers, I actually wasn't very good at crochet. I owe it all to her, really,' she added a little smugly.

'Really?' said Sarah, thinking somewhat darkly of Daphne's frightful plans for her cushion cover and wondering whether anyone should be grateful to poor Mabel or not. Without the woman's kind words of guidance, Daphne might have given up crafting, and crochet could have gone the way of most of her other enthusiasms. But never mind, Mabel had no doubt meant well and the patience and perseverance that must have been involved in those 'few pointers' probably said huge volumes about what a lovely lady she had been.

'Where to now, Daphne?' she asked her friend. A few minutes later, after Daphne had gone wrong a couple of times, they were drawing up outside a veterinary clinic near a roundabout on the main road out of Merstairs. Daphne had rung ahead while they were en route, so they were expected. Sarah bundled little Hamish up in his blanket, trying her best not to hurt his bad paw as she did so, and they were soon at the reception desk, explaining matters to a pleasant-looking girl in her early twenties, who was wearing a blindingly white pinafore that had 'St Francis Clinic' embroidered above her breast.

'Poor Hamish! You've had quite a morning, haven't you?' said the girl, ruffling the little dog's ears and immediately gaining Sarah's trust. She had such a natural way with her. 'The vet will see you as soon as he can. There's someone in with him now. Just take Hamish to a seat over there. I promise it won't be long.' Her smile was gently reassuring, and Sarah and Daphne sat down with Hamish lying in state on Sarah's knee, looking, Sarah had to admit, a lot better, though his paw was matted with blood. She tickled him under his chin, to distract him from licking at it and potentially making things worse.

Sure enough, as the receptionist had promised, a young couple carrying a cat basket came out of the consultation room with relieved expressions on their faces, and a few moments later the vet popped his head round the door and beckoned to Sarah and Daphne. Sarah scooped up the patient and they trooped in.

Anxious as she was about Hamish, Sarah took the opportunity to have a good look at Teddy Stanforth. He was in his late twenties or possibly early thirties, she guessed, and was an attractive, but not drop-dead gorgeous man, quite solidly built. It wasn't a stretch to imagine him on the cricket field, and something about the way he held himself suggested he'd be good with a bat. He had sandy, very curly hair and blue-green eyes, and wasn't tall, but nor was he short. He was the man she had seen at the Wittes Hotel with his mother, she realised. He looked good in his vet's scrubs and his manner with Hamish was irreproachable, a mixture of deft practicality and genuine compassion, though Sarah thought she detected an air of sadness underlying his professionalism. This was hardly surprising, she supposed, given that his fiancée had so recently been murdered. He must be trying to distract himself with work – something she'd definitely been guilty of in her time.

He parted the fur on the little dog's paw, trimmed it quickly and carefully, examined the wound and cleaned it thoroughly. The gash – a perfect forensic match with Mephisto's wicked, needle-sharp front teeth, she was absolutely sure – was quite deep. Daphne looked away, fanning herself. Sarah hoped that would be the last time she'd dismiss Hamish's ordeal as trivial.

'Quite a nasty time you've had, young Hamish,' Teddy said gently, and the little dog wagged his stumpy tail in response to the kind voice. 'Don't you worry, you've been a brave soldier and you'll be tickety-boo again in no time, my lad.'

Sarah couldn't help but prick up her ears. 'Tickety-boo' – the exact phrase Regina Stanforth had used, when she'd had that drink with them in the Jolly Roger and got covered in spilt tonic water.

'I've met your mother,' she said to Teddy with a smile.

'Occupational hazard, in a place like Merstairs. Can't go two steps without meeting someone you know,' Teddy murmured. 'I'm just going to give Hamish an injection of antibiotics,' he said, stepping away and preparing a fearsome hypodermic.

'Is that really necessary?' said Daphne weakly. She'd always been a bit of a wimp about needles, Sarah remembered.

'Cats do carry quite a lot of nasty bacteria in their mouths,' said Teddy seriously. 'Even the best-behaved ones,' he said with a smile at Daphne. Sarah, who had some trenchant views about Mephisto's manners, wisely remained silent. 'That can lead to very severe problems if you're not careful. I had to deal with a serious case the other day – the night of the Whitsun Fair, actually. I thought we might be too late, the poor cat was in such a bad way – he'd been bitten by his brother, of all things, and no one had seen the wound puffing up. That can happen in very fluffy cats. It took me a good couple of hours to debride the entire area,' Teddy said, shaking his head.

'How awful,' said Daphne, looking a little green.

'Yes... the night of the fair, you said?'

'Missed the whole thing,' Teddy said. 'Not that I could have faced going anyway...' he added, that deep sorrowfulness seeming to seep out again. 'Well, anyway,' he said with an effort. 'We wouldn't want Hamish to get a bad infection.'

'We certainly would not,' said Sarah crisply, rather glad that the vet had spelt out the dangers of a bite-happy menace like Mephisto so clearly – and given himself an alibi for Mabel's slaying at the same time. 'By the way, we were so sorry about Abi.'

Teddy, who had been advancing on Hamish with his syringe at the ready, faltered for a second. 'Oh. That piece of information is out in the public domain, is it?'

'I'm sorry, yes,' said Sarah quietly. 'I'm not sure whether I understand why it was ever a secret, though? You can't have been ashamed of each other.'

'Of course not,' Teddy said briefly, looking up from where he was finding a suitable injection site on Hamish's leg. 'It was just that... well, Abi was very soft-hearted. She was helping out a friend. I can't say more, really.'

'You mean Josh Whittsall? Oh, we know about that,' Sarah said. 'What I don't understand, I suppose, is why Abi didn't let her own mother in on the secret. I expect your mum knew all about it.'

Hamish whimpered as the needle went in, and Teddy patted him as soon as it was all done. 'Good boy, you've done so well,' he said. 'Mothers, eh? They can be very protective of their young. We see it all the time in the surgery,' he said lightly. 'He's a lovely dog. He should be fine, but I'll give you a short course of antibiotic tablets to administer at home. Just pop them into his mouth, or if that's hard to manage, you can mash one into his food every night. If he does have any symptoms, a fever, swelling around the wound site, anything like that, then just bring him back.'

'Oh, Sarah won't have any trouble about that, she's a doctor herself, you know,' said Daphne.

'Really?' said Teddy, looking at Sarah. 'Well, that's excellent news for this boy,' he said, ruffling Hamish's coat.

'Thank you so much for sorting him out,' said Sarah, feeling a lot happier now about Hamish's condition, and glad also that she'd managed to squeeze in a few pertinent questions about their case.

'Just one last thing,' Teddy said, turning back to her with a sheet of Perspex which he deftly twisted while he advanced on the little dog. 'Let's put this on, Hamish. Yes, that's right, it's the cone of shame for you.'

'Oh, poor Hamish!' said Daphne, and Sarah gave her a stern look. If it hadn't been for her dratted cat, Hamish wouldn't be in this ignominious position.

Hamish gazed up at Sarah with beseeching black eyes, clearly asking her what on earth he'd done to deserve this awful fate. But Sarah, while she felt for him, knew it was for the best.

'Come on now, Hamish. You'll just have to be brave. You know if you didn't have the cone you'd only be licking away at that nasty cut and making it much worse.'

'Exactly,' said Teddy. 'It's only until it's nicely healed. Keep an eye on things and I'm only a phone call away if you need me,' he said. 'There. You actually look quite smart in it, Hamish. Doesn't he?'

Sarah smiled at him, but as he turned away, she was pretty sure she saw exhaustion on the man's face. Was that because she'd pressed him for information all the time he'd been working, was it the effort of keeping up a brave face while he was grieving – or was there something else going on?

FORTY-TWO

Sarah tried not to wince as the nice receptionist handed her the bill for Mephisto's morning's work. Goodness gracious. Judging by these rates, if she'd been a vet instead of a GP, she'd have been able to buy Francesca's house several times over, if not quite the Wittes Hotel. But she couldn't regret it. Working for the National Health Service hadn't made her rich, but she knew she'd done her best to help people. She handed her credit card over with a brave smile.

'So, the vet was telling us about the terrible cat bite you had to deal with the other day?' she said conversationally as the girl keyed the figure into the handset.

'Oh my goodness, that was just awful. I have to say, I've never encountered a wound that had been so neglected,' she said confidentially. 'I'd been planning to go to my parents' place to eat, I always go on a Sunday. But it completely killed my appetite,' she said, handing the card back. 'Would you like your receipt?'

'Yes please,' said Sarah, hoping against hope she'd be able to claim this on her pet insurance. 'And thanks once again for seeing us so quickly.'

The girl beamed and Sarah and Daphne set out with Hamish in Sarah's arms. She soon had him installed on the back seat of the car, but he was in high dudgeon, every now and then shaking his head to try and rid himself of the plastic cone. All he succeeded in doing was rattling it horribly against his harness. Eventually he sank down on the seat and appeared to fall into a bad-tempered sleep.

'Poor old Hamish,' said Daphne. 'Still, it was great we got it all sorted out.'

Sarah couldn't help sniffing. Daphne wasn't a couple of hundred pounds out of pocket, or now the proud owner of a pet in a cone of shame. But she cheered up a bit thinking of the progress they'd made.

'I'm certainly glad we checked out Teddy's alibi for Mabel's killing. He does seem a nice man, though I still find it a bit odd that he went along with Abi's pretend romance with Josh.'

'Well, she was a lovely girl, as everyone keeps telling you. She'd always help out a friend. And wait a minute, I think I must have missed that about Teddy's whereabouts.'

'He told us he was dealing with a terrible cat bite on the night of the fair. I wonder if that was more of Mephisto's doing?' Sarah couldn't help adding a little pointedly, even though she knew it was the work of the victim's sibling. 'And just now, his receptionist said she'd had to miss a family dinner because she had to stay late and assist him. We know Mabel was dead by about six that evening, so I think that pretty much lets both of them out of it.'

'Well I must say, you did that very cleverly, Sarah. I didn't even notice you putting the questions,' Daphne said admiringly. 'You sneaky thing, you.'

Sarah didn't reply, as she had to negotiate the tricky corner coming up near the bandstand, but secretly she was rather warmed by the praise. It hadn't been a great morning – especially for poor Hamish – but at least they had made some headway.

There was one thing that was niggling her about the whole episode with Teddy Stanforth, though. If only she could put her finger on it. Oh well, she thought. Long experience had taught her that the more she puzzled, the further away she'd get from the source of her unease. The answer would come to her in its own good time, she was sure of that.

* * *

After a long day, during which Hamish was almost as needy and demanding as he had been when he'd arrived as a tiny puppy, Sarah was finally in bed. She'd always slept blissfully in Merstairs, which she put down to the sea air and really quite an unexpectedly hectic lifestyle. But rest, for once, would not come.

It was as infuriating as having a word on the tip of your tongue, or bumping into someone whose name you just could not remember. There was information – crucial information – but it was locked in her brain somewhere, tantalisingly out of her reach.

She kept replaying the scene at the vet's. Teddy Stanforth, reassuring but sad, in his spotless white tunic. The smiling, kind receptionist. The posters in the waiting room featuring gambolling spaniels and extremely well-behaved cats, looking as unlike Mephisto as it was possible to be. Everything was as it should have been. But something was wrong.

FORTY-THREE

After a restless night, Sarah sat at her breakfast table with gritty eyes and the makings of a headache. She massaged her temples with her fingers, then gave in and went to the cupboard where she kept her scant stock of painkillers. For a doctor who'd prescribed endless drugs for her patients, she was usually curiously reluctant to medicate herself. But today she took a blister pack of paracetamol and popped out two tablets, pouring herself a cup of tea from the pot on the table.

Some toast, that was what she needed. She'd managed to get a seeded wholemeal loaf from the Seagull Bakery yesterday afternoon, and now she cut a slice and shoved it into the toaster. Normally she would spend ages selecting a jam, but today she just got down a slightly crusty jar of marmalade. When the bread popped up, piping hot and a lovely golden brown, she took up her knife, and was about to slather the toast with butter, when she was suddenly arrested by the sight of her own hand. It struck a chord in her memory. It was to do with yesterday, in the vet's surgery.

Hamish, watching from his basket, in the cone which had been annoying him all night long, whined gently, as if to prompt

Sarah to get on with it before her toast – and Hamish's crumbs – grew cold. But Sarah just sat, knife in hand, willing the thread of thought to come back to her. She'd been holding Hamish steady, when Teddy Stanforth had taken that giant syringe, and prepared to inject the dog. She'd asked him about his mother – and it was then, she realised, that it had happened. His previously rock-steady hand, and his controlled and poised demeanour, had both faltered. Hamish had whined, just as he had done now, because the injection, instead of being smoothly administered, had actually jabbed him slightly.

Teddy Stanforth had some kind of problem with his beautiful, elegant, floral silk-clad mother.

What on earth could it be, Sarah wondered, her toast now totally forgotten. The butter pooled and congealed on the bread, and the marmalade remained in the jar. Instead, Sarah shot out of her seat. 'Come on boy, let's go and fetch Daphne.'

Fetch was one of Hamish's favourite games, and a word that was only slightly lower in his hit parade than the perennial top dog, *walkies.* Instantly, the cone of shame was forgotten – or at least put to one side in his mind – as he devoted himself to showing his mistress that she'd had a Good Idea. As for the toast crumbs, well, never mind. He might be able to get his paws on them later.

But the little dog soon found things weren't going as planned. First off, there was no sign of a nice stick or even one of his favourite tennis balls in Sarah's pockets this morning. Secondly, he found himself being chivvied up the path to her friend's place – which, in case his mistress had forgotten, was the scene of the heinous attack on him perpetrated by his wily orange foe. Hamish felt he had no choice but to make his feelings plain, and therefore put on the brakes. A moment later, he found himself being unceremoniously hoisted up and tucked under Sarah's arm, and the rest of the journey to Daphne's was carried out in this humiliating manner. Even his strongest objec-

tions resulted only in an offhand suggestion that he 'Hush now.'
Well, really!

Daphne, when she eventually answered her front door,
seemed even less enamoured of the whole idea than
Hamish was.

'What do you mean, there's something funny about Regina
and Teddy's relationship? And good morning to you, too,' she
said, rubbing the sleep out of her eyes. She was dressed already,
which was a big plus, but she showed no signs at all of wanting
to rush over to Regina's place to work out what Sarah's hunch
meant.

'He had that moment of hesitation, you know, when he
was... tending to Hamish,' Sarah said, with a significant glance
in the dog's direction. Hamish was already a bit peevish about
his cone. He'd backed himself into Mephisto's fleecy bed again
but he didn't seem to be enjoying this illicit pleasure as much as
usual, keeping a wary eye on the cat flap and sniffing the air
suspiciously every now and then. She didn't want to keep going
on about the injection, in case he began to associate the word
with pain, and therefore became sensitised about visiting the
vet. Medical phobias were a problem, as she knew. She'd had
quite a few patients who weren't at all keen on doctors, despite
the evidence that they were wonderful people, and she'd had
her work cut out to win them round.

'Well, maybe his hand did shake – but that could have been
about a thousand things, Sarah. It doesn't have to be anything
about Regina. Maybe you've been reading too much Freud.'

'No. Up until that point, he'd been supremely professional.
I'd been really admiring his bedside, or kennel-side, manner. I'm
not sure what you call it with vets. And then, well, it was still
only a tiny thing. But it was a real lapse in his composure. I
think there's something there, I really do, Daphne. And it's not
like we've got a million things to go on, at this point.'

Daphne sighed. 'Well, I suppose you're right about that.

This whole business has been very odd. There's never seemed to be anyone who really wanted to do Abi in, and yet she died on my doorstep. And the same with Mabel. I mean, you couldn't come across a nicer, more unassuming woman. Yet someone obviously didn't like her, in a big way.'

'Well, exactly,' said Sarah eagerly. 'That's why we should check this out.'

'But why should there be any connection between Teddy wavering over a shot, and two lovely women dying? I just don't get it.'

'Well, we were asking Teddy about the case. That has to be it, there must be a connection.' Sarah lifted her palms.

Daphne kept on looking at her steadily. 'I'm not convinced. But I suppose it won't hurt to pop round. It'll be interesting to see what you make of Regina's place, anyway.'

'Why, what's it like?' Sarah asked, gathering up her things and clipping Hamish's lead back on.

'Oh, let's just say it's, um, quirky,' said Daphne with a maddening smile. 'You'll see.'

FORTY-FOUR

As the two trotted along the seafront – a walk that had now become so familiar to Sarah she felt she could do it with her eyes shut, though then she would miss the magnificent sight of the waves crashing on the Merstairs shore – she started to speculate about what Regina's house might be like.

Of course, all things were relative. For Daphne, her own home was the norm, so any place that wasn't full to the brim with an astounding array of flotsam and jetsam, much of it with some sort of mystical feel, might be considered eccentric. Sarah knew Daphne considered her own place next door to be distinctly colourless, for example.

Yes, it was more than likely that it was just that Regina's own taste didn't dovetail with Daphne's, and that was what her friend considered strange, reflected Sarah as they plodded on. The weather was glorious today, a spring morning that was a harbinger of a perfect summer ahead, with that simmering sense of heat building that had already ensured the beach was busy with dog-walkers, wild swimmers and early birds getting beach equipment out of the pretty huts near the pier.

When they reached the end of the esplanade, Daphne and

Sarah ploughed straight on, following the road that climbed slowly upward towards the cliffs above Merstairs. Hamish cheered up at the thought of novelty and picked up his pace. Sarah soon realised that, despite all the walking she felt she did these days, she was much less fit than she had hoped. Before long she was breathing heavily, while Daphne at her side was panting almost as much as Hamish.

'It's deceptively steep, isn't it?' Sarah puffed, when they paused for a moment halfway up.

Daphne just nodded, and then plodded onwards. The view was certainly amazing from here. They were that little bit closer to Reculver, and Sarah could finally see the details of the ruined castle that so often appeared shrouded in mist early in the mornings. With a lazy circle of seagulls flying round it, she could almost imagine the time when its walls had been intact and its garrisons had helped to see off invasions from the turbulent seas which surged all about it.

'Not much further now,' said Daphne, her cheeks glowing pink and clashing with her vivid hair.

'I'm beginning to see why you weren't so keen on this outing,' said Sarah, who had a bit of a stitch coming on. Down on the beach, she suddenly caught sight of a familiar lanky figure which, though tiny, could only be Charles. He was walking a dot that must be Tinkerbell. She waved enthusiastically. 'Has he spotted me?' She hadn't seen much of him since his abortive attempt to ask her out and wondered when – or whether – he'd ever get up the courage to finish his sentence.

'The whole of Merstairs has seen you, you look like you're practising semaphore,' sniffed Daphne and they turned away and carried on up the hill.

There had been no houses along the path for quite a while, as they ascended the cliff. Now they came to a last, steep climb, during which there was silence apart from quite a lot of heavy puffing. Finally they reached a short terrace of three or four cottages, rather like Sarah and Daphne's own homes far, far below.

'Wouldn't you know it, it's the last in the row,' huffed Daphne.

'Wow, the view from here is spectacular,' said Sarah, peering way out to sea now. As well as the boats and their attendant knots of seabirds, there was the small island offshore that only appeared at high tide, and way out on the horizon, a strange group of metal structures which she knew must be the Shivering Sands army fort, constructed in the Second World War as an anti-aircraft defence. It looked rather unearthly, like a row of metal ants stalking through the waters.

'Come on, Sarah, you're the one who wanted to see Regina. Let's get it over with,' said Daphne.

Sarah was surprised, her friend was never usually tetchy. But the climb up the hill at this early hour had been taxing, it was true. 'OK, OK, we're here now,' she said soothingly, as Daphne adjusted her headscarf with a series of jerky movements. 'Shall we knock on her door?'

They were finally opposite the last house in the row. All were built of uncompromising blocks of local stone, probably cobbled together a century or two ago with extra-thick walls to withstand the winds whirling around the little promontory, and still standing against the odds.

'Regina always says these were the coastguards' cottages,' Daphne said, one hand holding onto her scarf.

'I can well believe it,' said Sarah. Anyone looking out from here would have a perfect vantage point for seeing ships in trouble in the bay. She wrapped Hamish's lead around her hand. Though she knew there was precious little chance of a breeze spiriting away his solid little body, she didn't want him scampering over the edge of the cliff to the white swirling waters of the sea far below.

The path to Regina's front door was stony, the garden

largely untended, though Sarah did wonder what on earth would grow up here anyway, in the winds. She was lucky further down at her place, protected from the elements, where the soil was much less salty and weather-beaten. She thought for a moment of her trampled and then replanted flowerbeds and felt an overwhelming urge to rush straight back there right now to check how her precious peonies and lavender bushes were doing. Don't be silly, she told herself. They were here now. They'd just straighten out a few things, then they could be on their way.

Meanwhile Daphne had her hand on the heavy tarnished brass ring of the door knocker. She hesitated, for one uncharacteristic second, then she let it fall with a loud thud. There was silence, apart from the whistling of the wind.

'Maybe try it again, Daphne? A couple of times?' Sarah encouraged her. She knew how her friend felt, it no longer seemed quite right to be dropping in on the stately Regina without a firm appointment, but they were literally on her doorstep now. The sooner they got this over and done with the better.

But there was no need to knock again. The door suddenly swung open, and there was Regina, resplendent in one of her flowery dresses, its hem instantly ruffled by the breeze so that it looked like a summer field in motion. She looked taken aback for a second or two, then her customary good manners kicked in. 'Ah, it's you two,' she said with a gentle smile. 'Do come in. Just passing, were you?'

FORTY-FIVE

'Is anyone ever "just passing"?' Sarah said mildly to Regina Stanforth. 'You're quite a long way off the beaten track.'

'Yes, I suppose that's so,' Regina replied with a little moue of sadness, as she led the way through into the small sitting room.

At once, Sarah could see what Daphne had meant about the place. The room was simply bursting with references to Regina's previous, much more exalted status, as chatelaine of the grand manor house that Francesca Diggory was now inhabiting. There was a huge walnut tallboy, bristling with drawers and brass knobs, looming over the small room, as well as two matching bookcases almost blocking the small windows. A credenza by the other wall edged into the passageway which must, Sarah imagined, lead to the kitchen. There was a vast, handsome desk in the opposite corner. A full chintz three-piece suite was crammed into the middle of the room and this was where Regina led her guests to sit. Each chair had not one but two fiddly piecrust tables flanking it, while the sofa had a very large buttoned footstool positioned in front of it which made it difficult to access.

Regina threaded her way gracefully through the furniture

maze, but Sarah barked her shins on the desk and Daphne nearly crashed into the tallboy. As Daphne finally sat, her huge bag almost knocked one of the side tables over, and Sarah dived to stop its fall. Then she deliberated about where to sit herself, not sure how to get onto the sofa without hurdling the footstool. Eventually, Hamish decided for her, leading her to the other chair which, in a less cramped room, might have sat by the fireside, but here stood uneasily with its back to it, cheek by jowl with the bookcases, tallboy and its chair twin. Regina skirted the credenza to enter the kitchen.

'You'll both take some tea, I hope?'

Daphne looked at Sarah with a rather hunted expression, but Sarah had no hesitation in saying yes. Hamish had curled himself up under one of the side tables, apparently seeing nothing odd at all in this jam-packed assortment of furniture. There were more antiques here than in Charles's shop, Sarah thought, and these were of far better quality. She levered herself out of the chair and went to help Regina in the kitchen. This was partly due to her usual desire to make herself useful, and partly the result of a growing feeling of claustrophobia.

The kitchen, she wasn't entirely surprised to see, was also stuffed to the rafters. As well as a highly polished dining table rammed into the corner, with no fewer than eight spoon-backed upholstered chairs jostling around it, there was a large Welsh dresser crammed with a full ironstone dinner service, including soup tureens and a flotilla of gravy boats. There was hardly room for a sink, a tiny cooker and Regina herself.

'Um, just wondered if I could lend a hand,' said Sarah, gazing around with a rather stunned look on her face. She wasn't sure she could live like this for a day. 'Have-have you just moved in?'

'Twenty years this summer,' said Regina with a smile. 'Could you reach down the cups and saucers for me, please, my dear?'

Sarah stared at the mountainous pile on the dresser. The cups were placed inside one another in an arrangement that looked extremely precarious. She was terrified she'd shake the pile and the whole lot would fall and smash on the stone-flagged floor, which she could just about see under an assortment of rugs which must be a major trip hazard. She gulped, and lifted three off the top, holding her breath as she safely transferred them to the table.

'And the saucers!' said Regina, as though Sarah had committed a major boo-boo. As these were located underneath the tottering pile of cups, Sarah was very reluctant to move them.

'Oh, um...' she said weakly.

'Here, come round to this side and I'll do it,' said Regina, ushering Sarah over to the other half of the room. There was therefore space for her to shimmy past the table to the dresser, and nimbly pluck three saucers from the stack without incident. Sarah breathed a sigh of relief from her vantage point with her back against the sink. She shot a glance out of the window, where the skies were blue and the wind seemed to have dropped a bit.

'You've got, um, quite a nice space outside,' she said, longingly. She had the awful feeling that if she moved either elbow too suddenly she would shoot through the window or decimate a pile of crockery.

Regina, now bustling about and making the tea, moving around the many obstacles with no apparent problem at all, just nodded at this. 'While it's so lovely to have visitors up here in my eyrie, I do rather wonder why you two have come?' she asked conversationally.

'Oh. Oh yes, of course. I see quite why you would be puzzling over that. Shall we wait until you've made the tea, and Daphne and I can tell you about it?' Sarah said uncomfortably.

'No need,' said Daphne from the sitting room. 'I can hear

you perfectly well from here,' she said, hardly raising her voice at all.

'Well, as it happens everything is ready, if you could just get that packet of biscuits?' Regina said to Sarah.

Sarah looked around wildly for a moment, seeing everything but biscuits: a matching set of Le Creuset pans, a selection of food mixers, two coffee machines, some sort of large milk frother, a slow cooker... It was a bit like being in the small appliances section of John Lewis.

'Oh, I'll get them,' said Regina, grabbing a packet Sarah hadn't noticed at all from the middle shelf of the dresser. 'Right,' she said, stepping into the sitting room and starting to distribute cups and saucers to the various small tables and popping the tray on the footstool, before slithering back into her seat. 'I'll pour, shall I?'

Daphne and Sarah looked at each other. 'Um, lovely,' said Sarah, picking up her cup and saucer and edging towards Regina while trying not to kick Hamish, trip up herself or knock anything over.

Daphne, looking askance at the whole procedure, declared, 'Do you know, I think I'm fine without tea. But if you could pass the biscuits, Sarah, that would be great.'

The bourbons, which Regina had fanned out daintily on a bone china plate matching the cups, were duly passed and Daphne nibbled the corner of one a lot more cautiously than she usually would.

There was something about the whole of this cottage interior that made the place extremely unrelaxing to be in, Sarah decided. And that something was about three hundred tons of excess baggage. Goodness knew what Regina thought she was doing, keeping this lot with her, when she could surely have downsized without too much trouble and the cottage would have been a perfectly liveable space. She could even have put a lot of this stuff into storage, though keeping it there for twenty years would certainly tot up. But there was no telling other people. And who knew what psychic wounds all these possessions were soothing?

While Sarah had encountered a few hoarders in her work as a GP, usually when they had sustained injuries due to their collections, Regina didn't really fit into that mould. There was nothing insanitary about the way Regina was living. That did not mean, however, that her way of life could be described as normal.

Sarah felt herself recalibrating her views of Regina, in the light of her home. If she had to make a diagnosis, she would speculate that Regina had not adapted as well as she had previously assumed to the loss of prestige that had occurred when the family had gone broke. But that had been more than a generation ago, by all accounts. Shouldn't Regina have got used to the status quo by now?

'Sarah? Sarah, Regina's asking you something,' said Daphne through a mouthful of biscuit. Regina smiled, seeming oblivious to the spray of crumbs that ensued. But maybe, thought Sarah suddenly, she wasn't nearly as unaware of things as she seemed. Perhaps she noticed everything, and a lot of it didn't go down that well at all.

Despite the gathering heat in the room, from three bodies in a small space – four, if one included the now-slumbering Hamish, which Sarah very much did – she felt a chill down her spine. It was disconcerting, when someone you'd marked down as perfectly civilised, rather charming, and above all normal, suddenly revealed themselves to be no such thing.

'I was saying,' Regina repeated with punctilious politeness. 'Just idle curiosity, I know, but what has brought you two ladies up to see me on this fine day?'

'It is a fine day, isn't it?' Sarah remarked brightly, though actually precious little light was coming into the sitting room through the largely blockaded windows. 'This is a wonderful spot. You have quite a vantage point. You must be able to see all sorts of comings and goings,' she said, her eye lighting on a tele-scope perched on one of the well-stocked bookcases. She got up carefully and clambered over to take a look, and Regina got to her feet too.

With an 'after you, no you go first' series of gestures which served only to slow things down, Regina eventually backed far enough away to allow Sarah to squint through the telescope. She felt a little thrill of alarm when she saw that it was trained not on the open sea, but on the coast road up to Regina's house – and the little parade of shops down in Merstairs, including Daphne's Tarot and Tealeaves. Sarah adjusted the focus and the doorstep where Abi had died shot into sharp relief. It was almost as though she was down there herself. She could see the flickering candles of the growing shrine, lit even this morning, and could almost make out the wording on the cards left with the various wilting floral tributes.

Sarah turned from the telescope and looked Regina full in the face.

FORTY-SIX

Regina sat down on the sofa with a deep sigh. It was quite an art, the way she managed to slot herself in so neatly behind the enormous footstool. But then, Sarah was beginning to suspect there was an awful lot that was artful about Regina.

'Did you like Abi?' Sarah asked abruptly. Daphne, sitting opposite quietly munching her way through the plate of bourbons, coughed slightly as a crumb went down the wrong way.

'Like her? Of course I *liked* her. Silly word, that, like,' said Regina, in a faraway voice. 'I like all sorts of things. The opera, dogs, even Daphne here. They're all likeable. But you're missing the point, Sarah. I *love* my son.'

'Is that why you knocked that tray flying in the Jolly Roger? You didn't want to discuss their relationship?'

Regina smiled. 'I thought I'd convinced you it was an accident. But it hardly matters. Yes, I had no intention of talking to you about something so vulgar.'

'I see,' said Sarah quietly. 'You thought he deserved better.'

'There was no thinking required. Of course he does, that's self-evident. He deserves the best. He's a wonderful vet, I'm sure you'd agree,' Regina said, looking up at Sarah almost cravenly, seeking praise for her best beloved.

'Oh yes, he's highly professional,' Sarah said. 'He was very good with Hamish here. Most reassuring.'

'Exactly,' said Regina, almost swelling with pride. 'Everyone says so. And if he had his proper inheritance – if my stupid grandfather, stupid father and stupid husband hadn't ruined our finances – then he'd be in the finest clinic in the county. Or a professor of veterinary science. Something befitting his status.'

'Status. Is that what all this has been about?' Sarah narrowed her eyes at Regina.

'Well,' said Regina, smoothing down her dress carefully. 'Don't you think it's important?'

'To be honest, not particularly,' Sarah replied.

'Oh come now, you're being disingenuous,' Regina said with a smile. 'You set great store by your position as a doctor, that's obvious. Or ex-doctor, I should say.'

'I'm retired,' Sarah conceded. 'But that was a qualification I earned, through hard work. It wasn't something I was born to. I think your problem with Abi, if we could bring things back to the matter in hand, was that her family background was just too ordinary by far. She had nothing to offer, did she? As far as you were concerned.'

'Oh, well, she was fine for a fling. A boy has to have his fun. But marriage? Of course not. When he finally told me she'd got her hooks into him – despite that ridiculous charade the girl went through with Josh Whittsall – well, I couldn't believe Edward had let himself get presumed upon like that. Not that he actually proposed, of course not. They were never engaged at all, despite her pathetic attempts to pin him down. Any chatter you might hear down in the town is wrong on that point, utterly so. But he shouldn't have had any sort of a relationship with her. It was bound to give her ideas.'

'Ideas "above her station", you mean?' Sarah asked.

'If you want to put it that way, then yes,' said Regina, completely unabashed. 'It was typical of him, he's just too kind. Always has been. So much compassion, for mangled stray cats and rabbits that should have been drowned at birth – and chits like that girl. Oh, I'm sure she was a super teacher,' she said, as Daphne showed signs of swallowing the last biscuit and protesting. 'But she was at a primary, let's not forget – not even a secondary school, and certainly not a university. She looked after the youngest children and provided the simplest lessons. In times gone by, she would have been a nursery maid, nothing more.' Regina flicked her fingers dismissively.

'And what could she ever make of herself?' she continued. 'If she was very lucky, in twenty years' time, she might perhaps have clawed her way up to become deputy head. But I don't think so. She had no ambition, no drive. My boy, shackled to that? When he could have had anybody?' Regina looked at Sarah, eyes wide. 'Well, what would you have done? It was all quite ridiculous.'

'Right. You thought Teddy should set his sights elsewhere.'

Regina nodded emphatically. 'Well, of course. The Diggory girl is the obvious choice. Arabella, you know. She's divorced, which isn't ideal. But her settlement with that banker ex-husband of hers should be quite healthy. It's only right, as Francesca's father was one of the many who swindled Grandpapa. All that money will come back into the family, once she's married to Edward.'

'But Arabella already has children, you know. I'm not sure all her money would end up with Teddy, even if they ever were to fall in love and get married,' said Sarah, trying to sound logical and measured, while becoming more and more sure that she was dealing with a mind which had left reason behind a long while ago.

'Oh, once she and Edward have their own children, those twins will be old news,' said Regina airily. 'Off to boarding school with them. Maybe a place in Scotland? There are loads of suitable establishments.' She glanced with satisfaction around her impossibly crowded home. 'Then all this can go back to its rightful place, our manor house. It's Edward's birthright, you know,' she said in conversational tones.

Sarah had to wait a beat before continuing. It was curiously disconcerting, speaking to someone who was so clearly mad, yet who was utterly convinced of their sanity, and the fact that their world view should reign supreme.

'Can you tell us how you did it, Regina?' she asked softly. Daphne made a strange, strangled sound, almost like a mew, but hastily stifled it. Hamish stirred next to Sarah and cocked an ear at her. She patted him as reassuringly as she could, hiding the slight trembling in her hand. She was just beginning to realise what a dangerous situation they were in. She now had no doubt that Regina had killed Abi, though she didn't know how. And what had happened to Mabel was just as much of a mystery as before.

Regina looked startled for a second. 'How I did it? Did what? Oh, you mean... oh yes, I see. Well, it was like this. The girl had to go. So I got rid of her.'

'But how?' Sarah persisted. 'What did you use, and how did you get her to Daphne's shop?'

'Oh, yes, Daphne dear. It was your shop, wasn't it? So sorry about that,' Regina said vaguely.

'Quite all right,' said Daphne automatically, then covered her mouth with her hand. 'That is... well, um...' she tailed off in horror.

'Did you ask her to meet you there?' Sarah jumped in. 'Very early that morning? I got there not long after dawn.'

'Yes, yes, that was it. I'd only just overheard the ridiculous gossip about the engagement. Naturally I wanted to talk some sense into her, get her to leave my Edward alone. She could hardly refuse a request from her future mother-in-law, could she? Or that's what she thought anyway. She claimed to be terribly busy, said we could only meet at that time as she had to rush off to the school. As if anything she did had any real importance. Poor deluded thing. How on earth could that girl think Edward would ever marry her? I mean, her mother, my dear. Have you met her?'

'I have,' said Sarah. 'A very brave, dignified woman,' she added, her hands curling into fists. Although she was suddenly terrified at what she and Daphne had taken on, anger at this woman's crimes and the way she was denigrating poor, bereaved Jennie Moffat was coming to her rescue, sharpening her senses, concentrating her mind. She scanned the distance to the front door. It wasn't far – but the route was obstructed by the huge amount of furniture everywhere. Mind you, Regina was a slight woman. No match, surely, for Sarah, Daphne and Hamish... or so Sarah hoped.

'Why did Abi have all those bags of clothes around her?' Sarah asked sharply.

'Clothes? Oh yes, that's easy. She was collecting for charity, planning to take them to the Save the Children store when it opened. I'd said I'd bring a few things down... well, not *quite* as much space here as one would like,' she said, as though it was a matter of a few full drawers, instead of the contents of a mansion jam-packed into a minuscule cottage. 'I agreed to meet her nice and early, saying it would be less embarrassing for me to drop my things off before opening time. She was always so compassionate, so caring,' sneered Regina.

'You say that like it's a bad thing,' faltered Daphne.

'It can be a weakness. In this case, it certainly was. Poor silly girl,' said Regina dismissively.

Daphne turned to Sarah with a look of wordless horror on her face. Regina, whom she'd admired so much, was turning out to be a monster. Sarah tried to smile reassuringly at her friend, but it was hard, when every fibre of her being was now shrieking that it would be an excellent idea if the three of them got up and ran full pelt for the door immediately. She needed to go on with her questions, though. She might never have this opportunity to get to the bottom of all this again, and it was too good to pass up.

'But what did you stab her with? They haven't found the knife yet,' Sarah said, trying to keep her tone light, and not inject all the repulsion and anger into it that she was currently feeling.

'Stab her? Oh yes, do you know, I've quite forgotten...' Regina said, looking blank.

Sarah raised her eyes to heaven. Really, this woman was so far off the scale of sanity, it was untrue. How could she forget a thing like that? Just then, she saw Regina's eyes flick over to the fireplace. Could the murder weapon actually be concealed somewhere over there? Sarah got to her feet and moved gingerly towards it, edging past the piecrust tables and the tray piled with tea things.

Once she'd got as close as she could, she stared at the objects clustered on the mantelpiece – a pair of Staffordshire china dogs, a carriage clock, an old-fashioned letter opener – aha! It must, surely, be that. She picked it up. It was shaped like a knife, about six inches long and looked pretty sharp. She turned to Regina, but the woman barely registered her, merely asking Daphne if she'd prefer coffee. Surely she would have shown more reaction if Sarah was on the right track? She looked again at the opener, and realised the blade was too thick to have caused Abi's wound, which Mariella had described as a puncture.

Daphne, who was stammering out a 'No, thank you,' to Regina's extremely polite offer of a fresh plate of biscuits, caught Sarah's eye and gave a strange tilt of her head, almost as though she'd developed a tic of some kind. While that wouldn't have been impossible, considering the stress they were both under right now, Sarah decided something else was afoot... her friend was doing her best to give her a clue.

She followed the direction of Daphne's head, to somewhere a bit nearer ground level. Here there were piles of old newspapers bundled ready to use as firelighters when the weather changed, as well as a full coal scuttle, a set of pokers which were too large and too blunt to fit the bill as weapons, and a few paperback books stacked up. She hoped those weren't going on the fire. She sighed in exasperation. This was like a game of hot or cold, and at the moment she felt she was definitely in the arctic.

'A glass of water, then?' Regina asked Daphne in the same icily polite tone, and Daphne took the opportunity to shake her head, her eyes again signalling wildly to Sarah.

Sarah looked around again. There was nothing else near the fire that could conceivably be a weapon. There were some slippers, true, but Abi hadn't been beaten to death. There were a few jumpers, but she hadn't been smothered or strangled. There was Regina's crafting bag, perching on a mound of colourful balls of wool which must surely be a combustion hazard in the winter, but Abi could hardly have been *knitted* to death... Oh. Wait a minute.

Sarah bent forward. Sticking out of the top of the bag was a pair of knitting needles. She stepped over a curious Hamish, grabbed the workbag and headed back to her seat, glancing gratefully at Daphne as she did so.

'Oh, oh, that's my project,' Regina remonstrated, turning at last from the teapot.

'Surely you don't mind if I admire it?' Sarah said quickly. She wedged herself back into her chair and removed the steel needles from their ball of wool. The scant light from the window bounced off them. They were long and thin, and tapered to sharp points at the ends. Sarah looked over to Regina, whose blue eyes were round and looking curiously vacant.

'Yes, oh yes, that. I do see,' she babbled. 'I do believe it's all coming back to me now...'

'Regina, is this what you used? To kill Abi?'

Regina smiled and opened her mouth to agree – when there was the sound of a key rattling in the lock.

'Who on earth is that?' said Daphne, looking round in consternation.

FORTY-SEVEN

Teddy Stanforth breezed into the jam-packed room, seeming to take in the little tableau before him at a glance.

'Ladies, how lovely to see you again. No, don't get up, Mumsy. Oh, and it's... no, don't remind me. Little Hamish. How are you doing today, boy?'

Hamish ambled over to Teddy, seeming to bear him no ill will after yesterday's injection, and threw himself on the floor for a tummy tickle, though he was somewhat hampered by his cone.

'None the worse for your experience, hey, boy?' said Teddy. 'Glad to see he's on such good form,' he said to Sarah.

Rarely had Sarah felt so socially awkward. On the one hand, she needed to thank this man for tending to her pet so successfully. On the other, she probably should break it to him that his mother was a double murderer. She cleared her voice, but Daphne beat her to it.

'Did you know what your mum was up to?' Daphne said to him conversationally. 'With the killings, and so on?'

'Oh, erm,' Teddy said, his face falling, looking from Regina to Daphne and back again. Sarah still had the mending bag on her lap and took the opportunity to slide her phone out of her pocket, hidden by all the wool. She went to dial Mariella's number, but nothing happened. She stabbed the number again, desperately. Then she saw the tiny letters at the top of the screen, *no service*. Good grief. They were so high up here, and out on such a limb, that there was zero reception. She went cold. She and Daphne had pushed it too far, this time.

But the next moment, she breathed a sigh of relief. Of course, Teddy himself was their best bet. He knew his mother so well, he had probably realised she was unhinged. With his help, they could get out of this in one piece and see to it that Regina got the treatment she desperately needed. Preferably in a top-security prison a long way from Merstairs.

'Teddy, your mother's been telling us how she stabbed Abi in the shop doorway, so that you could marry Arabella Diggory. I think she might need some specialised care,' Sarah said in gently matter-of-fact tones. 'It would be good if we could get some health professionals up here to look after her,' she said, not adding, we could also do with the Merstairs police. She gave Teddy her most meaningful look.

Immediately, he smiled back at her reassuringly. 'Of course, of course, well, don't you worry about that. I'll always make sure Mumsy is looked after. That's been a priority for as long as I can remember.'

'She has a very special dream for you, that you'll marry Arabella,' Sarah repeated. 'That's why she killed Abi,' she added.

'I know. So naughty of you, Mumsy,' said Teddy, wagging a finger at Regina.

Sarah and Daphne looked at each other now. Something was seriously off. What kind of man made a playful gesture like that at the murderer of his girlfriend? That cold feeling rushed into Sarah's stomach once more. She didn't like this. She didn't like it one bit.

'I don't think you understand, Teddy. Your mother *killed* Abi. She stabbed her,' Sarah said earnestly.

'Got you the first time,' said Teddy, wiping a strange smirk off his face. 'Terrible, terrible,' he said, shaking his head, suddenly adopting the slightly sorrowful demeanour she'd noticed at the veterinary surgery.

Sarah was baffled. Was it possible she had been wrong about Regina? Everything had seemed to point to the woman... but now she felt as though the world had turned on its axis, leaving all she had thought of as certain feeling infinitely shaky. She looked over at Daphne, who again seemed to be trying to signal something with her eyes. *Oh, for goodness' sake*, thought Sarah. *We've done all that. And this is not the moment to say you're getting a message from the Beyond.* She looked away, thinking quickly.

'There's one thing I don't understand. I see why you needed to get rid of Abi,' she lied to Regina. 'But what about Mabel? What was the problem there?'

Immediately, Regina's eyes flew to her son's face. Was she asking permission to speak... or was she checking something? Sarah realised with mounting dread that when Regina had spoken about the killings earlier she had been hesitant, and rather sketchy on the details. Was it possible? Surely it couldn't be? Was Regina taking the blame for her only son? Was *Teddy* the killer after all?

But why on earth would he want his beautiful girlfriend dead? And what about his unbreakable alibi, the cricketing mate who'd testified that Teddy had been at the Airbnb all night long? Then at her side, Hamish growled – not at Teddy, which at least would have shown good taste. But he'd lifted his paw to try and gnaw at it and been thwarted by the cone. Sarah remembered again that needle full of anaesthetic, the slight shake in Teddy's hand. Vets had unfettered access to drugs, just as doctors did. It was one reason why there were such high rates of addiction and abuse in both professions. She thought again about Mabel's death, from a fast-acting insulin injection. And even the neat, small hole in Abi's chest. And she looked again at the knitting needle.

'I just don't understand any of this,' Sarah said at last, in anguish.

Teddy laughed. It was an easy, assured sound – but for Sarah, it had the same effect as ice cubes pouring down her spine.

'The clever doctor, outwitted at last. You're so used to being in charge, aren't you? I've heard about you, getting everything ticked off in that organised brain of yours. Daphne talks too much to Mumsy, that's for sure. Well, some of us play the long game. Much more satisfying than the quick buzz of sorting out a few clues.'

'Maybe you could enlighten us,' Sarah said, shrugging her shoulders. 'Which one of you is the killer?'

To her astonishment, both mother and son laughed at that.

'Oh, that's a good one,' Teddy said. 'Can you really see my mother hitting the heart first time with a simple knitting needle? Um, I don't think so,' he guffawed, while his mother tittered along as though her boy had told the best joke ever.

Daphne's face was like thunder by now. 'How dare you! How dare you laugh about killing that sweet creature? Abi was worth fifty of you.'

'Don't be ridiculous,' said Teddy, offhand. 'She was nothing, cheap and easy. All right for a quick fling, but no more than that. While she was busy with that twit Josh Whittsall it was fine. But then she somehow convinced herself we were serious, and without even consulting me she ended the charade with Josh. And she expected me to step up! Frankly, it was laughable. I would never in a million years have asked a girl like Abi to marry me. That wasn't in our plans, was it, Mumsy?'

'Certainly not, Edward. I couldn't let you throw yourself away on her.'

'So why didn't you just break it off? People split up all the time, no one thinks anything of it. There was no need to kill the poor girl,' Sarah said.

'But don't you see?' Teddy said, as though talking to a simpleton. 'Abi had gone and got herself pregnant. And she was far too selfish to do the sensible thing about it. She kept bleating on about her religion, as if I cared about that. I would have had to support her until the brat was eighteen. There's no way Arabella would take me on, with that baggage. It's bad enough that she has kids of her own.'

Sarah and Daphne looked at each other. They hadn't heard a word about a pregnancy. Sarah couldn't help tutting. Mariella had picked a very annoying time to become the soul of discretion. If she'd had this nugget of information before... but no, Sarah couldn't kid herself that it would have led her to the Stanforths any sooner. She simply had not been bargaining for the twisted schemings of this evil pair.

'So you deliberately decided to kill your pregnant girlfriend?' Sarah couldn't keep the disgust out of her tone.

'Of course not, I'm no monster,' said Teddy. 'I gave her one last chance to do the right thing. Mumsy convinced her to meet down at that derelict shop—'

At this point, Daphne spluttered but Sarah managed to silence her with a look.

'We were going to get her to give the baby up for adoption. It was the obvious solution. She couldn't offer it any kind of life and I wasn't about to have my future ruined. But the silly girl was adamant. So she forced me into doing it, really.'

'Hang on, you killed her... and you're saying it was her fault?' Sarah was incredulous.

Teddy looked at Regina, then back at Sarah. 'Are you a simpleton, too? Of course I had to do it. She wouldn't see sense.

She had some fantasy about us bringing the kid up together. I wasn't going to do that, or pay child support for her brat either, was I? Mumsy was off to crafting later so she had her kit with her.' He shrugged nonchalantly. 'I admit, I saw red. It wasn't my finest hour, although I do think I was rather brilliant to improvise with the tools at hand.' He spread out his hands. 'It was necessary. I got the job done, then I had to rush back to join the cricket lot in their dingy Airbnb. Honestly, I don't think Abi really even felt a thing. It was over in a second, as painless as injecting your dog yesterday. You know how good I am with dumb animals.'

Sarah, who'd seen Abi's distress and watched her die very slowly, felt a flush creep up her face and shook her head. The man was disgusting. She couldn't speak for a moment. When she found her voice, she tried to keep the tremor of anger out of it. 'OK, but what about Mabel? She wasn't about to do you out of any money, she had no bearing on your social ambitions... she was just a little old lady who was very good at crochet.'

'Well, not exactly,' said Teddy.

'What do you mean?' Sarah was baffled.

'She was *too* good at crochet, that already had Mumsy's back up,' Teddy said, as though it was self-evident. 'But then she went a step further. She knew about my little bit of fun with Abi – silly Mumsy was a bit indiscreet there. And then she found out Abi had got pregnant.'

Regina nodded. 'I admit, I'd confided in her about Abi. I was just expressing my worries that someone of that type was latching onto my boy and trying to ruin his chances.'

'Mumsy, you really shouldn't have.' Teddy wagged his finger at her again and Regina simpered back at him coyly. Sarah felt nausea rising. The dynamic between these two was seriously off.

'Sadly, Mabel didn't take the situation seriously at all, she simply couldn't understand what the problem was,' Regina said.

'She kept saying Abi was a "nice" girl – that silly word again. I'd really thought better of her up to that point. But of course after that I never took her into my confidence again.'

'So what happened?' Sarah asked. 'Surely you didn't kill her just because she said Abi was nice?' Because, if so, there were shortly going to be two more casualties, as Sarah and Daphne had both given their opinions on Abi's loveliness.

Regina looked a little shamefaced now. 'No. The thing is, Mabel was with me at Edward's place. I pop in a couple of times a week to tidy for you, don't I, dear?'

Edward gave her that nauseating smile again. 'You're wonderful, Mumsy.'

'I probably don't have quite as much space as I need here,' Regina went on, and Sarah just managed to stop herself nodding fervently. 'But I always know where everything is. There's a system, and I've organised Edward's quarters in the same way. Mabel often tagged along. She would do her crochet, or sometimes help me out. This time, she was busy emptying the bathroom waste bin – I'm a little squeamish about some chores, I admit.'

Sarah now got a clear mental image of Mabel scrubbing away, while Regina sat around in one of her floral numbers and directed her. That seemed much more in keeping with this woman's view of the world and her place in it.

'I didn't even know what the little white stick in with the rubbish meant. But Mabel realised pretty quickly. She was congratulating me, if you can believe that. "Oh, you're going to be a granny, how splendid."'

Suddenly Sarah remembered Hannah Betts at the Beach Café. She said Regina and Mabel had been talking about sticks, and Regina seemed cross. So that's what it had all been about. Pregnancy tests, not knitting needles or crochet hooks.

'Such nonsense!' Regina was continuing. 'Mixing our DNA

with that fetid Moffat gene pool was *not* cause for celebration. It was a catastrophe, no less.'

'Of course, I see it with animals too,' Teddy said. 'Not every dog is a pure breed, like this handsome young man,' he said, tickling Hamish's tummy while the dog's tongue lolled. Sarah shut her eyes. She'd be having some words with her pet – if and when they got out of this mess. 'Pedigree matters,' he continued. 'In dogs, and in humans too.'

'I couldn't have said it better myself,' gushed Regina, clasping her hands together as she looked lovingly at her son.

Sarah swallowed, took a brief look at Daphne's anguished face, and carried on. 'So after Abi's death, how long did it take Mabel to start to suspect what had happened?'

Sarah was suddenly remembering that night in the pub, when she'd been introduced to Mabel, but Mabel had been distracted. She'd been keen to get Mariella's number, as she'd wanted to discuss something with her... If that had been her suspicions about Regina, then if Daphne had only passed her daughter's number on, Mabel might still be alive today. It was a horrible thought, especially as Sarah knew she now couldn't say a word about it. Daphne seemed to have forgotten, and Sarah was the last person who'd want to burden her with that guilt.

Regina gave Sarah a quick glance. 'It took Mabel longer than it should have done, I expect. She didn't have your enthusiasm for sleuthing. I did my best to seem devastated about Abi, of course, but silly Mabel couldn't understand why I wasn't more open about the fact that the chit had been dating Edward. She didn't seem to realise it was important to keep any whisper of the entanglement from Arabella.'

'And, of course, she was the only one who knew about the pregnancy,' Sarah said.

'Exactly. Poor old Mabel. She still trusted me, but she'd started to look at me a little oddly. It wouldn't have been long before she'd got it, and I couldn't sit around waiting for that to happen. I have my boy to protect,' Regina said, with a fond glance at Teddy.

'I saw my chance at the fair,' she continued. 'I noticed that charlatan Madame Grimaldi had nipped out for a cigarette or twenty – these frauds wouldn't be allowed within five miles of Merstairs if I had my way,' said Regina with a withering look at Daphne. 'It was the perfect opportunity, a nice dark tent with no witnesses. So I told Mabel she should go and get her palm read. I said it would be jolly good fun. Of course she was always so used to following instructions, whether it was me or one of her crochet patterns. I came up behind her and injected her with the insulin. Simple as that.'

'And you got the insulin from Teddy, I suppose?' Sarah asked.

'Full marks. I suppose that's what people like you crave, isn't it?' Regina sneered.

'And that was it?' Daphne was beside herself. 'You killed Mabel because she thought you were lucky to be a grandma? That's despicable, Regina, I feel so let down by you. Mabel adored you. And by the way, Madame Grimaldi is no fraud. Well, she may not be great at reading palms, and I think she improvises a bit when it comes to the Tarot – and let's not even talk about her fake handbags – but her heart's in the right place,' she said, shaking with rage.

Sarah was behind Daphne all the way – but she was also worried that this diatribe wasn't going to go down well with the Stanforths. What would they do next? They had form for murder, and as she now knew, they would carry it out on the flimsiest of pretexts. Sarah was beginning to feel that her days, and those of Daphne, were numbered. She hoped Hamish would be all right without her. She put her hand down to him unobtrusively and he wagged his tail trustingly. It should have been reassuring, but in fact it just compounded her feelings of guilt.

As she'd thought, Daphne's outburst proved to be the last straw for Teddy.

'I've seriously had enough of you two, and your silly questions,' he said. 'Mumsy and I don't need to answer to the likes of you. We know what we're headed for – and you are just two batty old dears getting in the way. With Abi tidied up, there's nothing to stop me marrying Arabella. Once we've moved Francesca out, we'll be back inside the ancestral home and things will be how they should always have been. And, as luck would have it, there's a very easy way to get you out of our hair.'

'There is?' said Sarah, deciding she should play for time. The longer they kept this mad duo talking the better the chances were that someone would wonder where on earth they were. But she knew there was little hope of anyone connecting them with this place, even if their absence was noticed. It was a horrible way to end things, at the hands of a couple of out-and-out psychopaths. It was, in fact, one of her worst failures of diagnosis ever. She'd seen Teddy at close quarters dealing with Hamish and had not spotted his tendency at all. The fact that many such killers were charismatic charmers was no consolation to her, none at all. And she had led poor Daphne into this mess. Daphne was now swivelling her eyes wildly at her again, and for a second Sarah wondered if she'd gone as loopy as their hosts.

But Teddy was evidently tiring of all the chat. He shot abruptly to his feet, and Regina followed suit, her pretty, girlish dress billowing.

'Get up, you two,' he snarled at Daphne and Sarah. They looked at each other, and for a wild second Sarah wondered what would happen if they disobeyed and refused. But then Teddy flexed his arms, readying himself to evict them forcibly from their chairs. She got reluctantly to her feet, and Daphne followed suit.

'Right, outside,' Teddy snarled.

'And take that dreadful little mutt with you,' said Regina.

Sarah turned to confront her. The woman had pushed her too far, now. Poor innocent Hamish, stuck in his cone but bearing it pretty well, did not deserve to be spoken about like that. But as she whirled round, she caught sight of something out of the corner of her eye. A movement, outside the cottage. She darted a quick glance at Daphne, who now had a very blank expression on her face – the sort she'd worn when telling massive fibs to prefects, back in the day. Something was afoot. Before she had time to work out what was going on, Sarah found herself being shoved roughly out of the cottage by Teddy, who was revealing more of his true colours with every ill-natured push and jibe. Hamish looked at him in surprise and whimpered.

'I know, boy. He really isn't very nice at all, is he?' Sarah said. Luckily, her words were whipped away by the wind whirling outside.

There was a relief in feeling the fresh gusts battering them. Even though Sarah knew danger was very close at hand, anything was better than the terrible claustrophobia of that cottage. But she didn't have long to think about it, before Teddy started up again with all the pushing and shoving. She tried to move as slowly as she could, without actively resisting him or antagonising him in any way. Daphne, with her scarf streaming out behind her in the breeze, was a bit less cooperative, though she disguised it well, pretending she had turned her ankle and developing an extravagant limp.

'Oh for goodness' sake, Daphne, stop play-acting,' said Regina crossly. 'There's no point resisting. People will just say it's a terrible shame that you and your chum here were hiking in such unsuitable footwear and came a cropper on the cliffs. It could really happen to anyone,' she said, poking Sarah in the back with her bony fingers.

'Wait a minute,' said Sarah. 'Yes, great idea about the cliff, but I just want to get one or two things straight...'

'Oh honestly,' said Regina. 'Don't you think we've chatted long enough? Anything you're still confused about you can ask God to explain when you meet him in a few minutes,' she added in an offhand manner.

Sarah was chilled but decided to persist. She had nothing to lose. 'But I really want to know what Abi's last word meant. What did she mean by "wits"? It doesn't seem to fit anything.'

Regina and Teddy looked at each other – then both burst into peals of chilling laughter.

FORTY-EIGHT

'Puzzling away to the end, eh, Sarah?' Regina said when she'd stopped giggling. 'Well, I'd have thought anyone could have worked that out. What is our crafting group called?'

'Um, Stitch and Bitch, Pat called it,' Sarah said, hoping the word wouldn't antagonise Regina further.

'Oh, that's just Pat. Daphne, don't you remember what it's really called? Though you hardly ever show up. You won't be much missed,' Regina said dismissively.

'Well, thank you, Regina,' said Daphne indignantly, trying to free her hand from the woman's grasp. 'To think I offered you a free card reading! It's always been called the Stitch and Bitch when I've gone along. And I'll thank you to know I've hardly missed a session...'

'Honestly, why I am not surprised that I'm the only one who knows the group's real name?' said Regina to Teddy.

'You're wasted on them, Mumsy,' said Teddy. 'It's such a good one, too, the Knit Wits.'

'Thank you, my dear. Though you might be a little biased,' Regina said, fluttering her lashes at her son in a way that Sarah considered revolting.

'*Knit Wits*,' Sarah said, enlightenment dawning. 'I wish I'd known that. It would have saved a lot of time.' And maybe even Mabel's life. Another thought struck her, though. 'Even if you're the Knit Wits, why would Abi say "wits" as she died, not say the name in full?'

'Maybe she didn't have enough puff?' Teddy said callously. 'But it was probably because of Mumsy and I having our special nicknames,' he said over the wind.

'Nicknames? What are those?' Sarah asked, hoping there wasn't too much desperation in her tone. Whatever movement she'd seen through the cottage window didn't seem to be resulting in any direct action, and the edge of the cliff was looming ever closer.

'Don't think I don't realise what you're up to,' said Teddy, with a twisted smile that for Sarah was even more sinister than his intent face earlier. 'But playing for time isn't going to help you. You're going over, and soon. But there's no harm in telling you this much. My little name for Mumsy is Nit, as she's such a nitwit sometimes,' he said, directing one of those sickly smiles at Regina. 'And she calls me Wits, as she says I've always had to live on mine. Just a little thing between us. I should never have mentioned it to Abi, of course. But only the five of us have ever known it. And in a minute, that five will be down to two.' He smirked again as he clamped his hand even more firmly over Sarah's arm and yanked her off the path that led downwards into Merstairs, forcing her instead towards the knife-sharp cliff edge, and the tussocky border between land and air.

Sarah dug in her heels firmly. 'Daphne, don't let Regina push you over. There are two of us, if we both resist, they can't do a thing,' she shouted, knowing she was being ridiculously optimistic. A healthy young man in the prime of life would have no problem at all in dispatching two ladies of a certain age. Admittedly, Daphne could probably take Regina but that was beside the point. Teddy would just chuck Sarah into the void and then go back for her friend. Just as Sarah was beginning to despair, as Teddy pulled her effortlessly forward, a little black ball of fur hurtled past Sarah and threw himself at Teddy. It was Hamish, and though he couldn't bite the man, thanks to the cone of shame, he jumped at him repeatedly, pushing him backwards with what had become a handy Perspex battering ram, while snarling for all he was worth. Sarah was astonished – even in his battles with Mephisto, he had never shown this level of determination or ferocity.

'Yes, go for it, Hamish!' shouted Daphne, renewing her struggles against Regina, while Sarah managed to wrench herself free of Teddy as the man was forced backwards by the little dog's bloodcurdling growls.

'Call him off, get that menace away from me,' screamed Teddy, but Hamish didn't back down, adding a cacophony of barks to his newly discovered attack repertoire. Teddy edged backwards, feeling behind him with his feet, not daring to take his eyes off the dog. 'That little tyke! When I get my hands on him—'

'Hamish! Careful,' said Sarah, as the man staggered a little and slipped to his knees. As he was trying to get up again, and the dog continued to bob forward at him, barking, there was a commotion behind her. Sarah wheeled round, to see Charles, Mariella and the two constables, Dumbarton and Deeside, advancing cautiously towards them.

'Stop right there,' said Dumbarton uselessly to Teddy. But Teddy couldn't stop. One of his legs had now gone over the edge, and he was scrabbling with his hands to get a purchase on the tufts of grass – tufts that Hamish was guarding ferociously.

'Hamish, here, now!' said Sarah. She couldn't bear the little dog to get too close to the edge – and didn't want him to be responsible for Teddy going over either. For that was what seemed to be happening. Despite all the man's efforts to pull himself up onto more solid ground, both legs were now swinging off the edge of the cliff, and the big policeman was demonstrably too frightened to approach.

'Edward!' Regina screamed. '*Edward...*' Sarah turned to look at the woman, who now seemed more demented than ever. And when she pivoted back to see what progress Teddy was making, there was nobody there any more. Just empty space, where he had been so frantically kicking and grabbing only seconds before.

FORTY-NINE

It wasn't until they were back down the hill, snuggly ensconced in the Jolly Roger, that Sarah began to relax. Hamish, the hero of the hour, was at her feet, an empty bowl of dog treats licked clean. Every now and then, someone would come up and ruffle his fur and pat him, and he would accept it as his due. He was officially a Very Good Dog, and everyone in Merstairs knew it. Even the awful cone couldn't dampen his joyous mood.

The fallout from the dreadful scene on the cliff face was something Sarah knew she would be processing for a long time to come, not least the terrible time lag between her first spotting movement outside the cottage through the window, and the belated arrival of the cavalry to save them. During those long minutes of struggle, Teddy had lost his life and Regina seemed to have parted with what remained of her sanity. She was now under sedation in police custody, awaiting transfer to a secure unit.

'What I don't understand is what you all thought you were doing, why you waited so long?' she said plaintively to Mariella – but in a way, her question was directed to Charles Diggory, who was sitting right next to her and rather furtively holding her hand under the table. While this warm clasp was a comfort, as had been his whispered invitation to dinner tomorrow night 'to see where all this is going,' she probably would have preferred it if he'd popped up sooner on the cliff and she hadn't been dragged to within a couple of inches of oblivion. That said, she was very glad he'd had the presence of mind to ring Mariella and toil up the cliff to Regina's cottage with reinforcements, after seeing them from the beach and realising something big was afoot.

'The trouble was, we have very little in the way of hard evidence,' said Mariella, with a touch of apology in her voice – but not nearly enough, as far as Sarah was concerned. 'Teddy still has that alibi for the night of Abi's murder. Though we're pretty sure he drugged his roommate on the cricket tour and that was how he sneaked back to Merstairs to meet Abi in the early hours with his mother, we can't prove it. The roommate was out of it, probably after a dose of ketamine, and Teddy avoided all the CCTV cameras on his way to Merstairs and back. He wasn't a fool. We needed his confession.'

'Couldn't you have got that out of him at the police station?' asked Sarah, who was still shivering, despite the warmth of the fingers entwined with hers.

'Why would he have cracked? He only told you what he'd done because he was about to throw you off a cliff,' said Mariella.

'Don't remind me,' said Sarah ruefully. 'And what about Mabel? Any proof of what Regina did to her?'

'No. It was the same. No witnesses, and insulin doesn't last long in the body, so there were only traces, and not enough to identify any particular batch. Of course Teddy had plenty of it at his surgery, as it's used for animals with diabetes as well as humans.'

'When I spoke to the receptionist, they said they'd been working on a cat all evening...' Sarah said.

'Well, that bit we have got straightened out,' Mariella said with a dash of relief. 'They were working on the cat all day, not all evening.'

'But she said she'd been going to eat with her parents and had needed to cancel because they took so long,' Sarah said with a frown. 'Wait a minute, do you mean—'

'That's right, she'd been going to her parents for lunch.'

Sarah shook her head. 'I assumed she meant dinner, because Teddy said they'd been working all evening. I've been such an idiot.'

'That's why good, old-fashioned police work is important, Aunty Sarah,' said Mariella.

Sarah nodded – and silently pledged to investigate more thoroughly in future. 'So Teddy was free to go to the fair and give Regina the syringe full of insulin.'

'I wonder if Teddy gave Hamish ketamine? He was certainly groggy after we got his paw fixed,' Daphne said.

Sarah remembered again the tremor in Teddy's hand when his mother had been mentioned – and how she had got completely the wrong end of the stick and thought Regina had killed Abi. In fact, Regina had only been responsible for Mabel's death, committing the murder to silence her friend about Abi's pregnancy and the horrific way it had been ended.

'Well, Sarah, I only hope this has all cured you of meddling with murder,' said Daphne, still looking pale on the other side of the table. 'I know you like a challenge, but this was more of a car crash than a nice orderly conundrum for you to solve.'

Sarah gave a rueful smile. 'I think you're right this time, Daphne. I really bit off more than I could chew – but on the bright side, sort of, at least we have the solution, now. And you really helped me identify the murder weapon.'

'I got a strong message from the Beyond,' said Daphne smugly. 'And then I saw the knitting needles glinting in the light from the window.'

'Well done. And I imagine Regina won't be let out for quite a while?' Sarah turned to Mariella.

'If ever,' said Mariella, shaking her head. 'The good news is that I will be joining the detective team, effective immediately.'

Daphne glowed with pride, and Sarah was every bit as thrilled. 'I'm so pleased for you, Mariella, that's brilliant news.'

'Well, that definitely means you can retire as an amateur sleuth. I mean, what else could happen with Mariella properly on the case?' Charles said, relief in his voice.

'Exactly what I said, Sarah,' beamed Daphne. 'There can't possibly be any more murders in Merstairs, anyway. Not after this one.'

Sarah just smiled and patted Hamish for the umpteenth time, while her other hand squeezed Charles's. Life in Merstairs had taught her a lot in a short time. And the biggest lesson of all was never to rule anything out.

A LETTER FROM ALICE

Welcome to Merstairs!

Thank you so much for reading *A Seaside Murder*, my second book featuring retired GP Sarah Vane, her Scottie dog Hamish, and her friend Daphne. I hope you've enjoyed it as much as I loved writing it. I've always adored the English seaside and it's been a treat to set a series in this wonderful part of the country. I hope you'll join Sarah and the gang on their next adventures. If you'd like to find out what they're up to, please sign up at the email link below. Your email address will never be shared and you can unsubscribe at any time.

www.bookouture.com/alice-castle

If you enjoyed this book, I would be very grateful if you could write a review and post it on Amazon or Goodreads, so that other people can discover Merstairs too.

I'm also on Twitter, Facebook and Goodreads, often talking about my own cats, who thank goodness are not quite as much of a handful as Mephisto!

Happy reading, and I hope to see you soon for Sarah Vane's next outing.

Alice Castle

KEEP IN TOUCH WITH ALICE

Alicecastleauthor.com

 facebook.com/Alicecastleauthor

 x.com/AliceMCastle

ACKNOWLEDGEMENTS

A big thank you to my fantastic agent, Justin Nash of KNLA, my wonderful editor Nina Winters, and all the team at Bookouture, for making Merstairs real.

PUBLISHING TEAM

Turning a manuscript into a book requires the efforts of many people. The publishing team at Bookouture would like to acknowledge everyone who contributed to this publication.

Audio
Alba Proko
Sinead O'Connor
Melissa Tran

Commercial
Lauren Morrissette
Hannah Richmond
Imogen Allport

Cover design
Tash Webber

Data and analysis
Mark Alder
Mohamed Bussuri

Editorial
Nina Winters
Ria Clare

Made in the USA
Las Vegas, NV
26 September 2024

95830739R00166